sisters of the heart

soul sister

friends forever

kindred spirits

sister-friends

SISTERCHICKS
on the Loose!

girlfriends

pals for life

chum

confidante

gal pals

ally

true blue

From one sisterchick to another...

"Robin understands the precious value of close friendships, and it shows in this sparkling new novel!"—Darlene Marie Wilkinson, author of the *New York Times* bestseller *The Prayer of Jabez for Women* and *Secrets of the Vine for Women*

"*Sisterchicks* by definition is a delightful thing—friendship in the raw...helping, providing, listening, laughing, and of course crying. Robin's *Sisterchicks on the Loose* takes us inside a longtime friendship to a place where we hear and see ourselves. If you've never experienced a sisterchick adventure...this is one trip you won't want to miss!"—Donna, Robin's original sisterchick

"Get ready, sisters, this is the real thing! There is nothing 'fluffy' about these lively sisterchick novels! And who better to tell such delicious tales of friendship and truth than Robin Jones Gunn, a woman who's been my cherished friend for years."—Melody Carlson, bestselling author of *Blood Sisters*

"Deliciously fun! The feel-good book of the season!"—Patsy Clairmont, bestselling author of *God Uses Cracked Pots* and *Stardust on My Pillow*

"After I happily tumbled through Sharon and Penny's story, I felt as though I'd traveled with a couple of sisters who shared my heart and knew my soul. Like a visit to the spa, the results were enriching and cleansing—and involved a fair share of giggles. I'd invite any woman who has ever dreamed of going on an adventure with her best friend to indulge in this delightful trek to Finland."—On the Loose in California

"I stayed up till midnight reading this book, and I hated to see it end. Sisterchicks everywhere will love it as much as I did!"—Linda

"I've been a sisterchick for years but never knew until now what I should be calling myself! *Sisterchicks on the Loose* took me on a refreshingly madcap jaunt in my own living room. I look forward to many more such memorable journeys with MY favorite friends as we read all the sisterchick novels together."—Jaynie

"I loved the way Sharon and Penny shared true friendship and community! I'm in my early twenties and found myself inspired to treasure the close friendships I have now and watch them grow into lifelong sisterhood."—Natalie, a newly hatched sisterchick

"How refreshing to read something so FUN!"—Lisa

"Sometimes you have to get out of your everyday circumstances (spelled *r-u-t*) to see what God is doing in your life and the world around you. *Sisterchicks on the Loose* is a real winner, and I can't wait to share this book with all of my friends!"—Marti

"*Sisterchicks on the Loose* is a lovely, joyous book. Sharon and Penny's experiences made me laugh and reminded me that God sometimes gives us more blessings than we ever thought to ask or hope for—including friendships that transform our lives. I'm looking forward to the next sisterchick book, and I hope there will be many more!"—Lisa

"Finally! A fresh, new novel about characters who seemed so real that I felt as if I'd made two new friends."—Meg

"Robin's book is so precious. It's truly a celebration of life and shows God's goodness to us. Don't miss out on this wonderful treat!"
—Julee

a sisterchick™ novel

SISTERCHICKS
on the Loose!

ROBIN JONES GUNN

Multnomah® Publishers *Sisters, Oregon*

SISTERCHICKS ON THE LOOSE
published by Multnomah Publishers, Inc.

© 2003 by Robin's Ink, LLC
International Standard Book Number: 1-59052-198-6
Sisterchick is a trademark of Robin's Ink, LLC

Cover design by Susan Rae Stegall of D/SR Design, LLC
Cover image by W. Jackson Goff Photography

Scripture quotations are from *New American Standard Bible* ®
© 1960, 1977, 1995 by the Lockman Foundation. Used by permission.

Multnomah is a trademark of Multnomah Publishers, Inc.,
and is registered in the U.S. Patent and Trademark Office.
The colophon is a trademark of Multnomah Publishers, Inc.

Printed in the United States of America

For information:
MULTNOMAH PUBLISHERS, INC. • P.O. BOX 1720 • SISTERS, OR 97759

Library of Congress Cataloging-in-Publication Data

Gunn, Robin Jones, 1955-
  Sisterchicks on the loose / by Robin Jones Gunn.
      p. cm.
  ISBN 1-59052-198-6 (pbk.)
  1. Americans—Finland—Fiction. 2. Women—Finland—Fiction. 3. Female friendship—Fiction. 4. Finland—Fiction. I. Title.

PS3557.U4866S57 2003
813'.54—dc21

                                                             2003000710

04 05 06 07 08—10 9 8 7 6 5

For Donna,
my original sisterchick,
who has been with me to Finland and back.
Next time we're buying more chocolate.

For Merja,
my favorite Finnish editor,
who opened her heart and home to us in Porvoo.
Kiitos, my friend, for letting me borrow your childhood
memories of Porosaari and for the night of the
unforgettable sauna in Hinthaara.
You sing the high notes better than any sisterchick I know.

And for Meg and Jaynie,
my dear PPCs,
who faithfully grabbed a booth at Branches
every Monday night where we met for months.
Thank you for patiently going over every word of
this story until we got it right or until
Jennifer started mopping under our feet.

Sisterchicks forever!

"We were like those who dream.
Then our mouth was filled with laughter
And our tongue with joyful shouting;
Then they said among the nations,
'The Lord has done great things for them.'"

PSALM 126:1B-2

Prologue

Kiitos Cottage
Maple Leaf Lake, Washington
October 12, 2003

When my husband, Jeff, tells this story, he says it started the day I dyed my hair green. He likes to tell how he found me on the bathroom floor with an airline ticket in one hand and a can of root beer in the other, crying my eyes out.

I prefer to start this story where it actually began—more than a decade before the green hair incident. One hot August night in 1982, my dearest friend of all time, Penny, and I were on duty in the church nursery. Seven of the sweaty children in the nursery that Sunday evening belonged to the two of us.

I was rocking my wailing daughter when Penny, in the middle of a diaper change, turned to me. "Let's make a deal, Sharon. When they graduate, let's go somewhere. Just the two of us."

"Where would we go?" I asked.

"Finland!" she spouted.

I stopped and stared to see if she was serious. She was.

I suppose I should back up this story to when Penny and I first met. Penny and Dave were married and expecting their first child. That's when they started to attend our conservative little church in Chinook Springs, Washington. They joined our home Bible study and pulled up that first night on a motorcycle, wearing matching suede jackets with fringe on the arms—but with no Bibles. Penny left her muddy boots by the front door and settled on my tattered couch as still as a tiger concealed in the brush. I'd never had such a potentially wild person in my house before.

The next week, Penny showed up with a burlap sack stuffed with freshly dug-up iris bulbs. She asked if I had a Bible she could borrow, and our friendship was off to a tender, unconventional start. That was twenty-four years ago.

Penny and I were in each other's everyday lives while raising our children. Our husbands swapped tools and went fishing on Saturday mornings. Penny and I never had a fight.

Then Dave landed the job he always had wanted at a big computer company, and the Lane family packed up and moved to San Francisco.

I was lost.

For a month I cried when no one was looking. Our phone bill went into triple digits. Penny kept saying we would get together, just the two of us, but nothing ever worked out. My separation anxiety lasted for two embarrassing years.

This is where my husband picks up the story. Jeff says that out of the blue, Penny decided to go to Finland. He doesn't remember the part about the church nursery where the idea was hatched more than a decade before Penny put wings to her plan. Jeff says he found me curled up against the bathroom wall, staring at the ticket and guzzling root beer.

I wasn't guzzling root beer. I'm pretty sure I wasn't drinking anything.

Jeff says I was sobbing because I was in shock.

I wasn't sobbing. I was sighing really loud. There *is* a difference.

Jeff likes to add a punch line here about how I dramatically pulled the towel off my head and—ta-da!—my hair was green.

That part, unfortunately, is true.

For almost eleven years now I've listened to my dear husband's account of the once-in-a-lifetime trip Penny and I took to Finland in February 1993. He loves to embellish, so every time he tells it, the story morphs into something that only vaguely resembles our real adventure.

Last Friday, Jeff had our new daughter-in-law in a state of stunned silence while going on about the night Penny and I accompanied two seventy-year-old women into a Finnish sauna. Jeff said we got all steamed up and then jumped in a frozen lake.

It wasn't a lake. It was just the snow. The snow and a single star. Jeff never includes the part about the star.

I got so mad at him. As soon as everyone left, I said, "I don't want you to tell stories about Finland anymore. You get it all wrong, and it's not even your story. It's my story. Penny's and mine."

A sly grin appeared on Jeff's face, and I immediately knew what he was thinking. He finally had succeeded in pushing me into the corner where a pad of paper and a pen had been waiting for me for years.

So here I sit, in my corner of the world, ready to tell the story the way it really happened…about how Penny and I jumped over the moon.

One

January 1993

Oh, Penny Girl, *what have you done?* That's what I was thinking when Jeff found me on the bathroom floor sighing. I truly thought Penny had gone too far this time.

For years the amazing Penny had blazed through life like a fearless comet in the vast summer night sky. I followed close behind as a cosmic DustBuster, content to collect her sparkling trail of wonder dust. Whenever Penny ignited a sentence with the words "what if," she took off soaring. I found bliss in the glittering possibilities that fell over my life in those moments.

Truth be told, we rarely did any of the things Penny dreamed up for us. I didn't think we actually would go to Finland. I thought we would talk big, buy travel guides, discuss sensible walking shoes, and in the end, cash in the tickets.

Penny, however, never doubted this adventure.

When she sent my ticket, she wrote with a thick, black marker across the front of the FedEx mailer:

SHARON, DO NOT OPEN! CALL ME IMMEDIATELY!

Thirty-five minutes earlier I had doused my hair with a

highlighting solution, and I knew I should be heading for the shower. But I went directly to the phone and dialed Penny's real estate office in San Francisco.

"Okay, Sharon, go ahead. Now you can open it. Read the itinerary."

The words, "San Francisco, London, and Helsinki," tumbled from my lips.

"And?" Penny prodded. "Did you notice the name on the ticket? Sharon Andrews. That's your ticket. We're going to Finland!"

"Penny, this is crazy!"

"Yep! Crazy like a daisy. February 25. Pack your bags, girl! We're finally going to run away from home!"

"But Penny…"

"We made a deal. You promised you would go with me to Helsinki and back. Remember?"

"Yes, but we were going to go after all our kids graduated. Tyler is the only one in college. It will be, what?…Eight more years before all our kids are out of the house."

"Exactly. And I can't wait that long. Life is too short. We need to go now."

I stammered and stuttered while Penny gave me instructions on obtaining a passport. By the time I hung up and dashed upstairs to the shower, the home coloring treatment had pushed my hair past summer sun highlights all the way to a disturbing autumn moss tone.

The strange part was I didn't have the emotional reserves left to process how I felt about my hair. I wrapped myself in the comfort of my old yellow robe and sank to the bathroom floor, staring at the airline ticket and sighing over the possibilities.

I had been on an airplane only once. I know that's unusual, but I led a small life. Jeff and I both grew up here in Chinook Springs, a quiet suburb in southern Washington State. We were high school sweethearts and married right after we graduated. Jeff and his brother ran a landscaping business. I was content to keep a tidy home for Jeff and our four kids. That was my life. It was a good life. I wasn't the kind of person who longed to see the rest of the world—or so I thought.

When Jeff found me on the floor, the first thing he said was, "The ticket came, huh? What do you think?"

"You *knew* about this?"

He nodded and repressed that sly grin of his. "Dave called me a couple of days ago. He said Penny wanted to surprise you."

"She surprised me all right."

"You don't look very excited."

"I'm still in shock. Why do you suppose Penny is so determined to hunt down her relatives in Helsinki?"

"She's Penny. This is how she does things."

"I know, but if she's going to go all that way to meet these relatives of hers, don't you think she should take Dave or one of their kids?"

"She wants to take you."

"Why? I mean, if we had this kind of money, I'd put a new roof on the house."

Jeff knelt down and kissed me good on the mouth. "Don't overanalyze all the fun out of this, Sharon. Go. Have the time of your life. Come home happy."

Jeff stood.

I reached for his arm. "Honey? There's one more thing I should let you know." I pulled the towel off my head and watched my husband's expression as my seaweed surprise made its debut. To his credit, Jeffrey Edgar Andrews held his tongue. Twenty-four years of marriage and four children had taught this energetic husband of mine a few lessons in the fine art of restraint.

All Jeff said was, "Must be January." Then, clearing a chuckle from his throat, he left me alone on the bathroom floor where I sighed some more and pondered my history of January bloopers.

Instead of making New Year's resolutions, I tend to make impulsive blunders. I suspect the dank January mornings in the Northwest bring on this temporary insanity. At the start of each year, I'm overcome with a restless passion to change radically a slice of my life. As soon as I try something, like turning my dishwater-colored hair to a lively summer blond, the madness passes, and I remain quite sane the rest of the year.

One January, after we had been married nine years, I decided I'd had it with our hunk-o-junk couch. As if on cue, I saw a Salvation Army truck pull up in front of my neighbors' house. I trotted over and told the driver that if he wanted, he could come take my couch, too.

Not only did he take my couch, but I also threw in a wobbly amber-colored floor lamp; a dented frying pan; two plastic candleholders; and our blender, which had a peculiar problem. The blender blended even when no one asked it to blend.

Once the blender started to blend at two in the morning. Jeff said it was an electrical short, and all I had to do was remember to unplug it. I always forgot to unplug it. Once we walked into the house with groceries, and there it was, filled with nothing but air, blending away.

I taped a note to the inside of the possessed appliance that read, "Needs repair," and handed it to the driver of the Salvation Army truck. He handed me a receipt and told me I was a "kind and generous person."

Euphoric over my benevolence and giddy over thoughts of a new couch, I called Jeff to share the great news. Jeff was…well, less than euphoric. I think that was our worst fight ever. It certainly lasted the longest. Seven wretched weeks passed before we finally bought a new couch on credit. Jeff's mother never forgave me for parting with the blender, which I had forgotten was a wedding gift from her sister.

In the Januarys that followed, I tried to confine my temporary lapses of judgment to areas that affected only me.

Penny used to say she liked it when I showed signs of entering my "New Year's Fit of Madness" because she could talk me into things I wouldn't normally agree to, such as the year we took a tap dancing class. We were the only students over the age of nine.

To our credit, we stuck with the dance class all ten weeks. To the relief of our husbands and children, we opted out of performing at the year-end recital.

I had to wonder if Penny calculated to the day when my fit of madness would strike this January. She cleverly timed her purchase of those two transatlantic airline tickets, sent them to arrive the very hour I was most vulnerable, and even prepared my husband ahead of time.

Even though I didn't think this—her most outrageous dream yet—would last until it was full grown, I didn't see the harm in playing along with it while it was still kitten-size.

I tucked the tickets into my top dresser drawer, dressed, and went through the rest of the day wearing one of my son's baseball caps. Curiously, no one at the dinner table ventured to ask about the hat. Either Jeff had said something to the kids, or my theory about being the invisible mom at our house was more accurate than I had realized.

The next morning I managed to get a nine o'clock appointment with Joanie at the Clip 'n' Curl. I told her about Penny's Helsinki scheme while she worked her magic on my limey mane. She shifted the color back to a blah-blah-blond shade, which was at least within the normal range for human hair.

I tried to tip Joanie a little extra. She slipped all the money back into my hand. "Please. Let this be my treat. You keep your spending money."

"No, Joanie, take it."

"Not this time, Sharon. Save it for your trip. If you want, you can buy me a souvenir."

Wide-winged guilt came swooping in and landed on the roof of my psyche. It was one thing for Penny and me to stir up a big cloud of dream dust, but Joanie shouldn't be turning down money because of it. I left the Clip 'n' Curl determined to pay Joanie double the next time I had my hair trimmed.

Most days, I pull my thin, straight hair up in a clip or a twist of some sort. Since Joanie had done such a nice job of styling it to gently skim my shoulders, I thought I might as well have my passport photos taken.

I drove to the closest mall, which was located twenty miles across the Columbia River in Portland, Oregon. I found a camera shop with a sign that read, "Passport photos while you wait."

The young man snapped my picture before I was ready.

"Are you going somewhere?" he asked, as I wrote out a check for the two small, not-so-flattering photos.

I looked up, startled, and heard myself say, "Yes." As soon

as the word leaked out, guilt flapped its molting feathers and cawed, "Liar! Liar!"

The young man stood still, eyebrows raised, waiting for the rest of my answer.

"I, um, I'm going to Finland."

"Cool. That's like, all the way over in Europe, isn't it?"

I gave a slight nod, paid for the photos, and went directly to the bookstore on the mall's lower level where I bought a travel book on Scandinavia. I didn't know that Finland was next to Sweden. I also didn't know that Finland bordered Russia. Helsinki was on the other side of the globe, half a world away from Chinook Springs. Did anyone there even speak English?

My next stop was the post office where my husband's partially deaf uncle has worked for thirty-seven years. Uncle Floyd was eager to help me organize everything and mail off for my passport application. Of course, I had to give him the details with my voice raised, so everyone within a two-hundred-yard radius heard me lie. This time I used words like, "I might be going" and "If it works out."

Uncle Floyd enthusiastically handed me a ten-dollar bill. "This is for you so you'll be sure to send lots of postcards home to everyone. Tell 'em to save the stamps for me. And try to get specialty stamps, will ya? Ask for the kind of stamps they don't use for everyday. Will ya do that for me, Sharon?"

I left the post office biting the inside of my mouth. How could I return the ten dollars to sweet Uncle Floyd after he and the rest of the world discovered this Finnish fantasy was a hoax?

Within three days everyone in my small life knew about the trip and everyone was excited for me. Everyone, that is, except Jeff's mother, Gloria.

Gramma Gloria and Grampa Max joined us on Friday night for our daughter's high school choir performance. Kaylee was a freshman and prone to wild emotional dips. As normal as that is for a fifteen-year-old, I didn't tend to be the most understanding mother. All I remembered about when I was fifteen was getting my braces off. I think I smiled a lot.

Kaylee seemed to smile at everyone but me.

Right before we were ready to leave for Kaylee's concert, she dribbled the slightest bit of apple juice on her white blouse. I tried to clean it up using the dabbing method with a wet cloth, but of course, that made it worse. The large wet spots weren't drying quickly enough, so Kaylee stormed upstairs, wailing that now she would be late.

Gramma Gloria shook her head. "This should be an eye-opener for you, Sharondear. How would your children manage if you took off for Iceland?"

Gramma Gloria made a hobby of conveniently forgetting the correct names for people and places whenever she wanted to cast a disagreeable light on them. My entire senior year of high school she called me "Sherrill" instead of "Sharon" even though she had known me since I was a child. Once Jeff and I were married, I became "Sharondear." I decided that was better than many other options, so I didn't try to correct her.

"Aw, the kids will manage just fine," Grampa Max said to Gloria, carrying the last of the dinner plates to the sink. "Isn't that so, Ben? You'll get along without your mom for a week or so."

"Twelve days," Gloria corrected him.

"Eleven," I said.

"Right in the middle of track season," Gloria added with a cluck of her tongue.

My reserved son, who was old enough to vote in national elections, wisely continued his chore of loading the dishwasher and didn't vote on this one.

Grampa Max motioned to our ten-year-old, who was trying to wedge his foot into his tennis shoe without untying the laces. "Come on, Josh. You can ride over to the school in my car. We'll save some seats in the auditorium for these slow-pokes."

I ventured upstairs and tapped on Kaylee's bedroom door. The distraught princess bid me enter. She had tossed the "ruined" white blouse on the floor. The very blouse I had washed, ironed, and sprayed with just the right amount of starch to make it perfect for her tonight. Ninety minutes of loving labor lay crumpled at her feet. Kaylee shot me a wounded look as if the apple juice disaster were my fault.

She had changed into a long-sleeved beige T-shirt that had once belonged to her oldest brother.

"That won't do," I said.

"I knew you would say that. But what else do I have?"

"I have a white blouse you could wear."

"I don't think so!" Kaylee rifled though her summer T-shirts. "I mean, no offense, Mother, but we don't exactly, like, wear the same size, you know!"

Kaylee yanked the beige shirt over her head, and I noticed that not a pinch of baby fat remained on my daughter's torso.

Where did it go?

She had the cutest little waist. Her 34A-size bra appeared too snug.

When did all this happen?

Kaylee was right. Nothing in my closet—not even my skinny clothes—would be small enough to fit her.

"I know you don't want me to wear a T-shirt, but I don't have any choice." She pulled the wrinkled cotton shirt over her silky blond hair.

"I could iron it if—"

"Mom, we don't have time! I'm supposed to be there in like five minutes!" Kaylee tugged the T-shirt over her black skirt and swished past me muttering, "Now my hair is so messed!"

That evening I watched with new eyes as Kaylee lined up on stage with the thirty other students. Nearly all the girls were wearing T-shirts. I counted only three white blouses in the choir.

Kaylee stood in the front row to the left. Under the bright lights none of the wrinkles in her T-shirt were as pronounced as I thought they would be. She blended right in. No one else in the auditorium would ever know how crisp Kaylee Andrews could have appeared onstage that evening. I wondered if I was part of a vanishing breed of mothers who owned an iron and knew how to use it.

I studied my daughter's perfect posture, her steady concentration, and the way her mouth delicately opened and her chin rose when she held the long notes.

She was beautiful.

And she was oblivious. Oblivious to her poise and her winsome beauty. All the way to school she had groaned about her impossible hair and moaned that her shoes were too tight. She even said she wished her legs weren't so long. Imagine!

From where we sat in the fifth row, all I saw was a gorgeous young woman blossoming in the right way at the right time, legs and all. Life would soon reveal the vast, wonderfully rich possibilities available to her. Gifted with an abundance of creativity, talent, and intelligence, my lovely Kaylee could become anything. She could go anywhere. Do anything. The possibilities were magnificent, and she was overwrought about speckles of apple juice; about long, silky, naturally blond hair; and about the "curse" of long legs.

When the choir came to the final number, I had to fumble in my purse for a tissue. I couldn't stop crying.

I don't remember what song they sang. Something patriotic that started with four boys in the back row singing in barbershop-quartet style. On the chorus, my Kaylee straightened her shoulders, tilted up her chin, and sang as if both she and Eve had never had a run-in with apples in any form. She was free when she sang. Free and beautiful. A vibrant young woman.

I cried because my Kaylee was unmistakably fifteen.

And that made me, unmistakably, forty-one.

Two

Two and a half weeks after the Helsinki ticket arrived, the glittering possibility of our adventure had grown to Milky Way proportions. I called Penny on the last Thursday night in January to tell her my passport hadn't arrived yet. I expected that by the end of our conversation we would come to our senses and agree the dreaming and scheming was fun while it lasted, but it was time to tell ourselves and everyone else the truth.

"People keep slipping me money and loaning me travel gear," I told Penny. "This trip has become a big deal. A very big deal."

"That's exactly what it's supposed to be. A very big deal. You and I are going to Helsinki, Sharon. Listen to me carefully. We...are...going...to...Helsinki."

A pause followed. If Penny wasn't going to speak the words that would begin the dismantling process, then neither would I.

The lovely delusion continued another week. That was the week everyone started to give me advice.

The clerk at the grocery store told me a terrible story about her sister. She went on a Caribbean cruise, but when she boarded the plane, she tried to heave her heavy luggage into the overhead bin and threw her back out. When they landed in San Juan, the paramedics had to wheel her from the plane on a gurney. She spent the week of her cruise lying in a Puerto Rican hospital.

Sufficiently motivated by her story, I drove around my neighborhood, measured a mile and a half on the odometer, then turned around and drove home. That became the three-mile course I walked every morning after the kids went to school.

Inspired by my determination, Penny bought some ankle weights and walked around her suburban San Francisco neighborhood. However, she outdid me by walking four miles every day and going on one of her protein shake diets.

"Have you lost any weight yet?" I asked Penny six days into her diet.

"Not yet. But I will. I need to. This always has worked before. It's just taking longer this time. I guess I have more weight to lose."

Penny and I were the same height and basically the same size. Her waistline was lower than mine, and she was larger on top. Over the years we shared maternity clothes and watched each other expand and shrink at different paces.

Penny's biggest complaint after she turned forty was the effect of gravity. She said she believed that putting a man on the moon had to be a hoax because gravity was, in fact, an irrefutable law. Things go down, not up. If any of the NASA scientists wanted to challenge her facts, she said she had secret evidence up her sleeve.

I didn't particularly like my size or the effect of gravity

either, but until this trip I guess I thought what was happening to my body was inevitable. Even if we never boarded a plane or hoisted luggage into an overhead bin, I liked the way I felt after I walked. That bit of motivation in my normally sedate life was worth the price of the tour book and passport—the passport that still hadn't arrived by February 6.

Penny called on the evening of the sixth to tell me her passport had arrived and she was sending me a tour book on Scandinavia that she had bought.

I asked why she was sending the book to me instead of gleaning the desired information herself.

"I don't have time to read it," she said. "This is supposed to be the slow time of year for real estate, but it's been wild around here. I might have another house in Moraga sold before we leave."

"That's great, Penny."

"I know. God must be providing us with extra souvenir money or something. I can't believe this year is off to such a great start."

I tried to image what life would be like with "extra souvenir money."

"I hope you're taking notes as you're going over the tour books," Penny said.

"I am."

"Good. Anything interesting yet?"

"Did you know more saunas are in Finland than cars?"

"Seriously?"

"According to the tour book the ratio is one sauna to every five people."

"Now that's useful information." I could hear Penny running the water in the kitchen sink. "Do you think you and I are going to upset the Finnish national sauna ratio when we show up and add two more people to the population for a week?"

"Finland isn't as insignificant as you think. You really should read this book, Penny. Finland is the only country that has ever fully repaid the U.S. for a debt."

"A debt?"

"We loaned them a lot of money after World War II."

"Sharon?" Penny had turned off the water, and her voice grew low. "You do realize, don't you, that this is supposed to be a *fun* trip, not a *field* trip? Immigration personnel will not make us take a test before we can enter their fine country."

"Very funny."

"What about fun places to shop? Tell me you marked those in the book, too."

"I have them all marked. Restaurants, too. I don't think you need to send me the other book."

"Okay. I might toss it in my suitcase, if there's room. All we have to do now is wait for your passport and a response from my aunt."

"You still haven't heard from her?"

"No, but I will."

"Did you try to call her?"

"I only have an address. She'll write back to me. You'll see."

The whole trip seemed to be hanging by a thread. I didn't want to be the one to snip that thread.

On Tuesday afternoon, the second week of February, Gramma Gloria stopped by with a laundry basket full of craft materials.

"You're the organized one in this family, Sharondear." She planted herself at the kitchen table and unloaded bits of red ribbon, Styrofoam balls, a glue gun, and white streamers. "You can help me figure out how to make centerpieces for the senior citizen sweetheart banquet at church on Saturday."

"What are you planning to make with all this?"

"Well, I don't know, Sharondear. That's why I brought it over. We need nine of whatever we decide on. We have fifty people coming this year. Isn't that sad? I remember when we used to have a hundred come each year. One hundred and twelve one year. Do you have any coffee?"

"For the centerpieces?"

"No, Sharondear. For me. I'd like a cup of coffee, if that isn't too much trouble. I don't want to be a bother."

This was one of my mother-in-law's favorite lines. After delivering it she would wait with one ear cocked until someone, usually me, replied, "It's no bother at all."

I had enough coffee left from that morning for about two cups, but the coffeemaker automatically had turned itself off. I knew the coffee would be lukewarm by now, so I poured a cup for Gloria and headed for the microwave.

"Don't heat it up, Sharondear. I burned my tongue the last time you did that."

"It's going to be cold."

"That's okay." Gloria took the cup from me. She had a sip and made a face. "Why, this is ice-cold!"

"I know. Here, let me heat it up for you."

"Oh no, Sharondear. That's okay. I can sip it this way. I thought perhaps you had a fresh pot going, that's all." With a grimace she pressed her lips to the cup's edge.

Jeff and I had spent not hours, not days, but the equivalent of weeks discussing the challenges we have with his mother. Gloria always has been opinionated and subtly manipulative. No one in town would disagree with that.

During the last few years, however, her comments had become more critical and biting. Everyone in our family hid a little scar somewhere that was inflicted by the jagged incisors her words now carried. There seemed to be no way of working through a disagreement with her once her mind was set. She was more determined than ever and at the same time disturbingly illogical in her thinking. We adjusted our relationship with her to what Jeff called "honor without homage."

While I'm sure this approach is a healthy way to deal with a person like Gloria, I usually diverged to the path of least resistance, and the cold coffee situation was one of those cases. I quietly started a fresh pot. Gloria protested, but I said, "It's no bother."

Satisfied, she fiddled with the ribbons. "It's Tuesday, isn't it? If you need me to, I can take Kaylee to dance lessons after she gets home from school."

"Kaylee doesn't take dance anymore."

Gloria looked up and blinked behind her large glasses. "She doesn't? You didn't tell me that. When did she drop out?"

"She didn't 'drop out.'" I clenched my teeth. "Kaylee chose to stop taking dance lessons a while ago."

"Well, no one tells me these things!"

More than two years had passed since Kaylee's last dance class. Of course Gloria had been told; the gaps in her memory were widening. I knew I should roll through the conversation rather than stop to correct her, so I excused myself, saying I needed to put the clothes in the dryer.

As I slipped out of the kitchen, I remembered years ago when Penny tried to correct Gloria when she used the phrase, "This is a fine kettle of kittens." Gloria defended herself to the end, saying that fish had nothing to do with this expression.

Everyone she knew said "kettle of kittens."

From that day on Gloria decided she didn't like my rude, uninformed friend. She started referring to Penny as "Daveswife." For some unspecified reason, Gloria adored Dave and thought we should have named our youngest son after him. She even said once, in front of our children, that she couldn't understand why Dave married Penny. Gloria said she doubted if Daveswife was "redeemed."

Joshua, who was four at the time, said, "What's that word mean?"

I will never forget Gloria's answer. *"Redeemed* means you stop being rude and become a nice person."

My innocent son tilted his head. "Gamma Gloria, are you redeemed?"

Grampa Max intervened by whisking Josh out to the garage in search of some phantom fishing pole Max said he had left at our house. Gloria changed the topic.

It had been six years since that incident. As I now lingered over the dryer, folding towels, I thought how Penny was more redeemed than the rest of us, if that's possible.

I'd grown up with God the same way I'd grown up with Jeff and all the other steady surroundings of Chinook Springs. When I was five years old, I prayed a simple prayer one night with my sweet mother. I asked Jesus to come into my heart. That was it. I never knew anything other than Christ's forgiveness and God's provision. Salvation had been handed to me by the same soft hands that had tucked me in under a fluffy comforter each night. I acquiesced to God at the simplest level of childlike faith, and His presence in my life was as comforting as the glow of the hallway night-light.

For Penny, salvation came after weeks of hand-to-hand

combat with the same hands that compressed the stars and sent them spinning across the galaxy. Once she grabbed hold of the tiniest piece of Him, she wouldn't let go until He blessed her. Penny sought God and fought God until He was all she could think about. She took long walks so she could argue with Him in private. In the end, I like to think she won His heart the same day she gave Him hers.

I returned to the kitchen with a stack of folded towels. The fresh pot of coffee was ready. Pouring a cup for my mother-in-law, I wondered about the real reason for her visit that afternoon. I placed the coffee in front of her and reached for the cup of cold coffee she had been sipping.

"Sharondear, you're not going to throw that out, are you? I told you I would drink it."

"It's too cold."

"Well, it's no wonder you kids are so low on money the way you throw away food. Do you know how expensive coffee is these days? I would think that with one son in college and another about to start in the fall, you would be more concerned about your finances."

"We're doing fine."

"I guess you must be doing fine. If saving money were important to you, I don't suppose you'd be wasting it on passport applications and travel books."

Bingo! This was what she really came for.

"I can't imagine how you and Daveswife came up with this irrational idea. I asked Jeffrey last night why he's letting this charade go on, when all of us know it's not going to happen."

"And what did Jeff say?" I tried to keep my voice steady.

Gloria turned away and muttered, "He said he thinks the trip is a good idea."

"It *is* a good idea." I smiled inwardly at the unwaning support of my darling husband. My mother-in-law might know the same language as the guilt vulture that had been circling for days, ready to devour the dream once it gave up its last breath, but my Jeff was speaking a different language over me. He chose to believe the truth even before I did.

"A good idea? Sharondear, how can leaving your husband and children to go gallivanting around Iceland with that Daveswife be a good idea? I never would have expected you to turn on your family like this and insist on taking this selfish trip."

That's when something inside of me snapped. Inwardly I was whooping and hollering, frantically waving invisible arms. Short of throwing a few sticks and stones, I set out to chase away this ominous spirit of shame that had been trying to feather a nest on the roof of my soul. I told that dark-winged mother of all guilt to fly away and take Gramma Gloria and her basket of Styrofoam balls with it.

The words that spilled from my mouth at that moment were a surprise even to me. "This trip is a gift to me, Gloria. I intend to accept it graciously, and nothing you can say will make me feel bad about it."

I felt strong. Strong enough to fight for the chance to get on that airplane in sixteen days and fly to the other side of the world, whether my mother-in-law approved or not.

When I related the incident to Jeff late that night in the soft glow of candlelight in our bedroom, he reached across the bed and rubbed his rough hand down my arm. He asked what his mother said to me after that.

"Nothing."

"My mother didn't say anything?"

"No, because Josh walked in the door right then with two of his friends. Your mom was sweet as pie the rest of the time she was here."

"What about the decorations?"

"Kaylee saved the day. She cut out paper hearts, which she turned into bouquets and stuck in the Styrofoam balls."

"Good for Kaylee." Jeff moved closer, and I drew in the faint scent of cedar trees that rose from his tousled brown hair.

This is what Jeff and I were good at, believing in each other. We had no trouble being close. We were still in love. We both knew I could leave him and the kids for a week and a half and have no reason to feel guilty.

"You know what I thought, when I watched your mother this afternoon?"

"Hmmm?" Jeff pressed his lips against my shoulder.

"I thought about getting old."

"You know you'll always be eighteen in my eyes."

I smiled as Jeff planted tiny kisses in an orderly, landscaped pattern across my shoulder.

"We have no guarantees when it comes to our minds though, do we?" I said. "Your mother is only in her sixties. She's in good health. But her mind has wandered off into a tangled forest. One day my mind might enter that same forest."

Jeff pulled back slightly. I turned to meet his questioning gaze.

"I was thinking this afternoon that once a person's mind enters that forest, she never finds the way out, does she? It's pretty dangerous."

"What are you trying to say?" Jeff smoothed my hair.

"I'm saying, I realized today that growing old is a risky

journey. I don't want my trip into old age to be the only risky journey I ever take."

Jeff looked confused.

"What I'm trying to say is…" I waited to hear the inner rustling of dark wings, but all was calm. All was bright. "I know it's risky, but I want to go to Finland, Jeff."

"You are."

"I know," I whispered. "Thank you."

With an eighteen-year-old heart, I gave myself freely to my husband as if it were the first time and the last time and the best time, all in one.

Three

The day my passport arrived, my son broke his wrist.

Benjamin, our normally reserved, mildly competitive, bright, athletic son claimed a burst of senioritis made him take the dare to shimmy up the flagpole after school. Three of the other guys on the track team had made it to the top, tagged the flag, and slid down unharmed. Ben tagged the flag but then had no idea how he lost his grip and fell to the cement.

I still picture Ben's guardian angel leaping in and cushioning the blow at the moment of impact. Ben easily could have broken more than his wrist.

"A clean break" was what the doctor called it. He predicted Ben would need to wear the cast for a month. Six weeks at most.

On the drive home from the hospital Ben said, "I just lost my scholarship, didn't I?"

I tried so hard not to cry in front of him. For two years Ben had his heart set on going to Rancho Corona University in Southern California. A track scholarship was his best chance for getting in. At the close of his junior year, he ranked third in the state for pole vault. Now he wouldn't be able to compete during the spring of his senior year. In that one moment, Ben's college plans went *poof!*

Jeff was silent at the dinner table that night. He seemed to be having a hard time finding a place to put his disappointment. Jeff was the one who wanted to name our second son Benjamin because it means "son of my right hand." Now his Benjamin had no use of his right hand and was making a mess of dinner with his left hand.

Over the next few days, homework became a problem. Morale was a problem. My husband wanting to yell at our son but holding it all inside was a problem.

I called Penny five days before we were to leave and said I didn't see how I could go. I thought she would understand and suggest a logical solution. Perhaps the trip could be delayed a month.

Penny was quiet for a moment and then said, "This will be the making of Ben."

I didn't like her tone, so I jumped in and described again how Ben had difficulty dressing himself and eating, not to mention being benched at track practice, and contending with my husband's simmering disappointment.

"Sharon, listen to yourself. You can't fix this. Benjamin is old enough to be in the army. He can handle this with or without you. You can't stay home just to button his shirts and cut his meat. Tell Jeff to yell at him and get it over with."

"Penny!"

"Well, it's the truth, Sharon. All this means is now you have to trust God in a bigger way than you did before this happened."

I had no strong, confident words to give back to her.

"Sleep on it and call me in the morning."

I didn't like what Penny had said. I didn't like Ben being old enough to be in the army. I didn't like the way I felt inside. And I especially didn't like the way Gramma Gloria stopped by wearing a smug grin and offering a plate of cookies for Ben while I was in the middle of my phone conversation with Penny. I had no fire left in my belly.

Instead of "sleeping on it," I lay awake and fretted until, by morning light, I finally felt exhaustion coming over me. As much as I didn't like it, Penny had spoken the truth. I couldn't fix Ben.

After sending the kids off to school, I called Penny at her real estate office. "Okay," I said firmly. "I'm going."

"You don't sound too happy about it."

"I'm not happy. I was awake all night."

"Practicing for jet lag?"

"Not on purpose."

"It's the right decision, Sharon. You'll see."

"I hope you're right."

"I am." Penny had to dash off to a meeting. She said she would call back that evening, but I didn't hear from her until the following afternoon when she called from her mobile phone on the way to an open house.

"Feeling better about Ben?" she asked.

"Yes, a little bit. Max came over this morning and said Gloria was having some abdominal pain. He's taking her to the doctor this afternoon."

"Do you think she's okay?"

"I don't know. Max looked concerned."

Penny paused. I thought the phone signal had cut out. "I

hope it's nothing serious, and I hope…" The line crackled, but I could guess what Penny was saying. She probably was questioning Gloria's timing and the validity of her sudden affliction.

It was better I didn't hear what Penny said because I'd probably jump in to defend my mother-in-law. No matter how irritating or bothersome my extended family could be, I rallied to the side of blood over water every time.

"Have you started to pack?" I asked once the crackling on the phone line subsided.

"I pulled a few things together last night, but I haven't thought through my clothes yet. We'll probably have snow. How about you? Are you taking boots?"

"Yes, my old brown pair. I sprayed them with some water-repellent stuff a few days ago. They're my most comfortable shoes."

"What about a bathing suit?" Penny asked. "Are you bringing yours?"

"I hadn't planned on it."

"Bring it. I'm taking mine in case we end up at a hotel that has a heated pool or hot tub. Dave thinks I should take a flashlight and a travel alarm. I put them on my list. I'm going to do some shopping later this afternoon. I still need to buy film for my camera, and—oh, did I tell you? The house in Moraga closes tomorrow."

"That's great, Penny."

"I know. Money will be the least of our worries on this trip."

I wanted to believe that Penny's comment referred to my reluctance to leave Ben and my possible Gloria crisis. But I thought I heard something else in her tone.

I asked if everything was okay, and she said, "Couldn't be

better." I hung up thinking that Penny could be hiding a whole basket of worries and choosing not to tell me about them yet. She tended to be selective as to when and where she would allow a personal crisis to unfold. Our conversations for the past month had centered on our trip. Penny had said very little about Dave or their three kids, I now realized.

The good news was we would soon be together twenty-four hours a day. All would be revealed.

Wednesday night I couldn't sleep. My bags were packed. Everything was checked off my list. I couldn't have forgotten anything because the last two days had been consumed with thinking and checking and packing and rechecking.

Jeff was going to drive me to the Portland airport at five o'clock the next morning. I would kiss my sweet husband good-bye, board a plane to San Francisco, navigate my way through the airport, and somehow end up face-to-face with Penny in the international terminal. It would be the first time the two of us had seen each other in almost two years. Penny and I would board a plane together, and twelve hours and twenty-three minutes later, we would land in England. Another meandering through a huge airport and getting ourselves on another flight, and we would end up in Helsinki at two-fifteen in the afternoon, their time, on February 26.

My brain couldn't imagine it all. I worked through the details a dozen times while curled up on my side of our warm bed. I tried to think what could go wrong and what I would do in each possible disaster scenario.

Jeff slept deeply.

The night-light in the hallway kept me company through the long darkness, and then the alarm went off.

I showered, dressed, and double-checked to make sure I

had my passport and the airline ticket in my shoulder bag. With quiet steps, I went to each of our three children, who were still in their beds.

I had called Tyler, our oldest, at his dorm room the night before to say good-bye. He said he was proud of me for being such a cool mom and getting out there to see the world.

Our youngest, Joshua, cried when I kissed him. But he said it was only the sleepers in his eyes and that he would be fine while I was gone.

Benjamin bumped my head with his cast when he tried to hug me. I assured him it didn't hurt even though it did. It hurt something awful in the deepest part of my mothering heart.

Kaylee brushed my cheek with a kiss and reminded me about the list of items she wanted me to bring back for her. Her room smelled like fingernail polish and wild jasmine. I kissed her twice.

Then I tilted up my chin and walked down the stairs with my mouth open, as if I were about to sing the highest note I'd ever sung. I didn't look back. I was going to do this.

Jeff hummed on the way to the airport. He said twice that he was going to miss me and followed that line with, "But I'm glad you're going." We kissed four times at the gate before my row was called and I boarded an airplane for the second time in my life.

I didn't cry a single tear over the emotional upset of leaving my family until my seat belt was fastened and my tray table was in its upright and locked position. The seat beside me was empty, so I took the blanket and a pillow placed there. With my face to the window, I watched sheets of Oregon winter wetness smash against the tarmac. The plane backed away from the terminal. And then I cried.

By the time the airplane's wheels touched down in San Francisco, I had no tears left. I'd successfully completed the second airplane ride of my life all by myself. I was ready and steady. In a few moments I would see Penny. My Penny. My generous, outgoing, crazy friend who had selected *me* as her travel companion. Tears were not on the agenda from here on out.

I stepped into the bustling terminal firmly gripping my shoulder bag while I scanned all the signs. I arrived in plenty of time and stood there, searching each face that passed, waiting for Penny. My anticipation rose and fell during those eternal fifteen minutes. I think it was the closest I'd ever come to a panic attack.

What if Penny doesn't come? What if she's waiting for me somewhere else? What if the plane leaves without me? What if this was all a bad joke? What if…?

I realized that for years I had reveled in the sparking wonder of Penny's "what if" questions. The unknown elevated her. My "what if" questions were suffocating me with fear and pressing me deeper into myself.

At just the right moment, I looked up, and rushing toward me came the one face in all the world I longed to see. Penny's!

With a bulging bag slung over each arm and tugging a wheeled suitcase behind, Penny came charging toward me in a straight line. Her smile was huge. Her cocoa brown hair bounced with carefully coiffured fullness while her reading glasses slid from their perch on top of her head. She wore wide-legged black pants, a fire engine red turtleneck sweater, and a sleek, black raincoat that flapped open with every long-legged stride she took. She looked as if she did this sort of thing every day.

Dark-eyed Penny, with her gold hoop earrings and her wonderfully wild, sparkling eyes, grabbed me and planted her signature greeting kiss on my right cheekbone.

"Look at you! You're here! We're here! Sharon, can you believe we're doing this? You look great!"

"So do you!" I hugged her again.

"Your hair! I love your hair! You didn't tell me it was down to your shoulders now. And the color is great! Not a hint of green anywhere," she said with a wink. "It couldn't have been as bad as you said. I love your coat. Is it new?"

"No, this is the one you talked me into buying at an after-Christmas sale about six years ago. I just never wear it."

"It looks great! You look great! I can't believe you're here! Come on! We need to hurry. Our gate is this way."

And we were off. Penny blazed ahead. I trotted to keep up. The galaxy had fallen back into its proper alignment.

"You would not believe the morning I've had!" Penny shouted over her shoulder. "I was running so late that I was afraid to check my baggage. I didn't think they would get it on the plane in time. I'm so glad you checked your suitcase and only have one bag. Would you mind carrying on one of mine so they don't tell me I have too many pieces?"

With the overhead bin story in mind, I opted for the smaller shoulder bag and let Penny keep her wheeled suitcase and the gym bag.

"How did you get everything in one suitcase?" Penny asked. "I kept thinking of more things to pack. I can see it already—I'm going to have to buy a bigger suitcase the first day there."

We were in line to check in at the gate and receive our seat assignments when Penny caught her breath. She looked at me, and I knew something was going on.

"What?" I asked her.

"What do you mean, 'what'?"

"You're about to spring another surprise on me."

Penny looked crushed. "How did you know?"

"Your left eyebrow. It goes up whenever you're about to reveal a secret."

"Oh yeah. I forgot you were onto that." She touched her left eyebrow. "You and Dave are the only two who tell me that."

"So what's the surprise?"

"I got us in business class," Penny said. "That's why I was running late. One of the guys at work offered me his flight upgrade coupons, but I had to go to his house this morning to pick them up."

As if this whole trip weren't luxurious enough, Penny and I were among the first group to board the wide-bodied aircraft and settle in with our extra legroom. I was by the window again with a pillow and a blanket. Penny adjusted herself in the aisle seat, and we kept on chattering as comfortably as if we were sitting at my kitchen table.

"I was up all night getting everything together." Penny shook her head and reached for her reading glasses, as they were sliding down her forehead. "I can't believe how unorganized I was at the last minute." She fished in her large purse for her glasses case. "I suppose you were all set to go by eight o'clock and got a good night's sleep."

"Are you kidding? Not me. I was packed, but my brain wasn't ready to shut off. I barely slept."

"Did you leave notes for your kids?"

"No, I woke them up to say good-bye. Did you leave notes?"

Penny nodded. "I ended up writing long love letters to each of them and Dave, too. My plan was just to leave little one-liners on their pillows. Then I started to write Nicole's first, thinking that would be the easiest. Was I wrong! What is it with our daughters? Did you feel this way when Kaylee was eleven? I feel as if every step from here on out needs to be guarded carefully. Do you know what I mean? It didn't feel like that when Noah was eleven."

"I know. Having only one daughter makes a difference, too, somehow."

"Exactly!" Penny agreed. "It's as if I have one shot at reinventing myself—and before you say anything, I know I'm not supposed to project all that on Nicole. She is not my second chance at a happy childhood. It's just bizarre how much more intense my mothering instincts are with her. The boys are easy. But then, they have a great dad."

I smiled because she was watching me, waiting for the smile. Dave loved his wife and kids intensely. Penny always wanted everyone to love Dave as much as she loved him.

One time, about five years ago, Penny told me she wondered what it would be like to sail through marriage the way I did with Jeff, rather than take every bump along the road as she had with Dave. She said Jeff amazed her because nothing fazed him. Whenever something disturbing, like Ben's broken wrist and lost scholarship, would come into our lives, Jeff would burrow deep inside himself. He rarely reacted outwardly. His emotions seemed to churn and sift through a dozen filters. Then one morning he would wake up, and nothing would be left to filter. He would be back to his usual steady pace.

Dave, however, was all out in front. If he had an opinion

about something, he would share it. If you needed something, he would go out of his way to get it for you. If he was mad, he would articulate why and quickly forgive. If he loved you, you knew it. And you never doubted it.

The plane had taken off while we were in the midst of our discussion. Penny opened her mouth wide and rubbed behind her left ear. I felt compelled to do the same, even though my ears weren't popping.

Penny continued to talk about the love notes she had worked on all night. She described how surprised she felt over her last-minute reluctance to leave her family. "I didn't expect to feel this way. And you know what, Sharon? I have to apologize for a couple of things. First, I want to apologize for being so cold when you were going through the trauma with Ben. I didn't understand. I think I do now. Sorry I wasn't more sympathetic."

"It's okay. I needed to hear what you said. You were right. I'm glad I didn't back out of the trip."

"Really?" Penny's left eyebrow went up.

"Yes, really. Why do you ask? What's the surprise?"

"Is my eyebrow up?"

"Yes."

"Rats! I'm going to have to work on that. I do have another little surprise, and I think you're going to need to read all my facial quirks when I tell you this."

I looked hard at her. I'd forgotten how intense Penny's gaze could be. She had a way of seeing into people as if she were shining a light so the person could search for something lost along the way. I don't know why I let her do that to me. I could turn away and listen sufficiently without looking. But I didn't. I allowed her dark eyes to shine their amber-flecked light on me because Penny knew things. She saw things way before I did. Right now she was looking for something. Apparently I had it.

"This is the other thing I was going to apologize to you about. We don't exactly have everything lined up in Finland. Which I think is fine because all our options are open. But I didn't want you to feel…," Penny searched for the right word, "…uncomfortable."

"That's okay. What needs to be worked on? I have the tour book. We could do some planning now."

"Yes," Penny said slowly.

"What about your aunt? Did she give you any specifics in her letter about things to do?"

Penny's finger went up to her lips. "No. You see, I never heard back from my aunt. And before you say anything, Sharon, it's not that big a deal. We have plenty of money. We can stay at any hotel we want the whole time, if we need to. I wasn't necessarily planning to stay at my aunt's house. I just wanted to meet her. But I don't even know if she's still alive. It's not that important, though. We can try to track her down once we arrive. But if we don't find her, we'll just have fun exploring."

I didn't say anything right away. I'm certain both my eyebrows were down. Penny was watching me carefully.

"So, you're telling me that we got on this plane and we're flying halfway across the world, but when we arrive, we don't have any idea what we'll do."

"Yes and no. We'll take a taxi and find a hotel. Or rent a car. And we'll find a restaurant and have some dinner. Or lunch, or whatever mealtime it will be then. And," she added on an upbeat note, "we'll pray and see what God puts in our path."

I wanted to scold her. I wanted to say, "Penny, people like us don't just show up in big foreign cities in the middle of winter and start looking up names of reputable hotels in a phone book!"

Before I could speak, Penny said, "I know I should have said something earlier, but I kept thinking I'd hear from my aunt at the last minute. I brought all the information I have about her with me. We'll take each step, each day as it comes. Like I said, we've got plenty of money." Penny's eyes were ablaze with dancing sprinkles of hope. "Whatever happens, I know it will be an adventure."

I reminded myself that "adventure" had been Penny's objective all along, even in the church nursery so long ago. And I had told Jeff I didn't want old age to be the only risky trip I ever took. This was it.

Risky. Adventuresome. Ridiculous.

At this moment, the appropriate adjective didn't matter because when a person is thirty thousand feet in the air, seat belted in business class, she is, for all practical purposes, committed. Two months ago I never would have dreamed up any of this. Two days ago I was still trying to work up the courage to board that plane in Portland by myself. Two minutes ago, however, Penny's left eyebrow went up, and secretly I wanted it to. I wanted Penny to surprise me and make me uncomfortable.

"What do you say, Sharon?" Penny looked at me hard. "Are you okay with this? I know you like life to be organized, but the thing is, now we'll be completely at God's mercy, and nothing is more adventuresome than that!"

With a deep breath, I gave my dearest friend the gift she had always so freely given me, the gift she was looking for when she looked so deeply into my eyes. I gave her grace. "Sure. I'm fine with this. We'll figure it out as we go along."

"Perfect! I was hoping you wouldn't be mad. This is going to be great; you'll see. We're going to have the kind of trip they never write about in the tour books."

My better sense told me I should mention people had good reasons for not abandoning themselves haphazardly to God's mercy, and such erratic trips weren't written about in the tour books for good reasons. But I pressed my lips together and enjoyed the sensation of once again being in the wake of the fabulous, fearless, flying Penny.

Four

With our enthusiasm elevated, Penny and I listed our options. A nice but not too expensive, centrally located hotel in Helsinki would meet our needs. A taxi was preferred over a rental car because it could be snowing, and neither of us had driven much in snow.

We went through the tour book, circling potential hotels and finding a phone number for a taxi company. Until we arrived, we couldn't do much more.

I bent down to put away the tour book, and something extraordinary happened. The clouds, which had cushioned our flight for the past few hours, cleared, and a burst of sunshine spilled in through the window. I turned to lower the window shade and found myself staring *down* on snow-covered mountains. They looked like a row of little girls dressed for their first Holy Communion. They seemed to be waiting for their cue to begin the processional march. I'd never seen anything so pure and majestic.

"Penny, look."

She leaned over. "I wonder if those are the Canadian Rockies. Or would we be past them by now? We're traveling north, aren't we? Into the sun. Our winter day will be short. Canada is so beautiful."

Penny flitted through a recounting of a story I'd heard many times. I guessed it to be one of her favorite memories since she told it often. Two summers before we met, Penny and Dave rode his Harley from California to Banff, Canada. They lived on moose jerky and cheap beer. She wore the same pair of jeans every day for seven weeks and only had two pairs of undies. She never wore a bra, only halter tops. The skin on her shoulders and upper back had become permanently leathered from the sun and wind. One night, when Penny and Dave were sleeping under the stars, a bear ambled within twenty feet of them. The bear licked the gas tank on their motorcycle and then lumbered into the forest.

I listened with my gaze fixed on the magnificent world beneath my window. The world I was watching couldn't possibly contain lumbering bears or braless women on motorcycles. From my viewpoint, the world below was perfect in every way.

The serving cart arrived at our row, and we received the lunch trays that were offered to us. I noticed the classy-looking woman across the aisle from Penny as, in a British accent, she asked where she might dispose of her "rubbish."

I subtly observed the way the woman kept her fork in her left hand after she cut her chicken and then took a bite without switching the fork back to her right hand. She wore a honey-colored knit skirt with a matching sweater. The sleeves were pushed up to her elbows, and she wore a gold charm bracelet on her right wrist that shone on her dark, bare arm. Her skin was as dark as obsidian. I'd never been so close to a person who was the opposite of pale, blond, uncultured me.

"Do you want my sourdough roll?" Penny asked me, as she examined the meal in front of her. "I'm trying to keep myself to only one bread a day, and I ate half a bagel on the way to the airport. It was stale; I shouldn't have eaten it. This roll looks much better. But I'm not going to eat it."

"I don't care for it, thanks."

"I meant to ask you earlier, how's Gloria? What did the doctor say?"

"He's going to run some tests on Friday."

"Did you go see her last night?"

"Yes, for about five minutes. She went off on a tangent about how inconsiderate I was being and how she might not be alive when I returned."

"What did Grampa Max say?"

"He said he thought she would be okay. I asked him if I could do anything for them, and he said, 'Yeah, you can get outta here for a few weeks and let us fix our problems for a change. It's time you went and made a few problems of your own.'"

"I've always adored that man," Penny said with a broad smile. "It's too bad Gloria treats you the way she does."

"It's not that bad."

"Yes, it is."

I shrugged. "I can't change her, Penny. I've reached the point where I've decided that she can't hurt me anymore."

"Well! That's a new, improved approach. Good for you."

"It's this trip," I told Penny. "I don't know exactly what happened that day when Gloria brought over the Styrofoam balls and I stood up to her. But when I saw her last night, I was free. It didn't bother me that she was still against this trip. I didn't feel guilty at all."

"Good for you." Penny opened her small packet of salad dressing with her teeth. "We'll find a really fun souvenir for Gloria, and you'll come home a hero in her eyes. You'll see."

Penny chatted about her kids as we ate. I listened and kept checking the view outside the airplane window.

The waning sun was already behind us, low in the west. We rapidly headed into the night. Layers of thick, ethereal clouds formed a puffy, pink-tinted comforter beneath us as our 747 rose above it all.

I watched the night come. Or perhaps I was watching us race into the night. Every so often a bundle of clouds would open, and far below I could spot tiny gatherings of light, evidence of life.

Then I saw it. The moon. Round and unblinking, that mysterious silver orb seemed to race toward us, riding an invisible, celestial current. I watched the moon peek in the window at me. I imagined I could feel its cool, steady light, more fierce and determined than the glow of any night-light. The plane banked slightly to the right. I turned my head to keep an eye on the moon. I watched and watched and then suddenly, in a blink, it was behind us.

I silently recited Ben's favorite nursery rhyme, *Hey, diddle diddle, the cat and the fiddle, the cow jumped over the moon; the little dog laughed to see such sport, and the dish ran away with the spoon.*

I looked out the window again and was certain that the moon now was under us. Turning to Penny with what I'm sure was a look of dumbfounded marvel, I said, "Guess what? We just jumped over the moon!"

Penny laughed. "Like the cow?"

"Yes, like the cow. We jumped over the moon!"

The flight attendant reached to clear my tray, and Penny busted up. "Well, don't look now, but your dish is about to run away with your spoon!"

Our little jokes weren't that funny, but we were so tired they seemed hilarious. We laughed hard, but then I had to excuse myself and stand in line for the rest room. I shifted from right foot to left and looked around at the immense variety of travelers. Did any of them realize we were on the other side of the moon? None of the faces I scanned seemed amazed. I would have to be amazed for all of us. Amazed and delighted and a little bit nervous about being at God's mercy, as Penny called it.

When I returned to my seat, Penny was engaged in a conversation with the woman across the aisle from her. "Sharon, this is Monique. Monique, Sharon."

I nodded at the middle-aged woman. Her eyes were clear blue, like two pebbles in a mountain brook.

"She's from England," Penny said.

"You're from England?" I tried to change the incredulous expression that must have washed across my face. Monique was the first Brit I'd ever met. I'm sure it was evident I expected to meet someone more like the Queen Mum or at least someone with a British name rather than a French name.

"Yes, I've lived in England since I was sixteen." With a gracious smile Monique added, for my benefit, I'm sure, "I was born in Jamaica."

"Oh." I cleared my throat.

Penny rolled on with her customary openness, chatting as freely as if the three of us were clients lined up under the hair dryers back at Joanie's Clip 'n' Curl. "My mother used to tell me that my father was a pirate from Jamaica. She made up all kinds of gallant stories about him. I never knew my dad, you see, so I liked the way my mom turned him into a hero."

"I'm not sure my relatives would agree that a pirate from Jamaica should be considered a hero." Monique's accent was mesmerizing.

"When you're six, nothing is better than being told you're descended from a Caribbean pirate."

Penny didn't speak often of her childhood or of her father, who had died before she was born. When Penny was in her midtwenties, her mother passed away, and since Penny had no siblings, she and I became surrogate sisters and our children became adopted cousins.

"My mother was from Finland," Penny went on. "Sharon and I are on our way to Helsinki. I hope to track down my mom's sister."

"Won't that be lovely for you," Monique said.

Penny explained about not knowing if we would actually find her aunt, but after all, we were on an adventure.

Monique leaned forward to capture a full view of my face. "Aren't you the brave one?"

Had Monique caught on that Penny was the instigator of this madness, and I was just along for the ride? I managed a half grin in response to Monique's insight.

"I suppose it wouldn't hurt if you had a backup plan," Monique said. "If you don't care to spend your entire holiday in Finland, you might enjoy having a look around our bit of country."

"We just might have to take you up on that," Penny said. "Our schedule being open-ended and all…"

Monique apologized for not having a business card to give us. She wrote her phone number on the back of a beverage napkin and handed it to Penny. "If you do make it to England, please feel free to ring me at this number."

Penny and Monique settled into a pleasant round of small talk that included fingernails, the benefits of vitamin C when combating jet lag, and Monique's trip to San Francisco. My eyelids grew heavier and heavier as the long night wore on. When the second in-flight movie began, I pulled up the blanket to my chin, leaned the pillow against the window, and slept.

Penny slept a little during the long flight, too, which was helpful because when we landed at Heathrow, we needed all our energy to get us off the plane and onto our next flight.

Monique stayed with us until we parted ways at customs. She wished us well in our search for Penny's relatives and repeated the invitation to look her up if we ever came her way. I doubted that we would be in England again or that we would contact her. I was certain, though, that her beauty and her graciousness would remain a strong memory for me.

When we reached the front of the line at customs, Penny went ahead of me. I noticed that the customs officer looked at Penny's passport and then appeared to be singing to her. I couldn't hear what was going on, but I did hear him burst out laughing.

Penny smiled and nodded politely.

I wondered if it was her passport photo. Was hers as unflattering as mine? Apparently not all Brits were as polite as Monique.

I stepped up to the window, preparing myself in case the customs officer found my passport photo equally hilarious. He glanced up at me for a moment, asked a few questions, and then I was sent on my way to join Penny. She had placed all her heavy luggage on the ground and was taking off her long coat.

"What was that all about?" I asked. "He wasn't laughing at your picture, was he?"

Penny shook her head and held out her passport for me to see. "I should have expected it. Look."

I scanned her picture and thought hers was much more flattering than mine. I didn't notice anything unusual.

"See?" Penny said. "You're immune to it like I am. Most people are in the U.S. But not in England, I suppose." A smile crept up her face. "It really is kind of funny, when I think about it."

That's when I remembered all the jokes Penny had made over the years about her name. She said the only annoying thing that had come out of her marriage to Dave Lane was that she became Penny Lane.

"I think I made that custom officer's day. He, of course, had to sing the first verse to me. Thankfully he stopped when he got to the chorus."

I laughed. I know I shouldn't have laughed so hard, but the expression on Penny's face and the craziness of having a man with a shiny badge and a snappy British accent singing to her as she entered this foreign country struck my funny bone. I couldn't stop giggling.

"I know, I know. Go ahead and laugh," Penny said. "It is funny. I suppose I'll laugh later. I'm too tired now to appreciate the humor of this situation. Come on, we better get a move on."

I reached for one of Penny's heavier pieces of luggage. "I can carry this one."

"Are you sure you don't mind?"

"No, it has to be heavy for you."

"I really appreciate it, Sharon. You're right. This stuff is starting to weigh a ton. If we were on a ship, I'd throw the excess overboard. I bet you're glad you checked your suitcase."

"I don't think it would have fit in the overhead bin. I probably brought as much excess as you did, but I put it in a larger suitcase."

With each step I took, Penny's luggage seemed to gain weight. I was perspiring heavily by the time we reached our seats on the flight to Helsinki. Fumbling in my purse, I found a small perfume sampler and dabbed the flowery potion generously on my wrists and the back of my neck in an effort to camouflage the unpleasant odor. In my haste to dress that morning, I think I'd forgotten to use any deodorant.

Penny sneezed twice. "What is that stuff?"

"I'm not sure." I tried to read the rubbed-off letters from the small tube. "Eau de something."

"Eau de phew!" Penny sneezed again. "Seriously, Sharon, I can't handle that, whatever it is." She twisted all three of the overhead airflow nozzles so that they blew on me in an effort to diffuse the fragrance.

Penny and I had an empty seat between us that apparently was assigned to a tall gentleman wearing a gray suit and carrying a briefcase. He stood in the aisle, holding his boarding pass and looking at Penny, who was settled in the aisle seat.

"Would you like to sit here?" Penny offered, as if his silent glare had charmed the words out of her. "I can take your seat in the middle." She slid over and tilted the center air directly on her. The gentleman gave an appreciative nod and without a word folded himself into the aisle seat.

The seat space allowed each traveler was definitely not as wide as it had been in business class. I knew Penny had to be miserable, squashed there in the middle and suffocating from my perfume. I barely could smell it, but I tried to wipe any hint of the fragrance off with a tissue. Would Penny have preferred my body odor? I noticed that Penny and I were pressed against each other, hip to hip.

She sneezed again.

I'd forgotten about Penny's bionic nose. We used to tease her when the kids were little because it would about kill her to change a diaper. She could smell a cat at fifty yards and our old dog, Bosco, even when he was outside. The windows at Penny's house were open nine months out of the year.

I tried to make myself small. It was impossible. We had to endure the bumpy flight with all its inconveniences and did so by both pretending we were sleeping.

My thoughts wandered to small luxuries like snack food, pillows, and a hot bath. I was glad that none of Penny's relatives were meeting our plane and taking us to a private home where it was likely we would stay up all night talking. A quiet hotel room sounded wonderful. Room service sounded like a dream.

All my private little dreams scattered when the pilot announced our plane couldn't land in Helsinki due to icy high winds. We circled for almost an hour before an announcement came that we would land at a different airport.

"This can't be good," Penny muttered under her breath.

I reached for the guidebook and found a map. "Do you suppose we're going to Stockholm? It looks pretty far away."

Penny studied the map. "Russia looks closer, doesn't it? They wouldn't fly us into Russia, would they?" It had only been a short year or two since the breakup of the former Soviet Union, and Russia wasn't a travel destination for the average American.

Our landing was rough. The plane came down with a thud on the tires and then bounced up again for three seconds before reconnecting with the runway. Inside our cramped quarters, the passengers responded with a group gasp.

Outside, the sleet came toward us at an angle. As the plane rolled forward, I could barely make out the small terminal's outline.

From all around us came the click of seat belts being unfastened.

The flight attendant spoke over the intercom in three languages. English was the last. By the way people around us were groaning while the message was delivered in the first two languages, we surmised the news wasn't good.

"We ask that you remain in your seats," the voice finally said in English. "We will not be deplaning at this airport. The latest weather reports predict a clearing in the storm. Our pilot has requested clearance to return to Helsinki."

I stared quietly at my hands. The large hook-shaped scar on the back of my right hand looked larger than usual. It had turned a pale, oyster gray color.

I got the scar when I was fifteen and fell against the side of a tractor at my summer job, picking raspberries at Gelson's farm. It took twenty-five minutes to reach the hospital, and I gushed blood all over the front seat of Mrs. Gelson's new powder blue Ford station wagon, even though I was holding the dish towel and pressing hard like she told me to.

Sitting on this icy runway felt a lot like sitting next to Mrs. Gelson in the emergency room. Whatever happened next couldn't possibly be pleasant.

Five

We sat on the runway of the small mystery airport for more than an hour. The flight attendants came by offering coffee.

"Is it okay if we use the rest room?" Penny asked.

"Of course. Please return to your seat, though, as soon as possible. We expect to receive clearance for takeoff soon."

I decided I better go to the rest room with Penny while I had the chance. The gentleman on the aisle stood silently to let us out. All the stalls were occupied. Penny and I stretched without speaking to each other or making eye contact.

"Penny." I touched her shoulder. We barely had spoken to each other during the past hour. "When we return to our seats, why don't you take the window seat? I know you said you don't like the window because it gets so cold, but you're welcome to use my coat as a buffer."

Her expression softened. "Are you sure that's okay?"

"Sure, I wouldn't mind. You need a few more inches of breathing space."

"Thanks, Sharon."

The bathroom stall door opened, and I motioned to Penny. "After you."

"Thanks. I owe you one."

That was a crazy thing for Penny to say. She didn't owe me anything. I was the one who was in debt to her for this whole trip.

I tried to lean against the wall to let a young blond woman with a crying baby join me in the crowded space. "He's not very happy, is he?" I asked.

She answered in a language I didn't understand, but when she slid the knuckle of her first finger into his mouth, I asked, "Teething?"

She gave me a weary look and said, *"Ja,"* before shifting the sobbing baby to her other hip. We were communicating in the universal language of all mothers: baby sympathy. My heart went out to her.

I reached over and gently stroked his damp cheek. "It's okay," I said softly. "It's okay." The tyke turned his round moist eyes toward me and stopped crying.

"That's better. You want me to hold you for a little bit so your mommy can have a break?"

I opened my hands, and the mommy gladly let her chunky bundle climb into my arms.

"How old is he?"

The mother shook her head. She didn't seem to understand my question.

"Is he about nine months old?" I shifted the curious fellow to my left hip and held up my fingers as if I were counting.

"Ah! *Ja, nio.*" She held up nine fingers.

"That's what I thought. My first two boys were solid like

this, too." I patted his back, and he released a tiny burp.

Penny stepped out of the stall. She looked surprised. "How did you manage to accumulate a baby in the last three minutes?"

"He likes me," I told Penny. "He stopped crying."

The mom spoke again and motioned toward the available toilet stall.

"You go ahead," I said confidently, as if I understood every word she had said. "I'll hold him for you."

Penny stood next to me, staring for a moment. "I'm going back to our seats."

"I'll be—" My response was cut short by a raging wail from baby boy.

Penny gave me a "he's all yours" look and left quickly.

I jostled the little one, touching his cheek and trying to comfort him by saying, "It's okay. Your mommy will be back in a minute."

He tucked his chin and leaned into my shoulder. I patted his back. "There, there. It's okay."

With a stifled sob, his head came straight up, knocking me hard on the chin and causing me to bite my tongue. Then, without warning, the little prince reared back and spewed partially digested airline pretzels and sour milk all down the front of me.

The stall door opened. I held out the baby and motioned with my head so his mom would see the disaster. With profuse apologies in whatever language she spoke, she took her son into the stall and closed the door, and there I stood, aware that a trail of baby barf had found its way under my shirt and was pooling in my bra.

Somehow, when your child throws up on you, it's never as

bad as when it's someone else's child.

The second stall door opened, and I rushed in, locked the door, and thought I might be sick from the overpowering smells in the small space. First I tried paper towels to clean up and flushed them before realizing I might clog the whole system. Oh, what a sorry sight I was, trying the dabbing method on my shirt but only making matters worse. I wet more paper towels and then gave up and stripped to the waist.

I had just wrung out my bra when a bright red light flashed. I stared at the light and then looked at my reflection in the mirror.

"What are you doing here?" I asked the woman who was standing topless in front of me in this suffocating, sour bathroom stall, trapped on the runway of some undisclosed airport, which was possibly inside the border of the former Soviet Union, in the middle of an ice storm.

The absurd looking woman in the mirror didn't answer. However, an invisible flight attendant did. In three languages, no less. "Please return to your seat," the voice said over the intercom.

"I would love to return to my seat," I answered politely. "But Houston, we have a problem here."

No one could hear me, of course, but my banter helped me to stay focused. "My shirt is ruined," I went on. "My bra is soaking wet. Can you smell me? I can smell me. If I can smell me, then Penny...well, Penny is..."

I tried to dry my bra by pressing it between two paper towels. Someone knocked on the bathroom stall door.

"Yes! I'll be out in just a minute."

"You must return to your seat," the heartless voice said.

"Okay. I'm coming right now."

I still can't believe I did this, but I had no choice. I put on my wet bra and slipped the rancid, damp shirt over my head. Unlocking the door, I made my way back to the center seat with my head down, certain that every eye in that part of the plane was fixed on me. Every nose was probably fixed on me as well.

Poor Penny! The look on her face! She turned away from me, staring out the window as I gave an abbreviated explanation.

I swallowed hard and tried to take tiny breaths. My tongue had swollen from when I bit it right before Junior was sick all over me. I could feel a cold, wet stream zigzagging across my middle and soaking the waistband of my jeans.

The man in the seat directly in front of me stretched to glare at me over the top of his seat.

"I know," I murmured in a tiny voice. "I'm sorry. This isn't exactly pleasant for me either."

Our takeoff was terrifying. The plane seemed to be flapping oversize, weary wings as we rose into the air. We bucked a dozen air pockets, rising and falling like a ship at sea.

Penny grabbed for the bag in her seat pocket and held it up to her mouth and nose. She didn't get sick, but I'm sure she felt she was about to.

We landed in Helsinki at 7:20 P.M. Without a word, Penny and I walked into the terminal and went directly to the rest room.

"Here." Penny wheeled her suitcase into the first open stall before I could grab some wet paper towels. "Anything you want to wear is yours."

I found a new sympathy for my daughter. *So this is how Kaylee felt when I told her she could wear one of my blouses to the school choir performance.*

Penny's underwear was large on me. Not too large. Just loose and funny feeling. The bra and panties were, however, silky black and a far superior quality to anything I ever owned.

The larger size of her clothes didn't matter because I opted for a baggy pair of sweatpants and a yellow sweater that were easy to pull out of the suitcase.

With my soiled clothes in a wad, I exited the stall to see a line of women waiting. Penny stood near the sinks. "You are going to throw those away, aren't you?"

I hadn't planned on it. I was going to ask if she had a plastic bag. Surely they sold good strong laundry detergent in Finland. I could soak these clothes back to life, if I had the right laundry soap.

Penny moved closer when she saw me stalling. "If I'm right," she said in a low voice, "your bra is at least eight years old, and it's about half an inch from self-disintegrating."

Penny knew all too well the areas in my budget where I'd scrimped over the years to keep four growing children clothed.

"And if I'm guessing correctly, that shirt found its way into your life in the mideighties. Its shelf life has expired, Sharon. You need to set the poor thing free."

Part of me was glad that Penny felt well enough to be flippant. That was a good sign. But I wasn't too happy about her painfully accurate comments about my wardrobe.

"I'm not trying to be mean," Penny said quickly. "Look, you said you packed plenty of clothes. And I packed way more than I need. We should be fine with what we have until your luggage arrives. If not, we'll go shopping and buy new clothes. Now wouldn't that be tragic?"

I opened the top of the trash bin, and against all my frugal instincts, I threw away a perfectly usable set of clothes.

"Didn't that feel good?" Penny said.

"No. Nothing feels good at the moment." I pushed up the sleeves of the baggy yellow sweater and went to work washing my hands and forearms. My sticky chest and stomach would have to wait. We had an audience in line, and I wanted to get out of there as soon as possible.

"Thanks for letting me borrow your clothes," I said as Penny and I followed the signs to baggage claim. The directions were in three languages, with English the last listed. I noticed how quiet the airport was.

"Of course, you're welcome to borrow anything you want." Penny's voice seemed unusually loud as she turned toward me. "I hate to tell you this, but I can still smell you."

"I know. I need to wash up some more."

"Why didn't you do it back in the rest room?"

"All those women were watching me," I said, lowering my voice.

Penny laughed. "But just think! You could have started your career as an international underwear model."

"Not in your black silkies," I muttered.

"What?" Penny's voice still seemed loud.

I shook my head and mouthed the words, "Never mind." In a whisper I added, "It's so quiet here."

Penny listened a moment. "It is."

We looked around at the people as we walked past the boarding areas. Some were looking back at us. Some were reading. Some were sipping coffee from white ceramic cups at small round tables. No loud announcements were being made. No elevator music filled the air like audio Novocain. We had landed in a somber place.

"This is spooky," Penny muttered. "I'm so used to background noise."

"I think it's serene," I whispered.

My voice must have been too low for her to understand my comment because Penny replied, "I know. It is a scream, isn't it?" She laughed. The sound echoed in the large terminal. Penny covered her mouth with her free hand, and we proceeded to baggage claim.

We didn't realize that we would have to go through customs again. This time they motioned for the two of us to step up to the window together, probably because we seemed to be traveling together.

The officer opened Penny's passport first. He looked up at her and carefully pronounced, "Penny Lane?"

Penny smiled and said flippantly, "Yes, yes, I know. I'm in your eyes and in your ears and under blue suburban skies and all that. Yes, that's my real name."

He didn't blink.

Penny smiled more broadly at the officer. "Aren't you going to start singing to me?"

Silence.

"The Beatles, you know? Penny Lane? Or did the Beatles never make it over here to Helsinki?"

I cringed.

The officer repeated, "Penny Lane?"

"Yes, that's my name. It's my real name. I am Penny Lane."

"Thank you."

"You're welcome."

"Visit to Finland for business or leisure?"

"Leisure."

"Length of stay?"

"About a week and a half."

Without changing his expression, the man stamped her passport and reached for mine.

"Sharon Andrews?"

"Yes."

Unshaken by Penny's vibrant monologue, the officer asked me the same string of questions.

Blessedly, we both made it through customs and arrived at baggage claim. However, my suitcase didn't fare as well. My luggage didn't make it to Helsinki.

By the time Penny and I had examined every unclaimed bag, waited in line, filled out all the paperwork, and talked with two polite airline representatives and one impatient one, the only hope we were given was a phone number to call for an update in the morning.

"What time is it?" Penny asked, as we trudged to the airport terminal exit in hopes of finding a taxi that would take us to the nearest hotel.

"I'm not sure if I set my watch right, but I think the local time is about ten-fifteen."

"At night?" Penny asked.

"Yes."

"And it's Friday here, right?"

"I think so."

"I'm so disoriented." Penny pushed open the door for both of us as we stepped into the deep, frozen Finnish night.

Until that moment, I had never known what the words *freezing cold* meant. An icy wind grabbed our faces with razor-sharp fingers and sliced through our clothes as if we were wearing paper bags.

Penny let out a muffled shriek. "Are we on the North Pole?

It's freezing! Where are the taxis? Over there? Come on!" She forged ahead with a fierce determination that had left me hours ago. "Sharon," she yelled over her shoulder, "get out the tour book so we can tell the driver the name of one of the hotels we circled."

Even in my state of frozen numbness, I found it ironic that I had the tour book. I had no clothes. No underwear. No deodorant. No pajamas. No toothbrush. But I had the tour book.

The driver threw Penny's luggage into the trunk, and Penny and I huddled in the black sedan's backseat, flipping through the tour book.

"This one." Penny pointed to one of the listings with the highest rating. "Man, it's cold."

I met the driver's gaze in the rearview mirror and tried to pronounce, "Hotelli Suomi on Mannerheimintie 8."

I rubbed my hands together and touched them to my cold nose and cheeks. The cab was warmer than outside, but not nearly warm enough for us.

The driver asked, "What part of America?"

"Are we that obvious?" Penny smiled professionally, as if she might sell this man one of her properties listed for more than half a million dollars. "I'm from San Francisco. Sharon here is from Washington State."

"You want a good disco?" He asked while he drove us out of the airport area. "A good place for dancing?"

"No, thanks," I said quickly. I couldn't believe he asked such a thing! Did the man have any idea how old we were?

Penny leaned forward in the seat. "Do you have a good rec-ommendation?"

My mouth dropped as the driver told us some complicated

name of a hot Helsinki nightclub and offered to pick us up at the hotel later.

"That's nice of you to offer," Penny said. I poked her in the side, and she finished with, "But we're much too tired tonight. Thanks, anyway."

He turned and smiled at Penny in a way that gave me the shivers. I already was shivering, but this was a heebie-jeebies sort of shiver.

Nothing felt safe. Not this car, not the driver, and certainly not the hotel, since he knew where we were going. What was Penny thinking?

I clenched the edge of the seat as Penny asked the driver about good places to shop and eat. It was too dark outside to guess what the icy world looked like beyond the backseat of this taxi. If necessary, though, I was prepared to leap into the black night dragging Penny with me if this driver tried anything funny.

He laughed at one of Penny's quirky comments about a sign we drove past and expressed his condolences when Penny told him my luggage hadn't arrived. We made it to the hotel without my needing to employ any of my escape route plans.

A bellman opened the door for us and took our luggage. Penny pulled out a credit card to pay for the taxi.

"Have you any *markkas?*" the driver asked.

"You don't take credit cards?"

He shook his head.

"We forgot to exchange our money at the airport." Penny tried to figure out how she could get the cash to him. As we stood in front of the hotel, we were freezing, and none of the options were working.

The taxi driver pulled a business card from his pocket and

wrote an amount on the back. "Will you leave the money for me at the front desk?"

"Certainly!" Penny glanced at me as if she couldn't believe how trusting this man was.

I thought the driver was trying to work a scam on my overly trusting friend.

"I'll have it ready for you by noon tomorrow. Would that be okay?"

"Yes. Good." He nodded at me and returned to the taxi, which he had left running.

Penny and I dashed into the heated lobby of the luxury hotel. My cheeks stung from the contrast in the air temperature.

"This is nice," Penny said.

"Yes, it's warm," I said with a shiver. Visions of hot soup and a leisurely bath danced in my head.

We stepped up to the front desk. In her most professional tone Penny said, "Hello. How are you this evening?"

The uniformed young man nodded politely.

"We would like to check in. It's just the two of us. Double beds, please."

"Do you have a reservation?"

"No, we hoped we didn't need a reservation." Penny casually waved her hand.

She reminded me of our boys when they used to play *Star Wars* in the backyard. Penny's youngest, Nathan, had a strong affection for acting out every movie he saw. *Star Wars* was one of his favorites. One day Nathan came over wearing Dave's bathrobe and told me he was a Jedi master. As I watched from the kitchen window, Nathan pulled his hand out of the wide sleeve, waved it over our dog Bosco, and said, "These are not the droids you're looking for."

I love that memory of Nathan. He doesn't appreciate my telling it.

Penny's Jedi mind-manipulation move didn't seem to work on the hotel clerk. He tapped a few keys on the computer keyboard in front of him, and looking up with clear eyes, he said, "I do not show a double room available for tonight."

Six

"Would you be so kind as to check your system again?" Penny asked the hotel clerk.

I stood back, thinking it wasn't this poor kid's fault we hadn't made a reservation.

Penny looked cool as could be.

"Madam, we have a suite available, but no double rooms until Monday night. Would you like the suite?"

Penny paused. I thought she was thinking what I was thinking. A suite would cost far too much at a hotel like this. We could call a taxi—a different taxi—and go to the next hotel on the list.

Penny apparently had another tactic in mind. "May I speak with your manager?"

"Certainly, madam."

"What are you going to say?" I asked Penny.

"Don't worry, Sharon. I've got it covered. I deal with people like this all the time."

"People like what? Nineteen-year-old college students

working part-time as hotel desk clerks? We didn't make a reservation, Penny."

"That shouldn't matter. You know they have empty rooms."

"I don't know that. You don't know that either. We should have called for a reservation as soon as we got off the plane. If we hadn't spent so much time with the baggage claim people—"

"Exactly!" Penny cut in. "And that's my point. I'm going to tell the manager our peculiar situation."

"Our peculiar situation?"

Penny's gaze moved past me. I watched her expression soften as she put on an engaging smile.

"Hello." She greeted the approaching manager and extended her hand. He was an older, distinguished-looking gentleman in a dark suit. He didn't look like someone who appreciated being called to the front desk to hear about "our peculiar situation."

"How are you this evening? My name is Penny Lane." She paused, waiting for a response.

The manager's reaction was exactly what Penny seemed to be hoping for.

"Penny Lane?" he repeated with a controlled smile.

"Yes, Penny Lane."

"How may I be of assistance, Ms. Lane?"

"I need a recommendation from you. You see, we left San Francisco yesterday morning, and due to delays, we arrived in Helsinki late. My friend's luggage was lost, and as you might imagine, we are about to collapse."

She sounded controlled and professionally articulate. This was a side of Penny I rarely had seen.

"I'm hoping you can give us a recommendation," Penny

went on. "We wanted to stay with you during our week-and-a-half visit to Finland, but I understand you don't have any double rooms available until Monday."

"That is correct."

"I see. Well, would you be able to recommend another hotel here in Helsinki? We would like to stay in a hotel that's as nice as yours."

The suppressed grin on the seasoned manager's face grew to a genuine smile. "Have you stayed with us before, Ms. Lane?"

"No, this is our first trip to Finland. My mother grew up in Finland. I'm here to visit relatives."

"Oh, so you are from Finland?"

"My mother was."

"May I offer you our preferred rate?" He rapidly tapped the computer keys as the young man looked on with a surprised expression. "I have a junior executive suite available for roughly 10 percent more per night than our double room."

"Perfect!" Penny said brightly. "I think that would work out just fine. Thank you."

"My pleasure, Ms. Lane. Joona can complete the reservation for you. I trust you will have an enjoyable visit with your relatives."

"Thank you. We appreciate this very much."

The manager nodded at me and left us in Joona's capable hands.

"How do you say 'thank you' in Finnish?" Penny asked Joona.

"*Kiitos.*"

"Please tell your manager *kiitos* for me."

He nodded. "Will this be on a credit card?"

"Yes. And I also need to exchange some money to pay the taxi driver who dropped us off tonight. I told him I would leave the fare here at the desk so he could pick it up tomorrow before noon."

"I can take care of that for you," Joona said.

Penny handed him her credit card and the taxi driver's business card with the amount due written on the back.

Shifting from my right foot to the left, I noticed I was nearly thawed out. At least Penny hadn't talked me into throwing away my old brown boots at the airport bathroom just because I had a pair of tennis shoes in my suitcase. All my nice, warm socks were in my suitcase along with my favorite pajamas. As Penny completed the reservation, I felt sad that I was going to have to spend my souvenir and gift money on underwear and warm socks if my suitcase didn't show up.

A young bellman loaded Penny's luggage onto a wheeled cart and looked at me as if checking to see if I had any baggage to add.

"No luggage," I said meekly, holding out my empty hands.

He took us up the elevator to the junior executive suite and opened the door to reveal a spacious area that made me gasp. I had seen hotel rooms like this in movies but never had been in such an elegant room.

The modern decor included a leather couch and chair in a separate sitting area by the television. In the corner was a beautiful desk. The two beds were queen-size and covered with inviting, puffed-up down comforters.

"What would you like to eat?" Penny asked as soon as the bellman left. "I'm going to call room service."

"Anything. And the sooner the better. I'm starving! You wouldn't mind, would you, if I took a bath while you ordered?"

Penny looked up at me for one incredulous moment and

then burst out laughing. "Would I mind? Is that what you said? Would I mind if you removed all those hideous fragrances from your body?" She scooped a pillow off the bed and threw it at me. "No, I don't think I'd mind."

I threw back the pillow, laughing along with her. "I suppose you wouldn't mind if I used your shampoo then, either."

"Anything you want or need is yours. Help yourself."

I foraged through her suitcase looking for her cosmetics while Penny studied the menu.

"Can you hand me my purse?" she asked. "I can't read this without my glasses."

"I don't remember your wearing glasses before."

"I know. I just got them about six months ago. It's very sad to become so feeble."

"Penny, you are far from feeble." I handed her the shoulder bag, trying to keep a reasonable distance so she wouldn't have to smell me.

Flipping her glasses in place, Penny said, "Oh, much better. Here we go. How does *kalakukko* sound?"

"What is it?"

"Fish and pork pie."

I grimaced. "What else do they have?"

"Reindeer meat, but that's only on the dinner menu. We're too late for dinner." Penny leaned back in the chair at the desk and turned to the next page, as if she had found her interesting reading for the evening.

Gathering a few essentials, I headed for the bathroom, only to discover a wire-rimmed basket on the bathroom counter filled with everything I needed. The towels, white and fluffed up, were stacked on a shelf. Two thick robes hung from pegs on the wall.

"They have an assorted cheese and fruit platter for a party of six to twenty," Penny called out. "How hungry are you?"

"Don't they have something simple?"

"What were you hoping for? Cheeseburgers and fries?"

"No, of course not. I was thinking of something like an omelette."

"Excellent idea. I'm going to call the kitchen and see what they can come up with. It'll be a surprise."

I closed the bathroom door and paused a moment. *Oh, Penny Girl, you and your surprises!*

Turning the faucet, I watched as refreshingly clear water tumbled into the large, deep tub. Within minutes the bathroom filled with steam. I unwrapped a bar of almond-scented soap and let the water rise higher than I ever would have in my tub at home.

Stripped down to my weary flesh, I cautiously slid one foot into the water. The other foot willingly followed. With all the honor of a regal ceremony, I lowered myself into the pristine water until the blessed element covered me up to my neck.

It wasn't enough. Closing my eyes and drawing my breath deep into my chest, I sunk all the way under until I was submerged. I could feel the ends of my hair darting about my neck like tiny fish in a tropical lagoon. The shimmering waters carried my weight and lifted from me all that was rancid. I floated in a free, uncomplicated state of tranquility.

With my chin up, I lifted my head out of the water, gulping in the steamy oxygen. I tried to capture the floating bar of soap that was bumping against the tub's side. Adrift like a rowboat that had been torn from its moorings, the almond-scented bar had no choice but to release to me its cleansing powers. Contentedly I lingered in the warm, soapy water for what seemed like a long time. I didn't ask my mind to assimilate that this wasn't my bathtub and this water wasn't Chinook Springs water. It was better to be still and breathe and nothing more.

Fragrant, fresh, and free, I left all my tensions in the tub and watched them swirl down the drain when I released the plug.

I couldn't stop smiling.

It's only a bath! my mind chided, as I reached for the fluffy white towel.

Oh, but what a bath! my heart responded. The heart knows truths that the mind could never perceive, there in its ivory tower. Such a going under and coming back up can heal and soothe and bring back life.

I decided that if women ruled the world, such a soaking would be mandatory for all individuals before any major treaties were negotiated. Ah yes, after that all negotiations could lead directly to world peace.

Slipping into the luxurious robe, I exited my private Shangri-la with all the grace of a ruling queen.

"Do you take baths at home very often?" I asked Penny.

"No. And it's really too bad because we have a tub in our bathroom with whirlpool jets. Nicole uses it more than I do."

"Baths are marvelous," I said in my dreamiest voice.

"You certainly smell fresh and friendly. Like a fortune cookie."

I almost asked if fortune cookies really had a smell, but questioning Penny's bionic nose when it came to anything in the dessert category was pointless.

"Room service is on its way," Penny said.

I noticed she had unloaded the contents of all three suitcases onto a bed and was busy sorting and piling. She definitely had enough clothes for both of us. For a month.

"What did you order?"

"Omelettes and something else."

"What's the something else?"

"I don't know. I had a fun conversation with the woman in the kitchen. I told her this was our first meal in the land of my ancestors and we could go for something festive to top off the omelette."

"What if festive to her means pickled squid brains?"

"I suggested something chocolate, and she said she had just what we needed."

"*Chocolate* is a word that women universally understand, isn't it? Sort of like how I felt on the airplane while I was talking to that young mother. Chocolate and babies know no language borders."

"Yeah, what was the deal with that mom?" Penny asked. "Did she speak any English?"

"I don't think so."

"Then how did you end up with her baby?"

"I felt for her. That's what I meant by the unspoken universal languages of all mothers. Don't you remember what it was like when our kids were that small? We could never do anything without a little koala bear hanging on us."

"It seems so long ago. I don't remember things as well as I used to. I think I burned up too many brain cells during my wild years." Penny tilted her head. "Speaking of wild years, did you really think I was going to let that taxi driver take us to the disco?"

"I couldn't tell by the way you were flirting with him."

"Flirting with him! I wasn't flirting!"

"Then what was that?"

"That was public relations. That's what I do."

"And with the hotel manager? And the kitchen chef? Is that public relations, too?"

"Yes, public relations with a dash of schmoozing. Perfect recipe for success, don't you think?"

I didn't respond.

Penny put her hand on her hip. "What? Do you think I did something wrong?"

"I don't know. I'm not used to being around you when you're schmoozing."

"This is how I operate in the business world. I don't lie. I just creatively direct the situations to get the desired results."

I folded my arms across the front of my cozy robe.

"What?"

"It could be considered manipulation, Penny. You know how to get what you want. You always have."

"And is that a bad thing?" Penny asked. "I mean, tell me if you think I have an integrity problem."

"No, I'm not accusing you of having an integrity problem."

"Then what am I doing that's wrong?"

I thought about how Penny's "public relations" techniques weren't dishonest or cruel. She opened herself up and gave freely to others. I think she expected others to respond with equal generosity.

"I don't know," I said after a pause.

"Well, you think about it while I take a shower. You, more than any other woman, know me by heart, Sharon. If you see anything out of line, I want to hear about it."

Penny always had been open and teachable. But I couldn't remember a time that I ever asked anyone to evaluate my actions or point out any undesirable qualities in my life.

I thought back on when our friendship was young and Penny asked me to help her practice what she was going to say at her baptism. Our church was more accustomed to baptizing children than adults. I think Penny realized that she and Dave were an anomaly, and she didn't want to shock any of the old ladies with what she called her "spicy testimony." I stopped Penny before she could read me the four pages she had written out. I told her I didn't want to know all that stuff from her past. I suggested she limit herself to three or four sentences and focus on making it clear that she was now an obedient follower of Christ.

I think that was the worst thing I ever did to her.

At her baptism, Penny stepped into the water, working hard to keep her expression flat even though I knew she was ecstatic. All eyes were on her. All ears were listening. Calmly reciting a few generic phrases of Christianese, Penny plugged her nose and went under. Up she came, glistening and spilling laughter from her merry heart with her arms in the air. She was so full of life.

I knew then that I had robbed her and those in attendance of experiencing the real passion for God that was exploding in Penny's life. I had censored her. I diluted her spirit in an effort to make her more like my type of Christian so she would be acceptable to people like Gloria.

I told myself I'd never do that again. I'd never try to change Penny. She was a zealous woman, true. But she was also humble and teachable.

Unwrapping the towel from my head, I leaned back, shaking the water from the ends of my clean hair. *Why do I still feel it's my job to correct her and corral her, even when I made myself promise that I wouldn't do that?*

Hoping to find a brush, I reached for my shoulder bag and dumped the contents on my bed. My belongings formed a small mound. I looked over at the mounds on Penny's bed and back at my meager collection.

The contrast reminded me of when we first met Dave and Penny. When they started out, they had very little. They decided to get married when they found out they were expecting Noah. At the time they were living in a one-room converted farm equipment shed under high power lines beside a peach tree orchard.

The first time I visited their substandard housing with a box of maternity clothes, my oldest, Tyler, was with me. He was three, and he thought sitting on the potty to take a shower at Dave and Penny's was the most wonderful thing in the world. The soapy water ran under the lopsided bathroom door and down the linoleum floor to a drain. Tyler came home and asked Jeff if we could put a drain in the middle of the floor in our house, too.

My dear hubby quietly collected funds from a few church folks and arranged for Dave and Penny to move into a two-bedroom cracker box before Noah was born. Dave had a full-time job by then and was taking computer classes at the community college. Penny read a library book on real estate and found a way for them to buy their little cracker box of a house.

A year and a half later, with a toddler on her hip and another on the way, ever-clever Penny managed to finagle some creative financing. They bought a serious fixer-upper in a nice neighborhood while renting out the cracker box. Penny made good use of all my hand-me-down baby clothes. She stuck to a tight budget, and she and I worked for days trying to sanitize their terribly neglected fixer-upper. The house had four bed-rooms, and we were certain that three of them had been used to raise chickens.

Within fourteen months, Penny had turned that chicken coop into a cupcake, and before their third child, Nathan, was born, she had sold it for three times what they had paid. They bought a house six doors down the street from us and lived there for nine years. I think those were the best years for all of us. I didn't realize at the time what a gift it was to be so close. Our lives were meshed together, and that made both of our families stronger.

Then Dave was offered an incredible job in the Silicon Valley. Dave never finished college, but he was sought after because of his exceptional computer programming abilities.

When they moved to the San Francisco Bay area two years ago, Penny managed to buy and sell another fixer-upper to get into the neighborhood where they wanted to be. I hadn't been to their new house, which they had bought five months ago, but I'd seen pictures. By Chinook Springs standards, they were living in a mansion.

Just like the contrasting stacks of belongings on our hotel room beds, Penny and Dave now had a blessed abundance, and I was the one with the drain in the middle of my budget.

A knock on the door startled me. A young woman deliv-ered our midnight omelettes. Each plate was covered with a silver dome.

"Are you Penny?" she asked warmly.

"No."

"Please tell Penny we made something for you that is a nice chocolate. I hope you will like it."

"I'm sure we will. Thank you."

I lifted one of the silver domes and found a delicious look-ing omelette and a parfait glass filled with a swirled chocolate dessert and topped with a Finnish flag on a toothpick.

Penny opened the bathroom door. "Did the food come?"

"Yes, and wait until you see it. Our first meal in the land of your ancestors, and it came complete with a Finnish flag!"

"As long as it includes chocolate," Penny said, "I'm sure it will be memorable!"

Seven

After enjoying our room service banquet so late on that first night, we weren't sleepy. Penny decided to organize her clothes in the closet and dresser drawers. I turned on the television, and the two of us wearily sat on the edge of the bed with our jaws slack, flipping through the channels and not understanding a single word.

Around two in the morning, Penny decided we should call home to let our families know we arrived safely. On the West Coast our kids were just coming home from school. I talked to Kaylee and Josh for a quick five minutes and told them to tell their dad everything was fine with me. Josh asked why I hadn't called yesterday, and I tried to explain the time change and the long flight.

My tenderhearted ten-year-old said, "Mom, could you call us every day when we get home from school? Then I won't miss you so much."

"Honey, it's the middle of the night here. I won't be able to call you every day at this time because normally I'll be asleep.

I'm awake now because we just got here a little while ago, and we're still up."

"Oh. Well, can you call us other times?"

"Sure. I'll call you whenever I can, okay?"

"Okay. Mom, can we eat the rest of the cake?"

"What cake?"

"Gramma Gloria brought a cake over yesterday, but I didn't get any 'cuz Dad said I had to do my spelling homework first, but after I did it, he said it was too late, and I had to go to bed."

I was glad to hear that my mother-in-law was feeling well enough to bake a cake and bring it to my family. "Is your homework done for today, Josh?"

"Mom, it's Friday."

"Oh. How did you do on your spelling test?"

"Not good. But could I still have some cake?"

I couldn't remember a time I ever had parented like this over the phone. I was the one who always was home. Monitoring snacks and helping with homework was my career.

"Yes, you may have a piece of cake. And Josh?"

"No, Mom, it's me, Kaylee. Josh went to get some cake."

So much for my son's missing me!

"Are you and Aunt Penny having fun yet?"

I had to think about my answer. Had any of this trip actually been fun yet?

"It's been an adventure," I told her.

"Do you think Dad would let me have a few of my friends stay over tonight?"

"How many is a few?"

"Just four. Rachel, Laurel, Sarah, and Emma."

"What did your dad say?"

"I didn't ask him yet. I thought if you said it was okay, then he wouldn't mind."

"Kaylee, you need to ask Dad. He's coordinating all the schedules while I'm gone."

"But you always say yes."

"Dad will probably say yes, too. But you need to ask him."

Kaylee sighed. "Okay. Well, I hope you guys have fun."

"Thanks, honey. Love you."

"Love you, too. Bye."

Penny talked with her kids much longer than I did. She asked for specifics about their homework and Nicole's practice for a play she was in at church. Penny gave them all kinds of details about our trip, including the sick baby, my lost luggage, and our deluxe hotel room.

I realized I hadn't told my kids anything about what had been happening with me. I wondered if I never had specifics to talk about in my daily routine at home, and therefore they were used to everything being centered on them.

Penny's kids seemed to be more involved in her life. Was that because she had more of a life than I did? Or was it because she opened up more to her kids? What would Kaylee have said if I told her I threw away my clothes? It didn't seem like a topic worthy of pricey long distance phone minutes. But then, what had we discussed with those pricey minutes? Cake and friends coming over.

I remembered when our kids were babies and Penny would come to me for advice on everything. I liked being the expert. My first two were born before her Noah arrived, so I had plenty of advice when it came to diaper rash and preparing children for the first day of kindergarten. As I listened to Penny relating so openly with her three kids on the phone, I thought I could learn a few things from her. In all our years of friendship, I'm not sure I ever had that thought before.

Is it possible that arrogance can masquerade as being "more experienced"? Did I think all these years that I was better than Penny simply because I didn't have all the childhood and teen stuff to get over?

That was the last thought I had before falling into a deep sleep. When I woke the next morning, it was nearly noon.

Penny was propped up in bed reading her Bible. When she saw I was looking at her, trying to focus my bleary eyes, she pushed her reading glasses up to the top of her head and giggled. "Guess where we are, Sharon? We're in Helsinki!"

I smiled. Then I remembered my lost luggage and frowned. "Do you think it's too early for me to call the airport about my luggage?"

Penny gave me a sympathetic look. "I called an hour ago. I didn't think you would mind; you were sleeping so deeply."

"What did they say?"

Penny shook her head. "They said there's no sign of your suitcase yet. They told me to try calling again this evening."

I pulled the covers over my head.

"Don't go back to sleep. You know what this means? We have to go shopping for some clothes for you!"

"Don't you want to make some phone calls and try to find your aunt first?" I peeled back the covers and propped myself up on my elbow.

"We can come back and start those phone calls later." Penny hopped out of bed. "Times like these call for an adjustment of priorities! The top of our list at this moment is new clothes."

And off we went. Twinkle dust everywhere.

A nonflirty taxi driver drove us through the streets of downtown Helsinki under dark, gray clouds. I stared at the profoundly solid stone buildings. Some were old with domes and architectural details of an era long gone. Modern buildings sprouted in unpredictable gaps standing straight, uncompromising, and sleek as silver. Quiet hung over the city and over us.

The taxi driver dropped us off in front of a tall brick building, and Penny paid him with the Finnish marks she had exchanged at the hotel before we left.

We dashed into the department store before the cold wind had a chance to find us. Just inside the door, to the right, Penny and I both spotted a corner bakery and chocolate counter.

Turning to face each other, we grinned and said in unison, "Yes, please!" Laughing at our old joke, we headed for the sweets before exploring the store.

I bought two small cookies dipped in chocolate and a mocha truffle.

"Is this breakfast or lunch?" Penny asked me before placing her order.

"Both?" I suggested.

"That's what I thought. I'm getting double then."

We found our way to the elevator and rode to the fourth floor, nibbling on our goodies all the way.

We found the women's section and looked through racks of pants. The sizing on the labels was different than what we had in the U.S. We had no idea what the exchange rate was, so the price meant nothing to us either.

Penny held up a pair of black pants in front of me. "What do you think? Basic. Serviceable. They feel like they would be warm."

"I wonder where I try them on?"

A woman wearing tiny wire-framed glasses stepped over to Penny and me and asked something in Finnish.

"Sorry," Penny said. "We only speak English."

"How may I help you?" The woman easily slipped into our language.

It amazed me that everyone we had met so far spoke English.

"Is there a dressing room where she can try these on?"

"Yes. This way, please."

"Wait a minute," I said. "I think I'll look around some more."

The young woman nodded, reached for the pants to hold them for me, and then politely followed me around at a distance. I randomly selected two other pairs of pants, a long brown-and-red floral skirt, and five or six tops, including a cute red sweater that would go great with the skirt.

The only thing that fit was the "serviceable" pair of black pants Penny had found. I remembered all over again why I disliked shopping. What is that verse about "hope deferred makes the heart sick"? That's how I felt when I shopped. I'd find darling pieces that went together to make what I thought was a cute outfit. I'd have it all figured out. Then I'd try on the clothes, and all my hopes would scatter. Nothing ever fit the way I thought it would.

"Don't look so glum," Penny said. "We have plenty of time."

"An abundance of time is not what I'm glum about. It's the abundance of other things." I patted my hip. "You won't miss these sweatpants of yours if I wear them all week, will you?"

Penny tilted her head and looked at me cautiously. "No.

You're welcome to the sweats. But you are going to buy the pants, aren't you? And a few new tops?"

I let Penny talk me into a sky blue turtleneck and a matching sweater that hung long and buttoned up the front. I'm sure it was outrageously expensive because the knit felt softer than anything I'd ever owned. Cashmere, I think.

"Now you look like a world traveler," Penny said. "I wondered what I would get you as an early birthday present, and I think this would be perfect."

"Penny, my birthday isn't until October."

"So? I'll be early for once. Now all you need is some new undies, and you'll barely miss your runaway luggage."

The shopping clerk, who had been following at a measured distance, asked if my luggage had been lost by an airline. I said it had, and she said the airlines often pay for the cost of replacing lost clothing.

"My husband was on a flight yesterday," the clerk said. "They were rerouted because of the bad weather."

"Our flight was rerouted, too," Penny said.

The attendant leaned close and confided, "I was very upset because it was my name day on Thursday, and my husband said we would celebrate on Friday when he came home. But he was too late for my party."

"Yesterday was your birthday?" Penny asked.

"No, my name day. In Finland every day is name day for a different name. For instance, my name is Tuija. It means a green bush."

"A green bush?" Penny questioned.

"Yes, a bush that is planted in front of a house for beauty. On Thursday all of the women in Finland named Tuija celebrated their name day. Here, I'll show you." Tuija slid a calendar out from under the clear plastic countertop at the cash register area. She showed us the month of February and pointed to the twenty-fifth. "Tuija day. Do you see?"

"Well, happy name day, a couple of days late." Penny opened her bag of goodies from the bakery downstairs. "Here, celebrate with a chocolate."

Tuija laughed. "Thank you, but I'm not allowed to eat while I work."

"Then take it for later," Penny said.

Penny once again was responding to someone with her never-met-a-stranger sense of camaraderie. Perhaps I had been too critical of her public relations skills.

Tuija gave in to Penny's generosity and accepted a truffle to save for later. She added up the prices on my new pants and sweaters and asked, "Are you visiting for long?"

"Only a week and a half." Penny pulled out her credit card.

"That's a long time. Most tourists I meet are here for only a day or two."

"I'm hoping to visit some relatives," Penny said.

"Do they live in Helsinki?"

Penny and I looked at each other. I tried hard not to show the slightest shade of condemnation in my expression.

"I'm not sure." Penny launched into her story and even added that we were at God's mercy on this adventure.

Tuija stopped punching numbers into the computerized cash register and gave Penny a smile. "I think God has given mercy to you today."

"He certainly has," Penny said. "It's not every day that Sharon and I get to go shopping and have cookies and truffles for breakfast."

"No, no. There is something else. My husband works for

the government." Tuija swished her hand in the air and said excitedly, "I don't know the word in English, but he makes records of all the people in Finland."

"He's a music producer?" Penny asked.

"No, no!" Tuija's cheeks were turning red. "I don't have the right English words. He makes all the information of where people live. He keeps the information for the telephones and the houses for all of Finland."

Penny and I looked at each other, trying to understand our flustered Finnish clothing clerk. "What I mean is that my husband can find your aunt."

Tuija made a phone call and told us we could meet her husband at his office if we left right away. He wasn't usually in the office on Saturday, she said, but he had gone in to catch up on a few matters after his business trip.

I had to forgo the purchase of some new underwear as we dashed off to catch a taxi to the government office building.

"This has God's fingerprints all over it, doesn't it?" Penny said once we were in the cab. "What if you hadn't lost your luggage, and what if we hadn't gone shopping in that department today, and—"

"And what if you hadn't been so good at public relations?" I added. "What if you hadn't offered Tuija some of your chocolate?"

Penny grinned. "So not all my schmoozing is evil. Is that what you're trying to say?"

"Something like that."

We arrived at the government building and were greeted in Finnish by the guard. After Penny explained to him in English that we had an appointment, the guard asked us to wait. Soon a young woman came down the elevator and greeted us with, "Will you follow?"

She led us up to the third floor and motioned toward a row of straight chairs in a small lobby. Taking that as our invitation to wait for Tuija's husband, we sat quietly, casually observing the two women who were standing a few feet away from us speaking Finnish. It was the first time we had been in a room where everyone didn't switch to speaking English when we arrived. I shifted in my seat, ignoring the unsettling feeling I had of being a couple of foreign specimens waiting on a shelf until it was time for us to be examined.

"Did Tuija say if we had an appointment at a certain time, or was her husband trying to fit us in?"

Penny shrugged. "I don't know. I guess we just wait and see what happens. How did you remember her name?"

"Tuija?"

"Yes," Penny said. "I don't think I'll be able to remember it."

"Didn't your mom speak Finnish sometimes when you were growing up?"

"Rarely. She wanted people to think she was an American. I know she worked hard to eliminate her accent when she tried to get a job in the film industry."

"I didn't know that. Did she want to be an actress?"

"No, she just wanted to work for a big Hollywood executive. She did for a few years. I think I was in the fourth or fifth grade when she worked at MGM. Or maybe it was Warner Brothers. I don't remember. She told me one time it was all too political, and she was let go."

"That's too bad."

"She went to work for a surgeon after that, and she worked for him for probably fifteen years. Funny thing was, the surgeon's wife was Swedish. She and my mom became close friends, and they spoke Swedish to each other all the time."

"Your mom spoke three languages?" I asked. "That's amazing."

"I know. I can barely manage English. I think she could get by with her French, too, if she had to. Swedish is the second official language here. You figured that out, didn't you?"

"No. Is that what they were speaking on the plane?"

"That would be my guess," Penny said. "Do you remember the flirty taxi guy telling us that the signs at the airport were all in Finnish, Swedish, and English?"

"No. I suppose I blocked out most of our charming conversation with that gentleman."

"I didn't," Penny said with a wink. "I even remember where the disco is located. I don't remember the name of it, but I think I could tell another cab driver how to get us there."

I sat still, studying Penny's expression.

"Kidding!" She gave my shoulder a friendly shove. "I'm only kidding! I wouldn't take you to a nightclub. Unless you really begged me to go, that is."

One of the closed doors opened, and a slender man stepped out. He greeted us in English, and we followed him into his office.

Penny explained her quest, pulling from her purse the limited bits of information she had, all in photocopied form. She had copies of her mother's birth certificate, some sort of school document, and two Christmas cards from her aunt. Penny showed him the returned letter from her aunt, and he confirmed Penny's suspicions.

"Yes, this message on the envelope means that this person no longer lives at this address. It is possible she has moved. Or..."

He looked at me and then at Penny. "She may be dead. Is that a possibility you have considered?"

"Yes," Penny answered solemnly. "I'm sure it's a strong possibility. She has to be in her early seventies at least. If she's still alive, that is."

Tuija's husband asked if he could make copies of all the pieces of paper and the photos Penny had shown him. He had a deep voice and sounded like a serious detective when he said, "I will find the answer for you. Where may I contact you, Ms. Lane?"

Penny told him the hotel where we were staying and asked how long he thought it might take to find some leads.

He didn't understand her question and asked her to repeat it.

"When do you think you will know something?" Penny asked.

"I will put my attention to this on *maanantai.*"

We looked at him blankly.

"*Maanantai.* Ah…Monday. Yes, Monday I will try to see what I can find for you."

"Thank you." Penny shook his hand.

I added, *"Kiitos."*

"Ole hyvä."

As we exited the building, Penny said, "Aren't you Little Miss International Ambassador of Good Manners!"

"What? Because I said *kiitos?*"

"Yes. I'm impressed."

"Don't be. It's not that hard to pronounce, Penny. People seem to like it when you try to communicate with them in their own language."

"Right now my language is hunger, and I'm hoping you're interested in communicating with me about something delicious and filling because I have a rippin' headache, and I'm hoping some food will help."

"I'm hungry, too. I should have brought the tour book. We could have tried one of the restaurants we circled."

"Circled-schmirkled. Come on." Penny linked her arm through mine. "We'll go find a restaurant and write about it in our own tour book someday. Wouldn't that be fun? We could do it. I know a magazine publisher in San Fran."

"Of course you do."

"She probably knows a few book publishers. How about it? We could call the book *Finland on a Whim* or *Happy in Helsinki*. What do you think, Sharon?"

"I think you should stick to schmoozing and selling houses."

"Do you really?"

"Yes, I really do."

"Good, because that's what I plan to do. I was thinking you could be the one to write the book. I'll promote it. I know a terrific artist who could do a great cover for us and...what? What's so funny?"

"You. You crack me up."

"How?"

"Penny, I could never write a book."

With a sudden jerk of our linked arms, Penny stopped in the middle of that icy downtown Helsinki sidewalk and turned to me with her fierce, fiery gaze. I didn't turn away.

"Sharon Marie Andrews, I am only going to say this once, so you better be listening with both ears."

I didn't blink.

"You are gifted and capable beyond your wildest imagination. You have not yet begun to explore all the ways you can make your life count for eternity. Strength and dignity are your clothing. It's time for you to drop your bucket deep down into the well of possibilities that you've been ignoring all these years. Drop it all the way down and see what you pull up."

I let out my breath. A fluffed cloud of chilled air floated between us for a moment and disappeared.

"Okay." It was all I could think to say at that frozen moment. I knew I would return many times in my mind to this street beside the gray stone building. And when I returned I would not remember the cold or the wind or the hunger pangs. I would only remember the intensity of Penny's voice, the ignited amber flecks in her eyes, and the way she looked at me as if she had decided long ago to set her favor and her friendship on me and nothing in this world would ever change that. I would return to this moment, and I would ponder what a woman like me looked like dressed in strength and dignity.

But for now, I said "okay," and that was enough of a response for her. We walked, arm in arm, in search of a restaurant.

Eight

Penny and I walked for several blocks with our coats buttoned up and our arms linked in an effort to brace ourselves against the shards of icy wind that raced in circles around the tall buildings. Everything looked old and yet well preserved. A few bundled-up businessmen and women brushed past us walking briskly.

"Do you suppose we should ask one of them if they know a good restaurant nearby?" I asked.

"No. Let's keep going and see what we find."

My ears were stinging from the wind. I wore gloves, but my hands still felt cold. The February sky above us seemed to be slowly closing its cloud-thick eyelids. The day would soon be enveloped by the night. Being so far north, the light here seemed thin and shy. I wondered if so far we had seen more midnight than we had daylight.

"Here." Penny pulled me with her into a small restaurant. "This is perfect."

"It looks Italian. Are you sure you want our first meal in Finland to be Italian?"

"Why not?" Penny smiled at one of the waiters, as he approached us and said something in Finnish.

"Table for two?" Penny held up two fingers.

"Ah, yes." The waiter held up two fingers back at us. "Come, please." He led us to a table by the window, which was nice because we could watch the world from a warm, snug corner.

"Do you have hot tea?" Penny opened her menu.

"Yes." He turned to me and held up his two fingers again. "Two?"

I nodded and used my useful Finnish word again. *"Kiitos."*

He smiled and nodded.

"Have you noticed how clean everything is?" I whispered across the table to Penny.

She looked around. "What do you mean 'clean'?"

"The hotel, the department store, the office building, and now this restaurant. Everything seems clean to me. Clean and tidy."

"We've only been gone a few days, Sharon. Are you having a strong urge to vacuum something?"

"No, I'm having a strong urge to eat something. Do you suppose they have meatballs here?"

"I'm trying to figure out if they have lasagna."

Our waiter returned with two white ceramic pots of hot water and a tea bag in each. I pulled off my gloves and wrapped my hands around the small pot. Ah, the simple pleasure of warm hands.

We dined for more than two hours at our window to the world. The tea cheered us. The darkness of the evening came quickly. Tall candles in fat wine jugs were lit throughout the restaurant, and more people arrived to fill the tables. All around us rolled the low murmur of conversation delivered at a leisurely pace. It wasn't at all like dining under the fluorescent lights at Larry's Family Restaurant in Chinook Springs. We felt no need to hurry, only the sense that we should lower our voices. Penny talked a lot about her job at the real estate office and how she loved showing young couples around houses and watching them get starry-eyed over the dream of owning their first home.

"I always think of how it was for Dave and me that day we moved out of the one-room tractor shed."

"With the drain in the floor," I added.

"Yes, the drain in the floor. We have you and Jeff to thank for getting us out of there and into our first home."

Looking down and tucking my hair behind my ear, I brushed off her praise.

"I don't think there will ever be a way to thoroughly thank you and Jeff for all you did for us. I told Dave that was part of the reason I wanted to bring you with me on this trip. I wanted to say thanks. Thanks for your friendship, Sharon. Sometimes I wonder where I'd be without you, and that's a scary thought. I'd probably be dead in some gutter somewhere. Or at least in prison."

I laughed.

"You think I'm joking. Wolf predicted I'd be dead before I was thirty."

"Wolf?"

Penny didn't move. Holding her forkful of lasagna in midair, Penny's left eyebrow elevated. She offered me a closed-mouth grin like a peace offering. "I never told you about Wolf, did I?"

"I think I would have remembered hearing about someone named Wolf."

Penny put down her fork, folded her hands, and leaned across our small table there in front of the window that opened to a dark, hidden world. "Wolf was sort of my first husband."

I told my face to stay still.

"I never told you because it was part of my messed-up life before Jesus and before Dave and before I even knew who I was. You told me once that you didn't want to hear about all that stuff." She seemed to be waiting for absolution or, at the very least, an invitation.

"I don't mind hearing about it now," I heard myself say. "I'd like to hear about Wolf, if you want to talk about him."

Relief washed over Penny's face. "Well, he was wild. I was, of course, on the wild side, too. I was seventeen, and you know, my mom didn't know anything. It was the sixties, and a couple of my friends were driving up to San Francisco in their VW Bug the day school was out. I thought I'd be gone for a week, but it turned out I was gone all summer."

I had heard bits about her summer in San Francisco before, but Penny had never shared details.

"I met Wolf in the park our first day in San Francisco. He had hair out to here with little wire-rimmed glasses, bell-bottoms, hippie beads, the whole flower child outfit. He was something to behold. Tall, with big feet laced up in these leather sandals he had made himself. I took one look at him, and I thought he was the coolest guy I'd ever seen. He looked up at me from where he was sitting under a tree. He got up, came over, and said, "Hey, Moonglow, wanna dance?"

"Moonglow, huh?"

"Yeah, Moonglow. He said wolves liked to howl at the glow

of the moon, and he wanted to howl at me."

"Now there's a clever pick-up line."

"It worked. But then, I was seventeen. He also said he liked my shirt. It was one of those embroidered Mexican wedding shirts. Do you remember those?"

I shook my head.

"Well, anyway, Wolf said he liked my embroidered shirt and my long hair. I thought his John-the-Baptist look was very cool, but he was doused with patchouli oil. Do you remember patchouli oil?"

I shook my head again. Penny and I may have lived during the same era, but I obviously didn't experience it the way she did.

"I never liked patchouli oil. It's too strong and too smoky-green, sweet-mossy smelling. But anyway, we danced to some earthy flute music a girl was playing a few yards away, and my friends ditched me. I didn't know where they went, so I stayed with Wolf."

"For how long?"

"About three months." Penny looked down and stuck her fork in her lasagna.

"Wow," I said quietly.

"Yeah, wow. Crazy, huh?"

I muttered Penny's longtime catch phrase, "Yeah, crazy like a daisy."

"Are you sure you want to hear all this, Sharon?"

I hesitated only a second before saying, "Yes, I do. I want to know about your whole life, not just the parts I made you clean up before you told me. I thought about this last night, Penny. I never should have censored you."

"Censored me?"

"You know what I mean. Like when you were baptized, and I told you only to talk about what God did in your life and not talk about your past."

Penny gave me a surprised look. "That was a long time ago. And you were right. It was much better to put the focus on Christ and not on me."

"What I'm trying to say is that I want you to feel the freedom to tell me whatever you want to tell me. I don't want you ever to hold back because you think I might be too sensitive."

"Thanks for saying that, Sharon. It does feel good to talk about Wolf after all these years. My perspective keeps adjusting the farther away I get from that time."

"So what happened during that summer when you were staying with Wolf?"

Penny paused and looked at me as if offering one last out before she dove in. When I didn't move, she said, "Okay. The uncut version of the summer I was seventeen. I should say that Wolf did a lot of drugs that summer. I didn't. I've never done well on any kind of meds, and maybe it's my controlling nature or something, but I couldn't stand not having all my faculties at full performance level.

"Wolf and I argued about the drugs a lot. We made stuff and sold it every weekend at this place called the Hippie Market."

"What did you make?"

"Hemp bracelets, bead necklaces, and these macramé things for hanging plants. Wolf made leather belts and sandals. We were married at the beach sometime in July. The minister said it was legal, but I doubted it. Of course, it didn't matter much at the time. Our calligraphied certificate said, 'On this day Wolf and Moonglow were united by Bob, Minister of World Peace.'"

"Oh, Penny." I covered my mouth and tried not to laugh.

"I know. Go ahead, you can laugh. It seems incredible to me now. When Dave and I met five years later, I tried to make sure I wasn't still legally married to Wolf. I took my marriage certificate to the county clerk, and he pretty much laughed me out of his office."

"Whatever happened to him? Wolf, I mean?"

"We had a huge fight on a cold night in August, and before you say anything, yes, it can get miserably cold in San Francisco on summer nights. Wasn't it Mark Twain who said the coldest winter he ever spent was a summer in San Francisco?"

I shrugged.

"Anyway. I was done being a flower child. I wanted to leave San Francisco and go home. I told Wolf we could live at my mom's until we could afford a place of our own. Wolf said I was uptight, locked in to the establishment, and destined to burn myself out and die before I turned thirty."

"That was a pretty awful thing to say."

"I said worse things to him. It was so ugly, you know? We were trapped in this big deception that we were free and living in the summer of peace and love. But it wasn't free or peaceful or loving at all. It was dark and lonely and painfully stupid. My mother was a saint for taking me back without a lot of questions."

I gazed into the flickering candlelight at our table. "Do you ever wonder if Wolf is the one who ended up dead before he was thirty?"

"Good question. Who knows? Wolf could have discovered the computer industry like Dave did and now be Mr. Corporate America. He was very intelligent and great at figuring things out."

"Have you ever thought how strange it is that you and Dave now live in San Francisco?"

Penny nodded. "I like San Francisco a lot more now than I did then. The park is still pretty much the same. One time I was there with the kids, and I thought I heard flute music. I stood in the park thinking, 'Did my past really happen here? Or did I dream it up and the park just happens to resemble this one?' I'm such a different person now. She sighed. "So that's the scoop on Wolf."

"Thank you, Penny. Thank you for giving me your story."

"My story. Yes, that's what it is." She pushed away her dinner plate. "For better or worse, it's definitely my story. I can't change it. I'm just grateful God did."

We silently sipped our warm tea, finding solace in the candle's golden glow. Outside tiny snowflakes flung themselves against the window, as if they were trying to come inside and share our moment. I felt protected. Not only from the determined snowflakes, but also as if my whole life I'd been protected from the cold world out there.

The waiter placed the check on the table. Penny pulled out a credit card. "I would like to go to church tomorrow," she said. "How about you?"

"Sure." I remembered how limited my wardrobe was and added, "If I can borrow something nice to wear."

As it turned out, I wore one of Penny's long skirts with my new blue sweater set on Sunday morning; but I never took off my coat, so it didn't really matter. We sat toward the back of the sanctuary. A stiff chill raced underneath our pew and sent rows of goose bumps up my legs.

The traditional service included lots of standing and sitting, which kept the blood flowing to my feet. The liturgy was all in Finnish, of course, but read with such gentle rhythm that I closed my eyes and imagined the words to be a long, lovely poem.

What I loved was the solemnity of the worship. I loved the solid beauty of this old sanctuary and the way this was definitely a church every day of the week. It wasn't a multipurpose room with folding chairs and tilted-up basketball hoops like our church in Chinook Springs. We were sitting reverently in a holy place that had been set apart for one purpose, and because I shared that purpose with those around me, the language wasn't a barrier.

I stared at one of the stained glass windows that depicted Jesus standing on the shore, calling out to the disciples as they were fishing. I guessed it was based on the time when they fished all night and caught nothing. Jesus told them to cast their nets on the other side of the boat, and when they did what He said, they couldn't pull up all the fish they had caught.

The sunlight came through the window so clearly that the silvery fish seemed bright enough to jump out of the net and ride a yellow and green beam of light all the way into the boat. I thought about those trusting disciples. What an illogical command it was. "Cast your nets on the other side of the boat." Why? Why would there be a bounty of fish on one side when all night nothing had been caught on the other side?

My mind wandered as I thought about Penny's and my illogical trip. Is it possible that Christ commanded the same sort of thing from His disciples today? When we jumped over the moon, was Jesus asking us to cast our nets on the other side of the world to catch more…more what?

People getting up from the pews and going forward to take

communion interrupted my thoughts. As long as I could remember, communion had been brought to me; I didn't go to it. Communion was passed to me on a doily in the form of tiny, pressed pellets and plastic thimbles of grape juice.

Rising with the others, Penny and I made our way down the aisle while a soprano sang a cappella from the balcony. I felt as if we had been transported to medieval times and were participating in an ancient ritual.

Then I realized we were.

How many millions of believers for these thousands of years have come to hundreds of thousands of communion tables just like the one we were approaching? How many times had those believers done what Penny and I were about to do in remembrance of Christ?

On this solid table, covered with a pure white linen cloth, a single candle burned. An exquisite goblet stood round and tall beside a round loaf of thick-crusted bread. The bread had been broken in two. I watched how Penny partook, and then I stepped forward, broke off a piece of bread, and dipped it in the goblet. Closing my eyes, I silently prayed and touched the bread to my tongue. My mouth woke up.

That was wine. The goblet is filled with wine!

All my senses were at full alert as I followed the other pilgrims down the aisle. *Your blood, Jesus. Your blood. Shed for me. Your body. Broken. For me.*

I didn't expect the tears that came as I swallowed the small piece of sharp, holy remembrance. I knew that when I returned home, communion would mean so much more than it ever had because I was seeing the sacrifice of Christ with new eyes.

I sat with my head bowed, letting the tears drip on my folded hands. The congregation rose to sing a final hymn.

"Holy, Holy, Holy." I knew almost all the words in English, so I sang along as the tears continued to race down my cheeks. The service ended with a benediction, but I didn't want to leave. I wanted to linger in this holy place. I watched the faces of God's people as they exited. One elderly woman wearing a hat made eye contact with me. I smiled, and she smiled back.

I'll see you in heaven, won't I, Gentle Woman? I couldn't remember ever having thoughts like these at home when I went to church.

"I wish I had my Bible," I told Penny, as we walked three blocks to a restaurant we had spotted on the way to church.

"Is it in your suitcase?"

"No, I left it at home. I miss having it. Isn't that strange? I have nothing except the miscellaneous items in my purse and the clothes I'm wearing, but the only thing I miss is my Bible."

We talked about the church service over a simple lunch of yogurt, rye toast, and hard-boiled eggs at the deli-style restaurant. Penny had the same sorts of feelings I'd had.

I told her what I was thinking about when I looked at the shimmering fish in the stained glass window, and she said, "It sounds to me as if you did cast your net on the other side of your life today at communion. Look at all the shimmering bits of glory you're pulling in now!"

I liked that. Shimmering bits of glory. I liked the idea of living a life that was full of silvery, flapping bits of shimmering glory. I felt as if all the fences and filters were coming off my sheltered life. Penny was giving me her story, uncensored. I was partaking of communion, undiluted. All that had been shadows in my understanding were taking solid form.

For the rest of the day I felt the lingering beauty of the worship service and the piercing reminder that filled my mouth when I tasted the bread and the wine.

We toured two downtown Helsinki parks in the pale winter sunshine. When we were too cold to walk anymore, we found a little place that served thick, strong coffee with cubes of sugar and tiny silver pots of cream. Penny had a slice of cake with a puddinglike frosting, and I had an expensive bowl of arctic brambleberries with cream. Penny tried mine and said I definitely had made the better choice.

We walked back to our hotel after dinner and fell into bed feeling fully "sabbathed," as Penny put it.

Monday morning our first priority was to contact the airport to check on my luggage. The clerk on the other end of the phone said they had a possible lead on where my bag had been misrouted, but they hadn't been able to confirm it.

"Please call again this evening," the nasal-sounding voice said on the other end of the phone.

"I will. Believe me, I'll call again."

Penny thought we shouldn't contact Tuija's husband at the government offices until later in the afternoon. That left the morning open for more shopping. All the department stores had been closed on Sunday, and I was glad. It had caused us to slow down, walk in the park, and talk about a dozen things other than ourselves or our bodies.

Taking a cab back to the large department store we had visited on Saturday, Penny suggested we bypass the chocolate counter because she wanted to buy a lot and didn't want to carry it all over the store. We headed straight for the lingerie department.

I should let it be known at this point in the story that my whole life I have shopped for underwear at K. C. Lorren's, which was the only department store in our area for almost thirty years before they built the Westland Mall. I'm certain my mom took me to K. C. Lorren's for my first bra, and from then on, Lorren's was the only place to buy what my mother had referred to as "unmentionables."

I rode the elevator with Penny thinking, *How can I possibly buy unmentionables in Helsinki when I can barely bring myself to buy them at home? At least at Lorren's I know what to look for and where everything is located, and that makes it a quick trip.*

If I could have put off this task until I got home, I would have. But I didn't want to go another day sporting Penny's saggy silkies.

Selecting the panties turned out to be easy. Kaylee, whenever she helped fold clothes, referred to my style of underwear as "basic cotton Mom-o panties." Apparently they are a standard model available for Mom-os around the world because I found a package of white Mom-os right away.

"You and your Mom-o basics," Penny teased me. "Do you remember when we burned that pair of Mom-o denim jeans?"

"Yes! Those pants were pathetic!"

"I know. I can't believe we didn't save them and try to enter them into the *Guinness Book of World Records* for 'most worn pair of ugly pants.'"

The legacy of the Mom-o denims started when I was pregnant for the first time. The jeans were a strange color. Sort of a nasty faded khaki green. My sister-in-law, Bonnie, gave me the baggy pants when I was two months pregnant because she said she liked having something loose to wear the first few months before she needed maternity clothes and then again during the few months after the baby was born.

She was right. I appreciated the worn-in comfort and elastic waist. I wore them when I was pregnant with Tyler and Ben and then loaned them to Penny after she had Noah. We traded those hideous pants back and forth through all seven of our combined pregnancies. I mended them twice and was certain they eventually would disintegrate in the washing machine. But they didn't.

One clear autumn afternoon, Penny came over with the green Mom-o denims in a big wad. "Don't let the kids see us do this," she said. "But we're going to torch these Mom-o losers!"

"Why?"

"Our pregnancy days are over, Sharon. Neither you nor I will ever wear these hideous blobber-britches again. That's why they must burn. The world should never again be exposed to the sight of them."

We made sure the kids were all inside. Penny and I went to the far corner of the backyard by the huge rhododendron bush. With our backs to the house, we doused the wad with lighter fluid and each struck a match in unison.

"In the name of all that is decent and fashionable," Penny stated, "we hereby ignite these slacks and vow never again to cover our flesh with pea green denim."

"Agreed." I solemnly tossed my match in with Penny's and *kapoosh!* We could have roasted marshmallows over the leaping flame. I shoveled the remaining ashes beneath the rhododendron and told Penny we would have to pay attention the next May to see if the rhodies blossomed with a green tint.

"You aren't regretting that you threw away your old bra at the airport, I hope," Penny said.

"No. It had served its full tour of duty. You were right. It needed to be tossed out."

"Good. Now you can replace it with something stunning."

Penny kept holding up lacy, colorful numbers while I gravitated toward the basic cotton wide-strap Mom-o styles. The sizing was different than in the States, so I had to try on a variety of styles before I had a fair idea of what would work for me.

"Try looking for one that's the same size as this one." I handed a bra to Penny over the top of the dressing room door. "Only see if they have it in white."

"Are you sure I can't interest you in another color?" Penny asked. "I think I saw this one in bright orange."

"Just white, if you please."

"What about lavender or something blue to match your new sweater outfit? They have light blue, Sharon. That's almost white."

"Plain, normal white works for me," I said impatiently from inside the dressing room.

I was trying to figure out the front snap on a pink floral underwire bra when Penny irreverently tossed two more bras over the top of the dressing room door. Neither was white.

"Penny!" I opened the door a crack. "What's the deal? Don't they have any white ones in my size?"

"I'm declaring a boycott on white bras. Life is too short. You need to live a little." Penny slipped into the dressing room and closed the door behind her. "Hey, now that pink one is a winner! It looks great on you!"

"Hardly! I was only trying it on to get a better idea of the size I need." I glanced at my reflection. "This looks like the top of a bikini that would only be worn by someone who doesn't want to keep a lot of secrets."

"Jeff would love it," Penny said. "You should get it."

I felt myself blushing. "Jeff wouldn't notice."

"Oh, yes he would. All men notice their wives' undergarments. They might not ever mention them, especially if there's nothing particularly exceptional worth mentioning. But believe me, they notice."

I couldn't remember Jeff ever making a comment about my undies, positive or negative.

"I have a theory." Penny planted herself on the narrow bench in the dressing room. "Men who have affairs have them with women who wear memorable undies."

I turned my back on Penny and undid the pink bra so I could modestly try on the light blue one.

"Mind you," Penny went on, "the men don't know at the onset that the woman is wearing memorable undergarments. But the woman knows. She knows how good she looks under her clothes, and she walks around as if she has a secret just waiting to be revealed."

"Oh, Penny, I can't believe you're talking about this."

"It's my little theory. Part of what I've learned after the past two years of working in a large office." Penny crossed her legs and picked up the pink padded bra for closer examination. In a low voice she said, "I only worked there a month before I went out and upgraded my lingerie wardrobe."

I paused. Why was Penny telling me she upgraded her unmentionables? Slowly turning to meet her gaze, I said in a low voice, "Penny?"

She looked at me innocently.

"You're not trying to say that…" I knew Penny couldn't, wouldn't ever be unfaithful to her beloved Dave. "Tell me again exactly why you went out and bought new underwear?"

Nine

"For Dave," Penny said. "I decided to buy the cha-cha undies because my husband works at a big office, and you know dozens of women are strutting around there in memorable underwear. I spiced up my lingerie so that Dave would remember what he had waiting for him at home."

"Oh."

"Why? What did you think?"

"I wasn't sure what you were getting at."

"I'm suggesting that you spiff up your undies. It's for Jeff, not for you."

I looked in the mirror at my less-than-glamorous body. I won't go into details, but I will say that I had done very little over the years to "spiff up" the part of my person only my husband sees. Penny probably was right. My landscaper husband would appreciate a little color and lift in what he saw every day.

With a fresh eye, I evaluated the pretty, light blue bra. It looked softer and smoother than my standard, industrial-strength style. Plus, it had more support.

"I like this one," I said bravely. "I'll buy this one."

"Bravo! Now I'll go find matching blue panties."

"I don't need blue panties."

"Yes, you do," Penny said. "Where's the package of panties you picked up? I want to match the size." She started to leave the dressing room but stopped and with a grin said, "You really should buy two bras, you know. In case you have any more disasters with foreign babies."

"Penny, I'm not going to have any more baby disasters."

She wasn't listening. "How about a black bra and panties to match? Trust me, once you wear black, you'll never go back to white."

I bought two bras that day in Helsinki. One light blue and one black. With four pairs of matching panties.

Penny said she was proud of me and that I should consider my expensive purchases as souvenirs for Jeff.

All I could think of was the souvenir money I was carrying around for Uncle Floyd and Joanie from the Clip 'n' Curl. I was certain both of them had something other than underwear in mind when they blessed me with souvenir money.

With Uncle Floyd on my mind, I convinced Penny to take a detour to the stationery department before loading up our shopping bags at the chocolate bar. I found postcards and bought stamps there as well. I asked for specialty stamps, like Uncle Floyd wanted me to. I'm not sure exactly what I ended up with, but that evening I planned to write all ten postcards and mail them with the hopes that they would arrive home before I did.

However, none of the postcards was written that night because we had a promising breakthrough in our case of locating Penny's missing aunt. Tuija's husband at the government office agreed to meet with us at four o'clock. He greeted us with a professional demeanor and invited us to sit down.

"I have information," our deep-voiced detective said. "I have located your aunt, Marketta Järvenin. This is her phone number. I called her today, and she is eager to talk with you."

Penny jumped up and grabbed the slip of paper with the phone number. "My aunt is still alive?"

"Yes. Would you like to place a call to her now?"

Penny stared at the paper in her hand. "No," she said slowly. "I'd rather go back to our hotel and call her. This is such great news. Thank you so much." Penny reached for his hand and shook it eagerly. "You have no idea how much I appreciate this. Thank you."

Penny and I took a cab to our hotel. Joona was on duty at the front desk. Irrepressible Penny left me waiting at the elevator while she dashed over to tell him the good news. Just as the elevator arrived, Penny motioned for me to join her at the front desk.

"Joona is going to help me make the call in case my aunt doesn't speak English and I need an interpreter."

Ever-helpful Joona dialed the number on the phone at his front desk and handed the phone to Penny.

"What is this crazy sound?" Penny held out the phone and laughed nervously. "I can't tell if it's ringing or if she's electrocuting her cat."

She handed the receiver to Joona, who appeared to be trying hard to repress a grin. Apparently someone answered because Joona conversed in what sounded like serious tones. He wrote furiously on a hotel notepad. Penny and I kept looking at each other, about to burst with curiosity as the conversation went on. When Joona looked up at us, Penny was squeezing my arm.

"Well?"

"Your aunt would like you to come to her home tomorrow," Joona said.

"Tell her yes!"

"You may tell her yourself. She speaks English."

"You goof, why didn't you tell me that?" Penny grabbed the phone. "Hello?"

I stood by her side, smiling and watching Penny's face. A new galaxy of golden adventure dust sparkled in her misty eyes.

"Yes...Of course...Okay...Yes...Wonderful...Yes...Tomorrow afternoon... Okay. Bye!"

All aglitter, Penny turned to Joona. "She said you wrote down the information on how to get to her house."

"Yes." Joona tore off the page of notes and handed it to Penny saying, "Here is the information."

Penny looked at the paper and looked back at Joona. "It's in Finnish."

"Is it?" Joona grinned.

"Yes, it is. Would you be so kind as to tell me what this says?"

"Certainly. I will write the directions for you in English. Is there anything else I may do for you, Ms. Lane?"

"Yes, there is something else. You can tell me what the going rate is for tipping hotel clerks when they have been especially helpful."

"I cannot accept a tip," Joona said.

"How about gifts?" Penny held up one of her shopping bags. "I have chocolate, and I'm not afraid to share it."

He shook his head.

"Okay. Then I'll just have to tell your manager how helpful

you've been. Hand me a piece of paper there, will you?"

Penny wrote her glowing report of Sir Joona the Helpful while Sir Joona wrote out the information about Marketta in English for us.

Over the years I've noticed how Penny can look as if she's eighteen when the lighting is soft enough and when she tilts her head just right. All the necessary elements were working for her at that moment. She handed Joona her note and, with a tease in her voice, said, "Feel free to translate *that* into Finnish for your boss."

He gave a noble bow, as if Penny had just knighted him.

Penny pulled a business card from her purse and handed it to Joona. She suddenly looked well over forty. "If you ever come to San Francisco, you have a free place to stay at our home. Our neighbor has a son who is twenty-one. I'm sure he could direct you to all the hot spots."

I thought I caught a fleck of adventure dust sparkling from the corner of Joona's eye. "Yes. Thank you. I may come someday."

"Good."

With that, Penny turned, and we paraded through the lobby as she led me straight to the hotel restaurant. "Time to eat," she declared.

We were seated in the middle of the restaurant when I noticed Penny's hand was shaking. "Are you okay?"

"I'm more than okay. I'm ecstatic! This is incredible. My mom's sister is still alive. What a gift from God! It's pretty much a miracle, don't you think?"

"Yes!"

"Just think, Sharon. What if you hadn't lost your luggage? We wouldn't have gone shopping, and we wouldn't have met Tuija and…"

I didn't share Penny's enthusiasm over the major inconvenience of my lost luggage. But I did agree it was remarkable to have found Marketta.

Penny looked as if she were about to cry.

"Are you sure you're okay?"

Penny put down her menu. The first tear left the starting gate, followed by a dozen equally eager racers. "My mom's sister is still alive. I have a living aunt! I thought she was dead, Sharon. When her letter came back, I thought for sure Marketta was dead. But she's alive. I have someone left in this world!"

I'm not sure I fully grasped what Penny was saying through her tears. But I agreed. "You know what, Penny? You're absolutely right. This is a miracle. All of it. The lost luggage, Tuija, and her husband. Tomorrow you're going to meet your aunt."

"I know!"

"I think this calls for something extra special for dinner. We need to celebrate!"

"What did you have in mind?" Penny ran a finger under each eye and blinked away her final tears.

"I'm not sure yet." I scanned the menu.

"Here it is!" Penny said. "Reindeer."

I closed my menu with a dramatic sigh. "How will I ever explain to my Joshie that I ate one of Santa's helpers?"

Penny gave me an odd look, and then, catching on to my silly joke, she burst out laughing. "That has to be the dumbest joke you've ever told! Besides, it's reindeer, not elves. We're not going to eat Santa's little helpers!"

I laughed way too loud for a forty-one-year-old woman who was dining in a nice restaurant. An impolite snort followed my guffaw.

Penny looked at me with both eyebrows raised and then laughed. It was a mixture of nervous laughter and light-headed giddiness. She covered her mouth in an effort to quiet herself, but it didn't help. The laughter leaked out. She couldn't stop.

All during dinner we kept laughing. Penny would cover her mouth with her napkin, try hard to restrain herself for a few minutes, and then *boom,* the laughter bomb would explode all over again. Her shoulders shook, and the tears tumbled to the table.

I gave up trying to appear sophisticated and hold in my companion laughter. I allowed one shoulder-flinching chuckle to leak out, and it was all over. I couldn't stop laughing either. Everything was funny. Funny and miraculous and sparkling.

I suppose the reindeer meat was good. I was too busy trying not to choke from our laughter to notice how it tasted. If I remember correctly, it was a little tough. I liked the mashed potatoes and the lingonberry sauce that came with the specialty dinner.

Penny said her reindeer tasted like a wild Canadian moose and that got me laughing because I was sure she had an equally wild Canadian story to explain why she knew what moose tasted like.

"No," Penny protested. "I've never tasted moose steak. Just moose jerky. However, I have smelled a wild Canadian moose from rather close up, and this meat tastes the same as that moose smelled."

I attempted to say, "Oh, Penny, you and your bionic nose." What came out was "Oh, Benny, you and your myopic toes." That sent us over the edge. I thought Penny was going to fall off her chair.

I'm sure the few other guests in the restaurant that evening were convinced we were drunk. All we were drinking was mineral water. Penny said some giggle enzyme in the reindeer meat must have got us going.

I felt younger and freer than I'd felt even when I was young and free. Laughter, being a powerful elixir, can cloud one's reasoning. I secretly—very secretly—hoped Penny would bring up the taxi driver's suggested disco because the way I felt right then, I think I would have agreed to go with her.

However, Penny wasn't thinking of discos. She was thinking of Marketta and kept saying things like, "I can't believe she's alive!"

We returned to our room and pulled out the tour book to see how far it was to Marketta's town of Porvoo. Only twenty miles. Our trip tomorrow would be shorter than we first imagined.

While Penny organized her outfit for the morning, I called airport baggage claim again. Still no word on my luggage.

I asked about filling out the paperwork to be reimbursed for my loss. The clerk told me I had completed all the necessary paperwork, but they had one more day of checking for the luggage before they could file the claim. If the suitcase never appeared, the compensation check would be sent to my permanent address.

Donning the hotel robe as I climbed into bed, I settled in for a cozy night's sleep. My jaw hurt from laughing. I kept stretching my mouth open and closed.

"What do you think Marketta will be like?" Penny had scooped up her thick, cocoa hair in a clip so that her tresses appeared to spout out of the top of her head like a little fountain.

"She will be wonderful, I'm sure," I said. "What do you know about her?"

"Not much. She sent me handmade birthday cards when I was little, and she sent Dave and me a small painting of a mountain lake as a wedding present. You know the picture I'm talking about? When we were in the yellow house it hung on the wall on the left side as you walked in the front door."

"Oh yes, I remember. It had a frame made out of birch."

"Yes. That was from Marketta. I have two photographs of her. I should have brought them with me, I suppose. The first one is of my mom and Marketta holding up a fish. I think my mom was about twelve."

"I've seen that one. Didn't you used to have it on the dresser in your bedroom?"

"Yep. The other one of Marketta you probably never saw. It's a family photo that came with her Christmas card the year after Dave and I married. She looked so much like my mom in that picture. I was going to frame it, but I never did."

"Just think." I propped myself up in bed with the pillows under my elbow. "Tomorrow you're going to meet her face-to-face."

"I know. I didn't think this actually would happen."

"You really didn't?"

"No, I really didn't."

"Even on the airplane when you were so lighthearted about everything and telling Monique that it was all going to work out? Didn't you believe your own prophecy?"

Penny slowly shook her head. "I wanted to hope, but this whole trip and finding my aunt is much bigger than what I thought God would do for us."

"What did you think God would do? I mean, why did you still want to come to Finland after Marketta's letter came back undelivered? What did you think we would do while we were here?"

"See things. Smell things. Eat things. Pretty much everything we've been doing. I wanted to be in the land of my mother's birth to see her world."

Penny gave her answer with such feeling, it sounded as if it were a line from a play. A line she had practiced enough to deliver it on cue with finesse.

"Well, it's a good thing we came now because Marketta might not have been around if we waited until all our kids graduated from high school."

"Exactly. And who's to say that both of us will still be around eight or ten years from now?"

"We will be," I said confidently.

Penny grew quiet. She stretched out on top of her bed and lay still with her head on her arm. "You're changing, Sharon."

"I am? Why do you say that? How am I changing?"

"Subtle little ways. You're becoming more sure of yourself, and that's making you daring and courageous."

"You mean like buying blue underwear?"

"Yes, that and other things like the way you stuck with this trip even though Ben broke his wrist. You used to be more passive."

"More of a martyr? Is that what you're saying?"

"No, I don't think you ever played the role of Suffering Sue. You spent years graciously stepping back and putting your personal preferences on hold so you could accommodate others. Now you're getting more adventuresome. I think it's a good thing."

"Thanks to you and this trip. If you hadn't invited me to come with you, I wouldn't be more adventuresome. I'm sure I haven't said it enough yet, but thank you, my friend."

"You are welcome, my friend. You know what else I think?" Penny sat up and looked directly at me, as if she were bestowing a blessing. "I think the second half of your life will be much fuller than the first half."

I thought of Penny's earlier admonition for me to drop my bucket deep into the well of unexplored possibilities and to clothe myself with strength and dignity. Somehow that image linked in my mind with the stained glass picture of Christ's disciples casting their nets on the other side of the boat.

"What was it you said the other day, Penny, about our lives being full of shimmering bits of glory? I'm sure the second half of life will be rich for both of us." I was saying this to a woman who had lived a whole lot of life before she even turned twenty. Even so, I believed the future would be bright for the two of us.

Penny sighed, as if she were contemplating my comment. She didn't respond.

"Can't you see us on our return trip to Helsinki when we're eighty?" I painted a picture of a couple of white-haired, feisty chicks in white tennis shoes. "Of course, by then you and I will be wearing hot pink underwear with sparkles because, you know, we'll need all the help we can get in the glamour department."

Penny didn't laugh the way she had at dinner.

"Hey, I thought my joke was pretty funny."

"It was."

"Penny, what's going on with you? Turn this way. I want to see your eyebrows."

"You don't need to see my eyebrows. I'm not hiding some surprise up my sleeve. It's just that…"

"What?"

"I'm forty-six, Sharon."

"I know," I said sympathetically. I flashed back to the night of Kaylee's concert when I realized I was fully forty-one. "Reality hits pretty hard every now and then, doesn't it?"

Penny sat up straight and with precise words said, "My mother was forty-six years old when her heart suddenly stopped on an otherwise uneventful afternoon."

We sat for a moment in shared contemplation.

"You're healthy and strong and very much alive, Penny. I don't think you should assume that your heart will suddenly stop just because you're forty-six."

"Of course you don't think I should assume that. All your close relatives are still living. Your genetic disposition is full of promises of longevity."

I thought about my husband, our children, Jeff's extended family, my extended family, and suddenly I realized how rich I was in people. Penny was right. All of them were still alive. All of them were in my daily life. I never had considered how Penny's not being connected to any blood relatives could create a hole within her heart.

We talked deep into the night in our extravagantly comfortable hotel room. Penny suggested we pray together.

I fell asleep in the middle of her prayer. My dreams floated right on the surface of my sleep, like water lilies on a pond. The floating dreams were of Marketta. I pictured her as a round, cheerful woman just like Mrs. Coates, my fourth grade teacher, who used to call me "Little Lamb" and put gold stars on all my homework papers.

The Aunt Marketta of my dream lived in a gingerbread cottage and offered sweets to us. Penny was popping the candies into her mouth while I hid mine in my pocket because I thought I needed to leave a trail so we could find our way home.

I don't usually remember my dreams, but that one was so close to the surface and so vivid that I woke the next morning feeling as if this hotel room and my adventure with Penny were my real life. Jeff and the kids seemed like a pleasant memory from another time and another place.

While Penny took a shower, I tried to call my family but only got the answering machine. I waited for the beep and said, "Hi. It's Mom. Everything is fine. Actually, it's great. We found Penny's aunt, and we're going to meet her today. I love you guys. Bye."

Hanging up, I realized I hadn't said, "I miss you."

Do I miss them?

No, I decided that at that moment, I honestly didn't miss them. Not right then, at least. And I didn't feel guilty about not missing them, either. I couldn't remember ever feeling this way. I knew the homesickness with its spiny twinges of responsibility would return eventually, but for now I was a free woman.

Just then the phone beside me rang, and I jumped like a guilty cat. Perhaps I wasn't as unencumbered as I thought I was.

Ten

A woman's voice on the other end of the phone asked, "Is this Penny?"

"No, this is Sharon."

"I am Marketta, Penny's aunt."

"Marketta, hello! Penny is excited about meeting you today."

"This is why I called. Do you know what time you will be coming?"

I told her we had a bus schedule and had talked about arriving in the early afternoon, if that was convenient for her.

"Yes, that is good. And when will you be leaving?"

"I'm not sure. Before dinner, probably."

Marketta didn't respond. Did I say the wrong thing?

"I mean for you to stay with me for all the days of your visit. Not just the afternoon. Is that not your plan?"

"We don't have much of a plan," I answered plainly and then cringed at my honesty.

"You must stay with me. I have been making my home

ready. Please tell Penny I say you must do this. You must stay with me."

"Okay."

Just then someone from room service knocked on the door with the breakfast Penny had ordered.

"I'll tell Penny. We'll come to your home early this afternoon."

"With your suitcases!" Marketta said firmly before hanging up.

Well, at least with Penny's suitcases, I thought as I opened the door and motioned for the young woman to bring in our coffee and croissants. She nodded and left the tray on top of the desk.

"Is the food here?" Penny opened the bathroom door, and a cloud of fragrant steam followed her out.

"Right here. And guess what? Your aunt just called, and she expects us to stay at her house. She said she's been making arrangements."

Penny stood still. The thick hotel towel wobbled slightly in its twisted turban on top of her head. "She wants us to stay with her?"

"Yes. I couldn't say no very graciously."

"Why would you say no?"

"I didn't know if you wanted to stay with her."

Penny sat down and blew her nose. "Of course I want to stay with her. I want to wrap her up and put her in my pocket so I can have my very own relative for the rest of my life."

"She's expecting us early this afternoon."

"Perfect. Do you have any sinus medication in your purse? I think I'm getting a cold."

"Yes. Help yourself. The white ones in the plastic bag are the nondrowsy sinus pills."

The phone rang. Penny reached for it and listened. She

interjected a few words like, "Oh…Uh-huh…Okay…What?" Then she burst out laughing. "Yes, yes. I got it." She jotted down a few notes. "Thanks. Bye."

"Who was that? Marketta?"

"No." Penny sat down and laughed. "Are you ready for this?"

"I don't know. Am I?"

"That was baggage claim."

My heart sank. If Penny was laughing so hard, the news couldn't be good.

"Did they find my suitcase?"

"Sort of. You know how they print out the tags with three letters for the airport?"

"Yes?"

"Well," Penny laughed another twenty seconds before finishing her sentence. "Your suitcase tag was apparently printed with *H-E-K.*"

"Penny! Where is *H-E-K?*"

"China!"

I stared at her.

"Your clothes took a trip without you! They went to China all by themselves." Penny rolled over on the bed laughing.

"Where in China?"

Penny drew in a quick breath. "I wrote it down. It's some place called Heihe, China!"

I didn't think it was funny at all.

For the first time in my life, I wanted to tell Penny to shut up. However, being such a politely repressed best friend, I said nothing. I stood there, arms folded across the front of me, scowling like a crow.

Penny noticed my stance. She held up her hands and

pulled back her laughter. "I'm sorry. I shouldn't laugh. It's not funny." Then she motioned that she was zipping her lips.

I marched over to the breakfast tray, breathing deeply. With a knife in my clenched hand, I tore into my croissant as if it were a chicken I was deboning.

"Did they say anything else? Like when I'll get it back?"

"Apparently it's not easy to get luggage out of customs once it's in China."

"Ever?"

Penny shook her head. "I'm sorry, Sharon. It doesn't look as if you'll get your luggage back. The guy on the phone said they were going to file the claim for you. The reimbursement will go to your home address within a month."

I took a swig of coffee and returned the cup to the saucer with a clatter. "Did they say how my suitcase got there?"

"A typo?" Penny suggested.

"I can't believe this."

I pictured the wife of some Chinese customs officer trying on my clothes. Certainly she would rage that the next time her husband brought home some loot, it better be of more value than the items in my worthless suitcase.

"Okay." I allowed the slightest grin of irony to pull at the corners of my mouth. "I'm not going to let it bother me. I'll need to go back to the department store to buy a few things before we leave for Marketta's. Do you think we have time to do that this morning?"

"Sure," Penny said. "Do you need anything else?"

"A few cosmetics, and I guess I'll need a suitcase of some sort."

"Perfect. Onward we go! Are you going to take a shower?"

"Why? Does your bionic nose tell you I need one?"

"No, my bionic nose is out of order," Penny said with an exaggerated sniff.

I showered, Penny packed, and we checked out of the hotel before ten. Our departure was much less memorable than our arrival. The same was true of our shopping trip. I knew what I wanted and made quick decisions, putting everything on the credit card that I had brought along for emergencies. My decisions were a lot less painful than making purchases at home because I hadn't figured out the exchange rate, so I had no idea how much I was spending. Plus, I figured the airline would compensate me.

We caught the 1:05 bus to Porvoo. Penny was sneezing like crazy. One of our purchases when we bought my cosmetics was a box of tissues.

"I never took those cold pills this morning," she said once we were settled on the bus. "Mind if I fish them out of your purse?"

"Help yourself." I handed Penny my shoulder bag while I searched through my shopping bag for a pair of socks. I liked the new clothes I'd purchased. I liked my new underwear, even though I hadn't admitted that to Penny yet. I especially liked traveling light. I was amazed that I needed much less than I thought I did to function every day. Warmth was the key, and my new socks were a fuzzy dream come true.

Penny slept on the hour-long bus ride with her chin tucked to her chest, her head bobbing as we rolled down a smooth, modern highway. Tall evergreens and winter-bare birch trees shivered as we passed, sprinkling occasional flecks of snow left from the last storm. The afternoon sunlight spread a transparent picnic blanket over the passengers on the other side of the bus. All was leisurely and felt strangely familiar.

I decided that was because of the birch trees. We had eight

birches in our backyard that were at least thirty years old. I knew what birch looked like in every season. I imagined this stretch of road was enchanting in late summer, when these ancient birch trees rustled their leaves in wild applause for the dancing breezes.

We pulled into a full parking lot next to a small bus station. I noticed that the cars were all plugged in. A cord ran from under the hood of every car to a box on a pole, like a parking meter. The sight made me think of the old Riverside Drive-In Movie Theater we went to when I was a child. Every car at the drive-in pulled a sound box on a cord to the partially rolled-down window. Here, the cords went under the hood instead of onto the window.

"I wonder if all the cars are plugged in to keep their engines warm." I nudged Penny.

She kept sleeping.

"Hey, this is our stop," I told her. "Wake up, sleepyhead. We need to get off now."

Penny didn't budge.

I froze. A terrifying bolt of emotional lightning coursed through my body.

"Penny? Penny, wake up." I shook her. "Penny!"

"What?" She lifted her head slightly and gave me a snarling glare.

My hand thumped against my chest and covered my heart as if I were about to pledge allegiance. "You scared the patochy out of me."

"What's wrong?" She moistened her lips and looked up, squinting.

"We're here. You fell asleep, and we're at our bus stop. We're in Porvoo."

"Oh." Penny tried to stand up and had to grab for the seat in front of her. "I went under, didn't I?"

"Come on. The driver is waiting for us to get off."

I had to steady Penny as she shuffled down the aisle. As soon as we were outside in the biting air, waiting for our luggage to be removed from the bus's underbelly, Penny shook her head, breathed deeply, and said, "Okay. Which way? Do you see any taxis?"

"Are you okay?"

"I'm fine. A little tired. Come on, let's grab our bags and get out of this cold air. I don't think it's doing my sinuses any good."

We had to ask someone in the station to help us call a taxi. Fortunately, the driver spoke English, like everyone else we had met. Being limited to only one language was humbling.

Penny fell asleep on our ten-minute drive to Marketta's. The narrow streets were slick in some spots with ice, which kept our speed down. The houses were charming, lined up next to each other side by side like turn of the century town houses. Lace curtains covered thick-paned windows. Some of the slender front doors were painted deep shades of blue or burgundy.

It started to snow as the taxi pulled up in front of a tall, nondescript beige building that looked like an apartment complex but larger than anything we had in Chinook Springs.

"This is it, Penny. We're here. We're at Marketta's."

"Okay, okay." She shook her head and opened the taxi door as if she welcomed the cold blast. "How much do we owe you?" Penny paid the driver while I wrestled our luggage to the covered entry of the apartment complex.

We pushed the intercom buzzer and entered the number

of Marketta's apartment. Marketta's expectant voice echoed back, "Penny? Is that Penny?"

"Yes, Penny and Sharon."

"Good. Come!"

A buzz and click caused the front door to open, and we gladly entered the silent, warm building.

"Where's the elevator?" Penny put down her heavy bags and looked around. "No elevator? Only stairs?"

I hoisted my new, light travel bag over my shoulder and reached for one of Penny's. "Come on. This is why we took all those morning walks. We can do this."

Up we went, thighs burning, lungs aching, shoulders spasming. Up to the seventh floor. I thought for sure I was going to pass out.

We dropped our bags by Marketta's door. I leaned against the wall, catching my breath while Penny dabbed her forehead and flushed cheeks with a tissue. Then she blew her nose. "Go ahead," she said, motioning to me. "Knock on the door."

"No, you knock."

I can't explain why I said that or what I was feeling at that moment. Yes, I was a little timid about being in unfamiliar territory. But more than that, I felt as if this was Penny's trip. Her aunt. This was her door to knock on. I didn't want to take any of it away from her. She was the trailblazer. I was the one who always followed.

Penny gave me a peculiar look, half upset, half confused. Her eyelids fluttered and she said, "I feel…"

Before I could grab her, Penny swooned into a limp puddle on top of the luggage.

Eleven

The door to Marketta's apartment opened. A solid woman in her early seventies with short, straight, silver gray hair peered at us in astonishment.

I went down on one knee and was patting Penny's face. "Breathe, Penny! Open your eyes! Breathe! She just passed out," I explained. "The stairs…"

Marketta grabbed Penny under her arms and single-handedly hoisted her off the luggage. "Penny?"

Penny's eyes opened. "Oh, hello. Are you my aunt Marketta?"

Before Penny's aunt could respond, Penny swooned again, but Marketta had a secure hold on her.

"Take the foots," Marketta instructed me. "We will go to the sofa."

I was amazed at Marketta's strength as she pulled Penny across the floor and the two of us lifted her onto a dark green sofa.

Marketta went for a glass of water. I patted Penny's face

some more and spoke with her gently at first and then with firm demands. "Look at me, Penny. That's right. Open your eyes."

Penny's eyelids fluttered. "I should have only taken one," she mumbled.

"One what?"

"Cold pill."

"Oh, Penny, how many did you take?"

"Two. Two of the blue ones."

"Blue ones! Penny, you were supposed to take the white ones. The blue ones are for nighttime, and you only need one of those."

"Oh," Penny moaned.

I turned to Marketta. "She took some medicine."

"For sleeping?"

"Yes, for sleeping, but she thought they were for her cold."

Marketta offered the glass of water. "She will be okay?"

"Yes, I think she'll be okay. She fell asleep like this once on a camping trip when a wasp stung her. She took an antihistamine to keep down the swelling and fell into a deep sleep. One nighttime cold pill is enough to make a person sleep all night. She took two."

I wasn't sure if I was speaking too rapidly or if using words like "antihistamine" would confuse Marketta.

She turned to Penny with the sweetest expression. "Just like your mother."

I watched with a twinge of tender surprise as Marketta leaned over, kissed Penny on the brow, and placed the back of her hand on Penny's cheek, as if lulling a child to sleep. "Penny, Penny," she crooned softly. "You are welcome to sleep as much as you want. You are at my home. Aunt Marketta's home."

"Okay," Penny muttered without opening her eyes.

"You can give me your hello later. Sleep now."

"Okay. You two go ahead." Penny's words came out in slow motion. "I'll be right back. Don't wait for me. Tell her about the picture, Sharon. With the fish."

I knew she had to be okay because only Penny would be half-wittedly networking at a time like this. If she was thinking clearly enough to remember the picture of Marketta and her mom when they were girls, then Penny was fine.

Marketta covered Penny with a crocheted blanket, and we let the antihistamine-assisted slumber fairies complete their interrupted task of carrying Penny to the Land of Nod.

"I'll bring in the luggage," I told Marketta.

She followed me and helped lift the heavy bags, carrying them to a small room to the right of the kitchen area. The room had one double bed, a cupboard-style closet in the far corner, and a straight-backed wooden chair in the other corner. The bed was covered with a puffy ivory comforter. A single picture of a basket of roses hung above the bed. As soon as we dropped the excessive and bulky luggage on the floor, no room was left.

I stepped over Penny's largest suitcase and trailed Marketta into the kitchen, feeling like a duckling that had lost its leader and was trying to fall in line.

"A coffee?" Marketta already was opening a white cupboard door and reaching for a ceramic cup and saucer.

"Yes, thank you. If it's no trouble. Don't make a fresh pot of coffee on my account."

Marketta turned and gave me a strange look. I froze, realizing I sounded just like my mother-in-law. *I can't believe that came out of my mouth!* I thought of Penny's recent encouragement about how I was changing and becoming more confident. *Come on, shoulders back. Head high. Strength. Dignity. You are not going to grow up to be like Gloria.*

I vowed right then and there that I wouldn't allow myself to sound like a weepy, whiny, overlooked wisp of a woman. Ever.

Everything in Marketta's kitchen was simple and honest. A thick-legged wooden table dominated the area with its three straight-backed chairs. The chair in our little guest room obviously was the fourth chair to the kitchen set. I sat at the table and smoothed my hand across the green and white linen tablecloth.

"Milk and sugar?" Marketta asked.

This time I kept my answer simple, like all things should be in this kitchen. "Yes."

Marketta plugged a teakettle into the wall and prepared a painted tray with two cups and a French press coffeemaker. None of her movements seemed wasted. She placed the tray on the table and motioned that I should serve myself. I stirred a bit of brown raw sugar into my coffee using a small spoon that was adorned with a British flag.

"My mother collects decorative teaspoons." I didn't add that my meticulous mother hangs them in a display box on the wall and never uses them. I loved feeling as if I were special enough at Marketta's house to use one of her fancy teaspoons.

"Please," Marketta said, after she had seated herself across from me. "Take the spoon home to your mother. Tell her it is a gift from me."

"Oh, I couldn't do that."

"Why not?"

"It's your spoon. I'm sure it's special to you."

"I can get another. My daughter lives now in England. She

sends me whatever I want. If I miss the spoon after you take it to your mother, I will have Elina send me a new one."

Clearly the matter was settled in Marketta's mind.

"Thank you." I remembered my only Finnish word and added, *"Kiitos."*

Marketta's face lit up with delight. *"Eipä kestä."* She continued with a full sentence in Finnish, a question, I guessed, based on the inflection.

I shook my head. "I only know how to say *kiitos.*"

"That is a good start. You will learn more. For now, we will use English. Tell me of you."

I couldn't remember ever being asked such a thing. I tried to speak slowly and gave her an overview of where I lived, my family, and how I had met Penny.

Marketta listened. She seemed to catch every word the way the birdbath in my small garden caught the rainwater. I wondered if I was pouring out too much at one time and if she would overflow.

"And your loves?" Marketta asked. "Tell me of your loves in life."

I wasn't used to having all this attention. Marketta had a wonderful way of leaning forward slightly and focusing her gaze on me, as if each word meant something to her personally. I recognized it as a trait that had sifted down to Penny in a slightly different form.

"Do you mean my children? My family?"

Marketta smiled, revealing deep laugh lines around her clear green eyes. "Yes? You have a close family?"

"Yes, my children and my husband bring me a lot of joy. I have a good life." My answer made me feel noble, as if my life carried the same simplicity and calm that Marketta's home exuded.

"What about you?" I asked Marketta. "I've been talking about myself too much. Tell me about you and the loves of your life."

"My husband is gone. We can speak of him later. My first son lives in the north of Finland. My daughter lives in England with her husband. They have three children. I have made a good life, too, here in Porvoo. We have lived in this apartment only two years, and sometimes I miss my garden. But I am happy. My work has been making chocolates."

"Really? Chocolate. Penny and I have been eating Finnish chocolate ever since we arrived."

"You have then tasted some of mine, I am sure. I have made chocolate for thirty-four years. Suklaavuori is the best chocolate in Finland. It is made here in Porvoo. Would you like some?" Marketta rose, opened a box on her counter, and carefully took out a dozen small milk chocolate blocks that looked like chunks of fudge. She placed them on a small plate and explained how the chocolate was still made in the traditional way. "I am an expert on chocolate."

"Mmm. This is the best. You're right." I tried to picture Marketta in a white chef's coat and hat, stirring large copper vats of chocolate with a paddle. That would explain the strong arms.

Over our rich coffee and melt-on-your-tongue chocolate, Marketta and I settled into a comfortable pocket of friendship. She told me more about her life and especially about her childhood with Penny's mom.

"Do you remember going fishing when you were young?" I asked.

"Yes, of course. Many times."

"Penny has a picture of you and her mother holding up a fish."

"Ah yes, Elsa's big fish. Of course. That was at Porosaari. In the summers we went to our summer cottage before the war. Our family had a small house by a beautiful lake not far from here. Every year, on the day school was over, my mother took us children and our servants to the lake cottage. My father would come for the weekends and for Midsummer's Eve. Do you have midsummer festivals where you live?"

"No."

"It is a big celebration time here. When we were young, festivals were held every year. Everyone would come. All night there would be music and dancing and much food like pancakes, fish, sausages, and bear."

"Did you say 'bear'?"

"Yes, bear. Do you not drink bear at festivals in Washington?"

I laughed. *"Beer.* I thought you said 'bear.'"

"Oh no! We do not eat bear! Some persons may enjoy eating bear, but not usually. I have never eaten bear."

"Neither have I," I confessed. "But I had reindeer for the first time the other night at the hotel restaurant."

"Ah, then I have another Finnish word for you. *Poro.* It means 'reindeer.' The lake we went to for summer has a small island called *Porosaari. Saari* is, of course 'island.' *Porosaari.* This means 'Reindeer Island.'"

"Were reindeer on the island?"

"No, no, only ants. Many busy ants. This is the island in the picture. I have a good memory of this because Elsa caught the big fish on Midsummer's Eve. Our mother and father said we could go to Porosaari with our brothers. This was important because it meant Elsa and I were no longer the babies. Do you see?"

I nodded.

"The sun does not set, of course, on Midsummer's Eve. This makes it light all day and all night. It is not easy to explain how this feels unless you live with so much light, and then in the winter, you have so much dark. It makes you ready to have a celebration for summer and feel like you also have new green leaves growing on you, like the trees. Do you know this feeling?"

I nodded again, but in my heart I knew I had never fully opened up to the wonders of life and allowed myself to feel things as openly as Marketta was now describing her childhood memory. I was selective about what I celebrated. Summer and light had not yet appeared on my party list.

"The island is not so very close to our cottage. I think six kilometers. We took food, blankets, and our father's boat. It was not a boat with a motor. No, only a wooden boat with long oars and two strong brothers.

"I do not think my brothers wanted any girls to go with them. As soon as our parents could not see us from our cottage, my brothers began to make the boat like this…"

Marketta leaned from one side to the other, as if riding in a boat that was about to tip. "Elsa told them we would die in the cold water, and they would be arrested for making us fall in."

"Did you? Did they tip the boat and make you fall in the water?"

"No, my brothers only wanted to make us afraid. We got to the island, and a man was already there with a camera. He was from Scotland. He said he was taking pictures for a book he was making.

"My brothers were not happy. They wanted to have the island to themselves like they did other times. The man with the camera wanted to take pictures of our small fire and of us looking at the sky. My brothers thought he was silly. Elsa thought he was handsome. I think she wanted him to take pictures of her."

I could imagine Penny as a young girl being just like her mother and wanting the photographer from Scotland to have eyes only for her.

"I made a fishing pole from a stick." Marketta leaned back and looked proud of herself. "We took some of my brothers' hooks and string and told them we would catch a fish. We said they could sit and do nothing because Elsa and I were going to catch the fish for our breakfast."

"Did your brothers laugh at you?"

"Of course. They called us babies, but Elsa and I went walking away from them, around the shore. I was a little frightened, but Elsa was strong enough for both of us and took me to a place where she said the fish came to look in the clear water and see their own beauty."

Marketta paused, and a faraway glimmer appeared in her eyes. "Do you know how much magic is in a summer night, when the sun plays on the water like small, jumping fires and the wind makes music in the trees?"

I smiled.

"All night it is like that. The earth is wide awake, and everywhere there is a happy feeling. I don't think magic is the word I want to use. I do not know the right word in English."

"I think I know what you mean, Marketta. I've never been to a place far enough north that the sun hasn't gone down all day. But I know what you mean about sunlight on the water and wind in the trees. I can only image how beautiful it is here in Finland during that time of year."

"You must come again to see it."

I was touched by her kindness. Her simple, gracious invitation filled in all the spaces where I felt awkward being the substitute guest while Penny slept off her overdose. "I would like to come back some day. I would like to bring my husband."

"Yes, you must! I will take you to Porosaari and show you where Elsa caught the big fish with the fancy fishing pole."

"Do you mean the stick with the string and hooks?"

"No, that stick was not strong enough to catch anything but ants. All those busy ants! But the man with the camera also had a fishing pole. He saw us trying to catch a fish with our stick and felt a tenderness in his heart for these two young girls. Elsa could speak very good English, so he told her she could use his pole. Right away she caught the big fish, and he took our picture with Elsa holding it. He put the picture in his book."

"He actually had a book published?"

"Yes, three books. One book about Finland, one book about Scotland, and one book about Spain. Would you like to see the book on Finland?"

"Yes!"

Marketta slipped out of the room. A vaguely familiar feeling crept over me. I realized the feeling came from a memory of Gloria that I had pushed deep inside. About eight years ago at Christmas, Gloria mixed up the tags on some of the presents. I opened a shiny set of expensive mixing bowls, and Gloria let out a shriek. "Those are Bonnie's!"

My sister-in-law, Bonnie, was about to open the box that Gloria had intended for me. Gloria bustled over and swapped our gifts. My "correct" gift was a pot holder shaped like a big strawberry. "Your pot holders are atrocious," Gloria had said.

As I waited for Marketta to return with the book, I half expected her to notice Penny on the couch and let out a shriek when she realized that she had given her wonderful story to the wrong person.

But Marketta returned with a warm smile and placed the charming old book on the table in front of me.

I touched the cover and then looked up. "Thank you, Marketta. Thank you for telling me your stories."

She reached across the green and white linen tablecloth and patted my hand. "I have many stories. Perhaps I will serve you story and story until you have had enough. If I serve you too much, you must tell me."

I choked up. "I'm not full yet."

That's when I realized that my mother-in-law didn't fill me. She emptied me every time I was around her. I let her empty me. Or at least, for many years I had let her empty me. Why did I do that?

Page by page, Marketta and I went through the book from the Scottish photographer named Loch McCallum. He had captured a unique sense of place on that midsummer's night. The light from the midnight sun cast otherworldly shadows on the smooth, sandy beach of the pristine Reindeer Island. In the background, tall evergreens stood like sentinels guarding a deep, enchanting forest.

We sat with our feet beneath Marketta's sturdy kitchen table for more than three hours. She made more coffee and poured out more and more fanciful tales until I was the one being filled to overflowing like a birdbath in the rain. But I wasn't too full. I still wanted more tales from her.

"Penny is going to love hearing all these stories about her

mother. Elsa sounds like she was a wonderful woman."

"She was. I missed her with my deepest heart when she went to America. Our parents did not want her to go. She was in love with Hank, that I know for certain. Nothing could stop Elsa. She was young, and he was persuasive. I think that is the right word in English. He easily could convince people to do things, and in the end, they thought it was their own idea."

So, that's where Penny gets her persuasive skills. From her father. I'm sure she doesn't know that. I'm going to enjoy being the one to tell her.

Marketta looked into her empty coffee cup and then glanced at her watch. "I should be thinking of what I will feed my guests for dinner."

"I'd be glad to help you."

"Yes, good. I will make things ready. Should you check on Penny?"

I tiptoed into the other room and leaned over the couch. Penny's steady, ruffled breathing didn't alter as I stood there. I didn't have the heart to wake her, yet it seemed she was missing out on all the fun.

"Penny?" I whispered. "Penny, are you about ready to wake up?"

She didn't move an eyelash.

I returned to the kitchen and asked Marketta, "Do you think I should wake Penny, or let her sleep?"

"Let her sleep. She is comfortable. When she wakes on her own, she will feel better."

"I hope so. She took the medicine because she felt as if she was getting a cold. I just can't believe we came all this way, and now she's missing out."

"It is okay. Tomorrow will be a good day for all of us. My

sister, Elsa, could never take even an aspirin without getting sleepy. Penny is like her mother."

"Does she look like her mother?"

"I can't say yet. I will have a closer look at her when she is awake. She has her father's color. Her brown hair and brown eyes, those she got from Hank. He had warm skin like her skin. Brown and warm all over. That was Hank. Elsa was fair like me with blue eyes and blond hair."

"I know Penny is eager to hear anything and everything you can remember about her father."

Marketta turned to me and tilted her head the same way Penny did when she was trying to discern a situation. "Penny did tell you, did she not? Her father was a pirate."

Twelve

I tried to read Marketta's expression as she said the word *pirate*. Before I could figure out a delicate way of asking what she meant, Marketta added, "First Hank was brave enough to steal my sister's heart, and then he was more brave to even steal her. We never saw her again."

A relieved sort of laugh came out of my mouth. The poor man was guilty of being nothing more than a "pirate for love." Penny would appreciate the irony of the label.

Marketta didn't laugh. She rose and said we should be about our dinner.

"I'd like to help," I said.

"Yes, of course." Marketta tied an apron around my waist and explained that we were going to prepare a typical Finnish specialty, which was from the Karelian tradition. I told myself to look up *Karelian* in the tour book before the day was over.

First, we made egg butter from hard-boiled eggs. She had me peel the eggs and chop them. With a small wooden ladle, Marketta mixed the chopped eggs with soft butter. She added salt by the pinch, rubbing it between her fingers.

"I made the rice pudding this morning. You can get the bread from the freezer," Marketta said. "It is the package of ready-rolled bread dough of rye and wheat."

I pulled out something that looked like small, oval pieces of pizza crust.

"This is what we do," Marketta said. "Put the rice pudding in the middle like this while it is cold and spread it so."

I watched Marketta fold the edges of the dough so that the rice pudding could be seen in the middle. I helped a little and soon we were surrounded by the warm, delicious fragrance of "Karelian pies" baking in the oven.

Marketta poured three small glasses of dark berry juice and set the table with three plates and only flat knives. I assumed she was setting for three because she was planning ahead in case Penny woke up.

The bowl of egg butter went in the center of the table. The timer for the oven rang, and Marketta invited me to take a seat. Placing the Karelian pies on the table, she sat down, folded her hands, and said, "I will pray."

With my head bowed, my heart full, and surrounded by fragrant promises of the meal we were about to share, I listened as soft, lyrical Finnish words rolled off her tongue. Deep in my spirit I agreed with her. Silently I whispered my humble thanks to our gracious heavenly Father. I knew I would never forget this moment when all things eternal seemed so clearly reflected in simple, earthly elements.

I opened my eyes and realized the earthly elements set before me were, once again, bread and juice.

"I hope you don't mind that I pray in Finnish," Marketta said.

"No, of course not. I think it would be tiring to speak as much as you have in a language different from your own."

Marketta nodded and offered me the plate of bread. "It is making me tired. My brain has to work hard to find the right words."

"We don't have to talk while we eat," I said. "I feel comfortable just sitting with you."

"Yes. Okay. We can sit in quiet. But first, I have to tell you how you make this for eating." Marketta put her knife into the egg butter and spread the mixture in the open center of the warm bread. "There. Any problems?"

"No, I think I've got it." I spread the egg butter and took a bite. "This is delicious."

"Yes?"

"Yes. Delicious. I think this could easily become my new favorite comfort food."

Marketta looked as if she were about to say something when we heard the front door open. Her eyes widened, and she leaned to see through the doorway into the other room. She called out something in Finnish, and a male voice responded.

Heavy footsteps came our way. A broad-shouldered man, wearing a wool cap and jacket, entered the kitchen. He bent down and kissed Marketta while the two of them spoke to each other in Finnish.

I'm sure I must have looked like a Cheshire cat, sitting there, grinning nervously while my glance swung back and forth from him to her. *Marketta said her husband was gone. She said her son lives in the north, but this man looks too old to be her son. Is he her boyfriend? One of her strong brothers who rowed the boat to Porosaari?*

The man turned to me as Marketta talked to him in Finnish. A look of understanding came over his leathered face.

Without warning, the unidentified man leaned over me, smelling of sardines and tobacco. He planted a brusque kiss on my cheek with two very cold lips. Besides my husband, my father, and Grampa Max, I couldn't remember any other man ever kissing me.

"Sharon, please meet my husband."

"Your husband?" I smiled. What a fascinating face he had. "Hello."

"This is Juhani," Marketta said.

"Johnny?"

He repeated his name with the *j* making a *y* sound.

I tried to repeat it. "Juhani. It's nice to meet you."

"He understands English but does not usually speak it."

Juhani took off his jacket and talked in Finnish while Marketta was still completing her explanation to me. "He wants to know if you speak Swedish."

"No."

"Juhani has been to the coast for a week, fishing with his brother."

I decided to share my little misunderstanding with Marketta. "When you said earlier that your husband was gone, I thought you meant gone, gone. Not gone fishing."

Marketta began speaking in Finnish before I completed my sentence. I'd never been in a situation before where someone was translating my words. It was unnerving.

Juhani laughed heartily at my translated comment and replied in clipped English, "I am not dead yet!"

We all laughed together, as if we had been friends for years. I decided I liked this crusty man with the cold lips and his adoring Marketta with her blue eyes and deep laugh lines.

Oh, Penny Girl, you are missing all the good stuff!

After a leisurely dinner and the most confusing, overlapping conversation I'd ever been part of, I helped Marketta clean up. Juhani apparently had fish in the car that needed to be dealt with, and he disappeared.

Marketta and I concluded it would be best to leave Penny on the couch with another blanket since she didn't want to get up when we tried to rouse her. That meant I had the bed in the compact guest room all to myself when I retired for the evening.

I closed the door and realized that was the first time in many days I had been by myself. The quiet was refreshing. I slipped into my new pajamas and pulled out the stack of postcards I'd promised Uncle Floyd I would send home. All the stamps were the same, and I couldn't guarantee they were exceptional, but at least I was writing notes on the postcards. On each one I mentioned something different about what we had seen and done. I told Kaylee about the baby incident on the plane and wrote, "You won't believe this, but I threw away my soiled clothes."

On Jeff's card, I mentioned my lost luggage and added, "So the credit card will have a few unexpected expenses this month."

When I came to Max and Gloria's card, I wasn't sure what to say. Should I tell my mother-in-law that Penny was sacked out at the moment due to a drug overdose?

No.

How about if I told her that we ate reindeer?

Probably not a good idea.

What if I wrote that my practical tennis shoes, which she had insisted I bring on this trip, had returned to their country of manufactured origin?

The truth, as I now saw it, was that it didn't matter what I wrote. Gloria would find a way to bend my words in a negative direction. That was her choice. Her way of viewing life, or at least her way of viewing my life.

With a light heart I wrote, "We're having a wonderful time. Finland is a beautiful country. Penny's aunt is making us feel very welcome here. Love you both, Sharon."

Thinking back over the years, I realized that Max had loved me enough for both of them. I figured there was nothing wrong with my choosing to love them both. That was my choice. My new and improved way of viewing life. I could love my mother-in-law even if she didn't choose to or care to love me the way I thought she should.

I rummaged through Penny's suitcase and found her Bible. In the back of my mind, I was trying to remember a verse in the Psalms about how good it is when relatives dwell together in unity.

Opening up the Bible right in the middle, I flipped through the Psalms and was amazed at all the notes Penny had written in the margins. Her Bible looked like a workbook. I never knew anyone who had read so much of the Bible or read it as often as she apparently had.

I remembered years ago when Penny quoted a verse to me and referred to her Bible as her "owner's manual." At first I thought the term irreverent. Then she explained that she felt as if she were rebuilding her life after messing it up for so many years.

"It's imperative," Penny had said, "that I read my Bible to find out how to make my life work the way it was designed to work."

I noticed now, in my quiet guest room, that Penny had underlined the first few verses of Psalm 126. I read them with my lips moving, without making any sound.

"We were like those who dream.
    Then our mouth was filled with laughter
And our tongue with joyful shouting;
    Then they said among the nations,
'The LORD has done great things for them.'"

My sister-in-law, Bonnie, had given me a travel diary for this trip. I'd only written in it once, on the long plane ride while we were still seated in business class.

Reaching for the diary and a pen, I wrote, "Theme Verse for Trip" and copied the words I'd just read from Psalm 126. Then I added,

I love these verses! They capture the essence of our trip. I feel as if this journey is like a dream, and that Penny and I have been filled with laughter.

Yes, the Lord has done great things for us. Even Tuija said that God was showing us mercy. I know I will never be the same after this journey; I don't want to be the same. I want to learn how to drop my bucket deep into the well of possibilities and be strong and

Trying to quote Penny's admonition to me sent me to the last chapter of Proverbs because I vaguely remembered her words sounding a lot like a passage we had studied in our home Bible study group years ago.

I found the verse in Proverbs 31. "Strength and dignity are her clothing, and she smiles at the future."

I finished my journal entry with,

...full of dignity. That's it. I want to be clothed with strength and dignity, and I want to laugh with no fear of the future. I want to live each day with a full, open heart to the Lord and always be thankful for what He does.

I felt good as I closed the cover on my travel journal and thought about the future being filled with laughter. When Penny and I had a chance to be alone, I planned to tell her about our theme verse.

When the sun rose the next morning, wide-awake Penny was back on top of her game. She was at last experiencing the joys of being Marketta and Juhani's niece.

Seated at the kitchen table with Marketta, Penny was listening intently to her aunt's stories. The two of them appeared to have been up for several hours.

I watched Penny's face. She was soaking it all in. I felt so happy for my friend. This was it. Right here. The whole trip could be summarized by this connection between these women who were bonded by their blood and so much more.

I slipped out of the kitchen and returned a moment later with my camera. Before they realized what I was doing, I'd snapped a picture of them leaning in over the simple white ceramic coffee cups.

"Oh, please! My hair!" Penny held up a hand in front of my camera.

"Your hair is fine," I told her. "Keep talking. Pretend I'm not here."

"If you're going to take more, at least make sure you have both of us in the picture." Penny got up from her side of the table and went to Marketta's side. She wrapped her arms around her aunt's neck and pressed her cheek against Marketta's short, silvery hair.

You just wanted to hug your auntie, didn't you, Penny? Go ahead. Hug all you want. You are going to love having these photos.

I took several shots from different angles as the two charmers posed for the camera. Penny hugged Marketta, and Marketta hugged her right back.

Penny always had been a snuggler with her husband and children. She was the first woman I knew who regularly greeted me with a kiss on the cheek. My mom never had been demonstrative. My sister-in-law hugged on occasion. And you know about Gloria. Penny was the one who gave me that womanly gift of affirmation with her hugs and kisses.

I loved watching Penny get back some of the huggin' and lovin' she so generously gave to others.

I found my place at the kitchen table, and our day was dedicated to storytelling. Marketta pulled out a marvelous old photo album, and Penny studied every picture of her mother, listening with her entire being to each story that accompanied the picture.

A stack of old letters rested beside where I sat. The penmanship was feminine. I guessed these were letters from Penny's mother to Marketta. They were, of course, all in Finnish. It would be quite a job to translate them into English.

Around two o'clock I interrupted briefly to ask if I could fix some lunch for us. Marketta's voice sounded hoarse. I imagined she was weary from using English and talking so much.

"Of course!" Marketta said. "My guests must eat. The soup

is ready. I can make it warm for us now."

"I can do it," I said. "Please don't get up. I can figure it out. Is this it?"

"Yes. *Kiitos.*"

"*Eipä kestä,*" I replied tentatively.

"*Eipä kestä!*" Marketta repeated.

"Listen to you!" Penny teased. "I sleep through one day, and you double your Finnish vocabulary."

"She also can say 'Reindeer Island,'" Marketta said. "Show her."

"*Porosaari,*" I spouted with a cocky tilt of my head.

"Impressive. Where did I hear that before? Oh, I know. The island where my mom caught the fish, right? Marketta told me the story this morning."

"Did she also tell you that you get your skills in the fine art of persuasion from your father?"

"No, we haven't talked about my father yet. I have a question to ask you, Aunt Marketta. Did my father love my mother?"

Marketta paused. "Yes," she said at last. "Your father loved your mother."

I'm sure Penny had the same feeling I did. Marketta was hiding something. It was as if she were really saying, "Your father loved your mother, but…"

The phone rang just then. Marketta got up to answer it in the other room.

I turned the flame under the soup kettle to low and went over to Penny. "How's your cold?"

"Cured! Although I don't recommend my method of treatment. I can't believe I overmedicated myself! I'm so bummed I missed a whole day with you guys. Marketta said you are 'precious,' and she and Juhani loved spending time with you yesterday."

"They are amazing, aren't they? So full of life. And your uncle! I've never met anyone like him."

"I know. I love him. I love them both to pieces."

"Where is Juhani?"

"Off to market with his fish, or something like that, from what I gathered. My conversation with the two of them earlier this morning was a bit hard to follow."

"Yes, I know what you mean."

"This is so much more than I'd hoped for, Sharon. Being here and listening to all these stories. I think God outdid Himself when He answered this prayer for me."

I nodded.

"Marketta said her daughter in England could translate all my mom's letters for me. Can you believe that? I have a cousin in England."

I could see the glitter flecks gather in Penny's comet-riding mind. She was planning her next adventure. I secretly wanted to be her companion whenever she took off on that jolly lark. I told myself it was too much to wish. I needed to stay in the present and be content with this trip's abundance.

"Penny, how are you doing with all this? Is it overwhelming?"

"Yes, but in a good way. It's much better than I thought it would be, seeing Marketta and being in her home. She has been giving me bits of my mother that I never had before. It's so amazing to me. I feel as if I didn't know much about my mother at all. And you know what? The more Marketta tells me about her," Penny paused and took a deep breath, "the more I miss her."

The tears began to come.

"I'm so sad that my children never knew her. I'm so sad that I didn't love her when I had the chance. I never got to know her as a friend. Woman to woman. I just took her for granted. From the time I was fifteen, all I wanted to do was get away from her."

Penny buried her face in her hands and let the tears roll down her arms. I gingerly touched her elbow and gave it an awkward pat. I never was good at moments like this.

Marketta entered the kitchen and nearly flew to Penny's side. Wrapping her arms around Penny's shoulders, Marketta nestled her nose into Penny's neck and spoke to her in low, melodic tones.

"I miss my mother," Penny blubbered. "I miss her."

Marketta drew back her head. Tears were tumbling from her eyes. "Yes. Yes, I know. I miss Elsa, too."

I leaned back in my chair, sensing this was a hallowed moment between niece and aunt. The two of them clung to each other and cried big tears that came from deep caverns of their souls. Marketta slowly rocked Penny back and forth.

Then the tears stopped. The sobbing was over. Penny reached for a cloth napkin on the table and dried her eyes.

I was painfully aware of how controlled all the women in my family were. True, we hadn't faced a death together, or even remembered a loss together, the way Marketta and Penny had just done. I found their honest expression of grief compelling and a form of humility about which I knew very little.

They kissed each other on the cheek, and the outburst was over.

Marketta stroked Penny's hair. She looked at me with a little grin that resembled a shy sunbeam, wondering if it's safe to come out and play after the storm has passed.

"That was my longest friend on the phone," Marketta said. "We have been close to each other since we were twenty. I think we decided to become like sisters after Elsa went to America."

Penny looked up, caught my gaze, and smiled at me. Penny and I knew what it was like to be each other's longest and closest friend. We understood that feeling of one day deciding you've become like sisters.

"My Anni called to say she would like us to go to her house tonight for dinner. Just us girls."

"That's nice of her," Penny said.

"She lives in Hinthaara. In the country. I will get Juhani to drive us because I do not see well at night. We can sleep there, and a bus comes to Hinthaara tomorrow, on Thursday, so we can take the bus home. How does that sound to you?"

"Wonderful!" Penny said.

"Yes, wonderful," I agreed. "It's so kind of Anni to invite us."

"Anni has an old house, and this is good because she has the best sauna."

"The famous Finnish sauna," Penny said. "Sharon's been reading about your saunas."

"You can tell nothing by only reading about our saunas." Marketta turned to me, and I noticed her left eyebrow was slightly elevated. "Tonight you will experience sauna!"

Thirteen

Penny bathed and put on her nicest outfit to visit Anni. Then Penny handed me a few of her things to pack in my new bag so we would have just one piece of luggage for our overnighter.

I watched Penny curling her hair and thought back to when I was in sixth grade and received an invitation to my first overnighter, a slumber party at Lisa Bachman's house for her twelfth birthday. The big treat was that we had pizza delivered and root beer floats. We each were supposed to bring a clean, empty soup can so that we could curl (or rather, straighten) our long hair by gathering it on the top of our heads and rolling it on the cans.

I didn't bring a soup can because I was the only one with short hair. My mother believed all respectable preadolescent girls should wear pixie cuts with curls at the cheeks achieved by bobby pins and pink hair tape every night.

Since I couldn't roll my hair, I became the beautician for everyone else. My fingers were sticky with the green gel goop that came in a little round pot. Up went each girl's ponytail, on went the goop, and then I was at my very best, carefully rolling the soup can so that not a single hair strayed.

Connie Kidamon brought an empty frozen orange juice can instead of a soup can and arrived at the party with a big bandage on her thumb because she had cut herself when she tried to wash out the can. Everyone thought she was brave.

All the girls wore pajamas with a top and a bottom. I was the only one wearing a nightgown. Connie called it a "granny gown," and I didn't think she said it in a way that sounded as if she wished she had one.

All the girls were running around with green goop on their long hair and soup cans on top of their heads. I dutifully did my bobby-pin spit curls and taped them to my cheeks. No one copied me or asked to borrow my pink hair tape.

One's identity can be established from a few defining moments in childhood. I learned something about myself at Lisa's slumber party that stayed with me all these years. I learned that everyone liked me when I helped them. The girls didn't notice or admire me. They appreciated me because I was useful. My role in life was to be the facilitator.

Pausing over the half-packed overnight bag, I wondered if part of the reason I was drawn to Penny and part of the reason our friendship worked, even though we were so opposite, was because Penny made me feel almost cool. She listened to me and laughed at my jokes. Penny accepted me just the way I was yet wasn't shy about speaking up when she saw areas where I could stand some improvement.

Yes, I was still a facilitator around Penny. I was the one on the floor packing our bag while she curled her hair. But Penny always made me feel equal or even sometimes above her. She didn't look down on me. If Penny had been at Lisa Bachman's slumber party, I might have turned out to be a different person.

Then a thought struck me. *It's never too late. If Lisa Bachman's slumber party established my role in life for the past thirty years, why can't tonight's slumber party—or this whole trip— reestablish my identity and role in life for the next thirty?*

Those were bold thoughts. They were the kind of bold thoughts that usually came to me only during my stints of January madness. Was I really a different person deep inside, waiting for a chance to break out? Like a brave chick still inside her shell, I saw myself peck, pecking my way to the world outside.

"What do you think?" Penny turned to me with every hair smoothly in place. I thought she looked stylish and elegant enough to have tea with the queen. Or rather, the president, since we were in Finland. Marketta told us they had a woman president, and Penny and I were impressed.

"What do I think about what?"

"Do you think all our stuff is going to fit in that bag?"

"I think so."

"Did you pack our bathing suits?" Penny asked.

I turned and gave Penny my best poor-me pout.

"Oh, that's right. Your bathing suit went to China without you."

Marketta called to us from the hallway. "Ready to go? Juhani has gone to the car to make it warm."

"Okay, just a minute." Penny tossed me her one-piece bathing suit and stuffed her cosmetics into her shoulder bag. "We'll figure out something. Maybe Anni has an extra bathing suit."

We joined Marketta by the front door. She looked like the cutest, cuddliest, most lively grandma on the planet with her hand-knit ski sweater and stocking cap. Her gloves were a matching deep red and looked fuzzy and warm.

"Ready then?"

"Ready or not, here we go," Penny said.

Marketta led us out her apartment door and over to what looked like a broom closet door with a big sign on it. She opened the door, revealing an elevator.

Penny and I looked at each other and laughed.

"Guess I should have looked up the word for elevator so we would have known what the door said downstairs," I said.

"Ah!" Marketta said. "This now explains why you took all the stairs. The lift is faster."

It was. We were down all seven floors and out into the dark, crisp evening chill in a few quick minutes. Juhani waited with their small white sedan pulled up under the portico. He got out when he saw us and, with a big smile and lots of Finnish words, took our bags.

Penny and I slid into the scrunchy backseat. All the doors closed. Penny reached over and squeezed my arm. Her face silently screamed, "Get me out of here!"

I took one whiff and understood.

Juhani's fish.

The tiny car was permeated with the overwhelming stench of fish. He may have just hauled those flappers to market, but their poignant memory lingered.

Penny used the crank handle to roll down her window a few inches. She leaned over, stretched her chin up, and elevated her nose to the small opening, gulping in the icy winter air.

Juhani looked around, as if his comfort zone had experienced a breach of security. He used his large hands and punchy

Finnish words to notify Marketta of the situation. She answered in staccato words, and the two of them bantered briskly as we moved onto the main highway.

Marketta turned around and with a humoring expression said, "I am sorry for the fish. It is familiar to us. I think it might not be pleasant for you."

I was feeling overwhelmed, not only from the fish smells but also from the damp, slick seat I had just placed my hand on. I could easily believe that a few hours earlier a rather large, dead fish had occupied the space where I now sat.

Clearly Penny was in physical agony over the stench. "I hope it's okay if I keep the window open. I need some air."

Juhani and Marketta conversed. I tried to take tiny breaths and joined Penny in rolling down my window a few inches. It had begun to snow, and bits of the white flakes flew at us through the open windows. Marketta said we should "make ourselves with comfort," so we left the windows down.

We froze all the way to Hinthaara. It was either the fresh air or the warmth. We chose breathing over normal blood circulation. The noisy airflow made conversation impossible. I think Juhani and Marketta were uncomfortable. I noticed he had turned the car heater to full blast so at least their feet were warm up front.

All of us were relieved when the drive in the dark concluded at the end of a gravel road. A small cabin tucked under evergreens of primeval proportions awaited us. My dream at the hotel about the Hansel and Gretel cottage came to mind. Anni's home certainly had all the charm and ambience of a storybook setting.

Juhani retrieved our bags from the car's trunk and carried them to the front door for us. With a gruff kiss on the cheek for all three of us, he turned and left.

"Did we upset him?" Penny asked. "With the open windows, I mean. Did that make Juhani mad?"

"No, why should it? He is not angry. If he were angry, he would not kiss you, and he would make you carry your own bags." Marketta turned and waved to her husband. With a twinkle she said, "Juhani is himself, and no one tries to make changes to him."

The door of the storybook cottage opened, and Marketta's "longest" and "closest" friend greeted us with hugs and kisses. Anni welcomed us into her small home as if we were her long-lost daughters.

Anni reminded me of a bird, even though she wasn't small by any means. She had to be in her early seventies, like Marketta. Her quick movements, long nose, and keen, darting eyes made me think of a brilliant blue jay that visits my bird feeder every winter and upstages all the dull brown wrens.

Anni took our coats. "Please. Come. Sit. You are my guests."

The first thing I noticed was a round table covered with a beautiful lace tablecloth and set with china and crystal. An assortment of candles glowed from the center of the table. Boughs of freshly cut evergreen hung from the rafters. Bright flute music floated around us.

The four of us gathered at the sparklingly elegant table. On each plate perched a white cloth napkin, folded in the shape of a swan. Anni nestled herself snugly into the chair to the right of me and reached for my hand. For such a large woman, she had slim, bony hands.

"I would like to pray," Anni declared.

We all joined hands. I drew in a deep breath, as if I could absorb the meaning of Anni's lyrical words and hold them always in my heart. Her voice carried the same depth of sincerity and tender humility I'd heard in Marketta's voice when she prayed. These two women, who each held one of my hands, sat up straight, like warriors awaiting their marching orders, yet they both spoke as softly as handmaidens called upon to nurse a wounded soldier back to strength.

Anni said "Amen" in English and served us a generous spread of cold meats, cheeses, meatballs, thin rye bread, and some sort of creamy pudding. I watched her movements. She was strong, like Marketta. I could picture Anni chopping all her firewood each fall and stacking it outside in the snow. She didn't move or act like a woman in her seventies. Neither did Marketta. They were young in spirit and strong in body.

I wanted to be like them.

After we had eaten, Anni announced she had a song for us. Penny and I exchanged glances, not sure what that meant. Anni rose, went to the stereo and turned it off, then clasped her hands together. With her chin up, she sang in English a song I'd never heard before.

Her sweet voice rose passionately on the chorus. She lifted her hands, like an opera singer, palms turned up toward us, open and inviting. She was offering us her song as a special gift.

I cried.

When I tried to describe Anni's song a few days later in my travel diary, I couldn't find a way to convey the sense of honor I felt. I've heard many people sing over the years. I've been moved by many performances. But what made this so overwhelming was that Anni wasn't performing. She was simply giving. Giving us a song. That's why I cried. No one had ever given me a song before.

When Anni hit the last note, Penny rose to her feet,

applauding and shouting, "Bravo!"

I didn't want to clap. I wanted to say thank you, the same way I would say thank you if Anni had handed me a box with my name on it, wrapped in lovely paper and tied with silver ribbon.

At that moment, I felt as if my instincts were tapping on the shell of my life, urging me to respond to what my heart was telling me to do. And so I did.

I didn't clap along with Penny. I didn't follow or facilitate or hang back in the shadows. Instead, I got out of my chair, with tears still wet on my cheeks, and took three giant steps over to Anni. Taking her hands in mine, I looked her in the eye and said, *"Kiitos!"* Then I kissed her on the cheek.

Anni cried. She pressed her soft cheek against mine and murmured a string of words in Finnish. Switching to English she said, "A blessing on you for your kindness, young Sharon."

The moment ended awkwardly with my pulling away and bumping the table when I tried to sit down. Penny looked at me with both eyebrows raised as if to say, "Well, aren't you full of surprises?"

Marketta asked if either Penny or I had a song we would like to sing, and both of us shook our heads. I felt as if we had come to a birthday party empty-handed.

"No songs," Penny said, "but Sharon and I have a few small gifts for you." She went into the other room where our luggage had been placed. I couldn't imagine what Penny had in mind. I hoped it wasn't leftover Finnish chocolate from the department store. I wasn't sure if Penny knew that Marketta made chocolate and therefore wouldn't be impressed with such a gift.

Penny surprised me.

Again.

She had several small, gift-wrapped boxes, which she presented to Marketta and Anni. "Just a little something sweet."

The first gift was a package of five different Ghirardelli chocolate bars.

"From San Francisco," Penny said. "You'll have to tell me if you think it's as good as your chocolate."

The women seemed delighted. The other two small gifts turned out to be miniature-sized bottles of expensive perfume. Marketta and Anni's appreciation was evident. Suddenly I was on the receiving end of their squishy hugs of thanks, even though I had nothing to do with the gifts.

"And now for sauna," Anni announced. She suggested that she and Marketta clear the table while Penny and I got ready.

Penny carried in our bag, and Anni opened the door to a bathroom that didn't seem to fit the rustic cottage because the room was large and modern with tile covering the floors and the walls. I noticed that the shower fixture came right out of the wall with no separate, enclosed area to serve as a shower. On the left side of the room was a door.

"That is the sauna." Anni pointed to the door. "Would you wait until Marketta and I come back?"

"Yes, of course," Penny said.

Anni left us, and I made a brave decision. As Penny opened the bag to find her bathing suit, I announced, "I'm going to wear my underwear. The black set looks like a bathing suit. You even said so. I doubt that Anni or Marketta will think I'm immodest because I don't have a one-piece bathing suit. Besides, who cares? It's just us girls."

Penny slowly turned to me with the most wonderful expression on her face. It was a mixture of amazement and glee. Applauding, she shouted, "Bravo! Good for you!"

I felt proud of myself.

We did our customary turning of our backs to each other as Penny and I stripped down. I folded my clothes neatly and tucked them back in the bag. Ignoring the feeling that too much of my flesh was showing or that the black bra and panties did nothing to cover the lily-white rolls around my middle, I reached for a bath towel to hold in front of my stomach.

Penny pulled a shower cap from her cosmetic bag. "I hope they don't think I'm weird. I've never gone in a sauna before, have you?"

"Are you kidding? No."

"Well, I'm guessing that all the steam will make my hair frizz. I just washed it, and I don't want to have to mess with it after the sauna. Especially if Anni doesn't have a hair dryer."

I reached for another white towel and wrapped it around my hair in a tightly wound turban that pulled the skin back from my eyes.

Penny tucked her hair under the plastic cap. "Does this look really dumb?"

"No, not really dumb. Just a little dumb."

"Oh, aren't you the punchy one tonight." Penny checked her reflection in the mirror.

"I'm not punchy. I'm emerging," I declared with a broad grin. I pictured a fuzzy little chick pecking out of its shell. That was me. I was almost all the way through.

"I noticed," Penny said. "You sure surprised me when you gave Anni a kiss after her solo. I think she was surprised, too, but I could tell she liked it."

"I wanted to do it, and so I did! I'm changing on this trip, Penny."

"Yes, you are."

"We both are," I said quickly. "We're emerging into the women we're going to be for the next half of our lives."

Penny dipped her chin and squinted her eyes. "The next half of our lives, huh?" Her voice carried the same somber tone it had in the hotel room the night she reminded me that her mother had died when she was forty-six.

"Hallo, ladies!" A tap on the bathroom door announced that Anni and Marketta were ready for the sauna. The door opened. Penny and I turned around, and both the older women burst out laughing. They were laughing at us.

"Look at you!" Marketta chortled. "This is a good joke! You are both wearing bathing suits!"

Penny and I immediately turned our gaze away from the obviously free-spirited women.

In unison, Penny and I said, "And you are not!"

Fourteen

Yes, Marketta and Anni had prepared for the sauna by shedding their clothing and appearing at the bathroom door wearing their seventy-year-old skin and nothing else.

And they were laughing at us!

"Did you think we would go swimming first?" Marketta asked, still laughing. "Is that why you have on your swimming cap?"

Neither of us could bring ourselves to look directly at the saggy-baggy sisters.

"We've never been in a sauna," I explained.

"Oh, why did you not say this? I will tell you how this goes. One does not wear clothes in sauna. We sit. When we are warm, we go in the snow. If we had a lake, we would go in through the ice. But there is not a lake here. Only snow outside."

"No lake, huh?" Penny pulled the shower cap off her head. "No way to cut a hole in the ice and take a dip. Isn't that too bad?"

I subtly nudged Penny with my elbow and explained, "This is unusual for us."

Anni placed her hand on the wooden door that opened to the sauna, as if testing the temperature. Marketta gave me a puzzled look. She didn't seem to understand why we were hesitant.

Penny said, "Life is too short. When in Finland…" She slid out of her bathing suit and quickly wrapped herself in a bath towel. "You don't mind if I go in with a towel, do you?"

"You will be too hot," Marketta said. "Come. You will see."

Anni opened the door to the sauna and stepped inside, closing the door behind her. A wave of warm air filled the tiled bathroom.

I felt paralyzed for a moment. I had thought after giving birth to four children that I was no longer modest about any-thing. Apparently childbirth hadn't completely cured me, because this was definitely a stretch. It seemed to be all or nothing with these aged women, and Penny was willing to go for nothing.

Okay, this is it. I can stand here all night with my undies in a bunch, or I can be fearless and join the other flabby chicks in the Finnish sauna.

I chose to be fearless.

But I took the bath towel with me for camouflage.

The sauna was hot. Dry, desert, well-over-one-hundred-degrees hot. The "hot box" was made of wood with one wide, wooden bench for the four of us to sit on, hip to hip. None of us was narrow in the berth, so we filled the bench and all sat facing a rock-based heating element of some sort that rose from the floor next to a wooden bucket that was filled with water. Anni reached for the bucket, scooped a small ladleful of water, and poured it over the rocks. A dragon-sized hiss and puff of steam appeared.

No one spoke.

Anni, to my right, breathed in the steam and exhaled slowly. I tried to do the same. The heated air seemed to stretch my lungs and open my pores. I realized this was the warmest I had been since we arrived in Finland. I closed my eyes and felt the tension in my shoulders relax. My arms felt heavy. My nervous toes uncurled. My jaw went slack.

Oh yeah, I could see how this could be relaxing. I realized that the naked part was hardly an issue. No one was looking at anyone else. All four of us were silent.

Marketta was the first to speak. Her tone was hushed and slow. "Penny, did Elsa never take you for sauna?"

"No."

A moment later, Penny added, "I'm sure they have plenty of saunas at resorts and health clubs in the U.S., but I've never been in one, and my mom never had enough money to visit such a place."

"Did Elsa not tell you much about her life in Finland?" Anni asked.

"No, not much. If she did, I'm sorry to admit I didn't pay attention. I know even less about my father."

"Hank was a pirate," Anni stated firmly.

"So I've heard. He stole my mother away from here and away from her family."

"Yes. He also stole secrets from the U.S. government." Anni tossed another ladleful of water on the rocks.

A loud hiss filled the sauna. I could feel myself perspiring.

"Is that true?" Penny's voice sounded choked. I couldn't see her face without leaning over and craning my neck.

"We don't know," Marketta said. "Hank came to Finland after the war. We had learned for all those war years to be suspicious of anyone who was from another country. He worked at the embassy. Elsa met him there. Our parents did not want her with Hank, but Elsa was not one who did our parents' wishes."

"Did they elope?"

"I do not know this word."

"Did my mother get married without permission?"

"She was old enough to marry," Marketta said. "They married with the law."

"Legally?" Penny suggested.

I remembered how Penny knew a few things about not being legally married. How strange if her mother and father had been joined the way Penny was joined to Wolf.

However, that wasn't the case. Marketta assured Penny that her parents were legally married, but the ceremony hadn't taken place in a church.

"My parents never stopped being sad for that," Marketta said. "When Elsa left for America with Hank, she said they would come back one day. But Hank died from a short sickness. Then you were born, and no one had money to bring you and your mother back. Those were times without much money."

Anni spoke up. "You should tell her, Marketta."

Marketta answered Anni in Finnish, and the two friends exchanged swift words.

"Tell me what?" Penny asked.

I was perspiring like crazy. It felt like the truth was about to pour out of Marketta the way all the sweat was pouring out of me. I considered stepping into the bathroom to cool off, but I didn't want to miss a thing.

"Tell me what, Aunt Marketta? I've felt all along there's more to this than anyone has said over the years. I want to know."

"If your mother wanted you to know—" Marketta began.

"Know what?" Penny challenged.

Silence.

Anni shifted and spoke firmly. "Marketta, there are no secrets in sauna. Tell her."

That's for sure! Nothing else is covered up in here.

Marketta took a deep breath. "You were born five months after your parents married."

Silence in the sauna.

"I thought it might be something like that," Penny said in a low voice. "When I went through her things, I never found her marriage certificate. I wondered many times over the years if she really was married. For a while I wondered if she invented my dad just so she would appear respectable when she tried to get a job."

"Oh no, your father was real," Marketta said. "He was handsome and strong, and he was persuasive. Do you understand how it was at that time? How it was for Elsa? She would be the only girl in all our region and in our family to have a baby and not a husband. Hank wanted Elsa. He wanted you. He could not live here because of his job. If Elsa wanted Hank, she had to go with him."

"And she did," Penny said softly. "She left everything for him."

"I wish you could have known your father," Marketta said. "I believe Hank was a good husband to Elsa, even for so short a time. He would have been a good father to you."

Marketta paused. "Are you sad that you know this?"

"No, I wanted to know. Thank you for telling me. I was just wishing that somehow your parents could have accepted my dad so maybe things could have been different."

"Our parents were worried about Elsa's heart more than anything."

"Yes, I guess that's how it is with all parents, isn't it? Thank you, Aunt Marketta. I'm glad you told me everything."

"Say your thank you to Anni. She told me this information is the only gift you want to take home from Finland."

"It is."

Anni clapped her hands together. "This is good time for the snow!"

"Yes, come!" Marketta hopped up and opened the sauna's door. A rush of cooler air from the tiled bathroom blew in. I grabbed my towel and wrapped it around me.

Anni led us through the bathroom, past the lace-covered table in the room where the music was once again playing on the stereo, and out a back door into the snowy night. The dim light that shone through the kitchen window spread a transparent glow over the fresh snowfield. The open area extended only ten yards or so before the forest and darkness took over the landscape.

A few snowflakes fluttered in the frozen night air. I was so heated up I didn't feel them as they touched me. I imagined the snowflakes were like meteorites burning up as they entered Earth's atmosphere.

I stood there, incinerating snowflakes with my bare arms and watching as Anni and Marketta, with all the grace of prima ballerinas performing a scene from *Swan Lake*, lowered themselves into the untouched snow. Murmuring to each other the ancient language of best friends, they rolled in the pure white flakes. They moved with a dignified agility that matched their uninhibited spirits.

"Come, before you lose your hot," Anni said.

I laughed. *Before I lose my hot.*

Penny and I were both wrapped in our towels. I didn't feel cold. Only the bottoms of my feet were aware that I was standing in snow. They weren't complaining at the moment.

"It's now or never," Penny said.

"You first," I said.

"Let's go together. On the count of three, we'll drop our towels and run over there to the right. Do you see that open patch?"

"Yes. Okay. I'll count."

"No, I'll count," Penny said.

Marketta and Anni laughed at us again. "You two are good at making jokes together."

"Come on," Penny said. "One…"

I joined her. "Two, three!" We dropped our towels, burst out laughing, and splayed our unsuspecting hot bods in the fluffed-up snow.

Every pore in my body suddenly woke up and screamed at me. *What are you doing!?*

Go with it! I told my pores. *Experience this. Take it in.*

All around me and inside of me was silence. I remember looking up and seeing a single, brilliant star in the night sky. The rest of the stars, I suppose, were smart enough to cover their eyes from such a sight.

I didn't feel naked. I didn't feel cold. I felt very much alive.

"Back to sauna!" Anni announced.

Penny already had gotten up. She tossed my towel at me.

As I was rising and wrapping up in the towel, Penny threw

a snowball that missed me by a mere inch. I tried to pack a snowball to retaliate, but when I threw it, the snowball went *poof* like a dandelion in the wind. Penny had her second snowball ready. That one self-destructed as soon as she launched it. The gleaming particles of white floated to the ground.

We laughed deeply, standing there in the snow, wearing only our bath towels. Our breath and our snow-dusted hair were illuminated by the glow of the kitchen light. The air was so cold, our puffs of laughter seemed to crystallize and float to the earth on translucent clouds.

Penny caught her breath and said in her most naive, awestruck voice, "Sharon, are we in Finland?"

"Yes, Penny, I believe we are."

"So this isn't just an elaborate dream I'm having?"

"Nope. This is all real."

"Wow!"

"Yeah, wow."

Penny turned the handle on the back door. It didn't open.

"Try pushing it," I suggested.

Penny pushed with her shoulder. It didn't budge. "Hello!" Penny knocked on the door. "Can you hear me, Marketta?"

From inside we heard playful giggling.

"Who is out there?" Anni called from the kitchen.

"Why those little grannies! They locked us out!" Penny pounded on the door. "Let us in, or we'll huff and we'll puff and we'll blow your house down!"

More muffled giggles floated outside. I was thoroughly thawed out now and feeling the cold. The door opened an inch.

"Who is come to my door?" Anni asked.

"Two freezing snow bunnies. Let us in!"

Anni opened the door all the way. "How nice of you to come visit!"

"Make way," Penny said. "I'm heading for the sauna, and nobody is going to stop me!"

"Just like your mother," I heard Marketta say with a chuckle.

I couldn't wait to get back in the sauna and feel that extravagant heat. This time the heat made my cold skin feel prickly. All four of us immediately mellowed.

"This is making me sleepy," Penny said.

"You will sleep well tonight," Anni said. "Would you like the first shower?"

Penny showered and pulled on her pajamas. I was right behind her. We sipped small glasses of berry juice and listened to the soothing music on the stereo.

Anni showed us to her guest room. She had pulled back the fluffy comforters on the two twin beds and lit a candle on the windowsill. I stretched out and pulled the comforter up to my chin.

I couldn't remember how old I was. Or where I was. Or if I'd ever seen a star before tonight.

Sometime later, in the padded darkness, I heard Penny's voice. "Are you awake?"

"Hmm?"

"Sharon, are you awake?"

"No."

"It's morning, Sharon. Wake up. I have something to tell you."

I opened one eye. Penny was sitting up in the twin bed across from mine, but I could only see her shadow because the room was still dark.

"What time is it?"

"Almost six."

"Penny, why are you awake?"

"I could hardly sleep. I've been waiting for morning to come so I could tell you my idea."

"What idea?"

"Let's go to England."

"Okay." I pulled up the comforter over my shoulder and mumbled, "When we get home, we'll plan another trip. To England. I'll buy the tour book. You can buy the plane tickets."

"No, I mean today, Sharon. Let's go to England today."

Despite my better judgment, I opened both eyes and squinted in an attempt to read the expression on Penny's face. She was serious.

"Why?"

"I want to meet my cousin. Marketta's daughter, Elina. Remember? She lives in England."

"Don't you want to see more of Finland?"

"No."

"Penny..."

"I can't explain it, Sharon, but this trip to Finland is done for me. We have five more days before our plane flies out of Heathrow. What's to keep us from changing our connecting tickets and flying to Heathrow today? I'll call Elina to see if we can visit her. I can hand-deliver my mom's letters so Elina can start to translate them."

"Penny..."

"Before you say anything, just think about it. Think about how convenient it would be to adjust our plans."

"What plans?"

"Exactly! I knew you would agree with me. Our plans are flexible."

"Very flexible."

"We can do whatever we want."

"Within reason."

"This is within reason. Come on, Sharon. What do you say? Let's go to England today!"

I let out an exaggerated sigh. "Why not?" As if my opinion mattered for anything at this point.

Marketta was more understanding than I think I would have been if someone woke me by clomping around at six-thirty in the morning. Anni cheerfully made us breakfast. Marketta made a few phone calls, checked on bus schedules, and helped us to organize our crazy plan. She kept saying she was sorry to see us go so soon. I told Marketta I was sorry to leave, too, but Penny was barely aware of our conversation. She was on the phone with the airline and managed to arrange a flight that left at two.

Our hugs and kisses for Anni were brief at the bus stop because the bus was already there, waiting. Penny and Marketta sat beside each other on the bus ride and talked the whole time. I tried to catch a little more sleep.

Juhani was ready when we arrived at their apartment complex in Porvoo. While Marketta gathered the letters from Penny's mom and a few photos, Juhani put our luggage in the car. He drove like a wild man to get us to the airport in time. His car had aired out considerably, but we still rode with the windows down a few inches because of the lingering fish fragrance. I think Penny was too preoccupied to be bothered by the odor this time.

I found it difficult to say good-bye to Juhani and Marketta.

I wasn't ready to leave them or to leave Finland. I'd read about and marked in the tour book so many places of interest, but now we were leaving after seeing very little of Finland.

Once again, I reminded myself that this was Penny's trip, and she was the one to call the shots. I was merely the travel companion, and travel companions don't have much of a say in things.

The problem was that having "emerged" so much during the past few days, I found it difficult to fall in line behind my trailblazing friend. If it had been my trip, I would have stayed the rest of the time with Marketta and Anni and let them show me the Finland they knew and loved.

But Penny and I were boarding a plane, and barring possible ice storms and layovers at unnamed airports, we would be in London before our next meal.

Fifteen

The best part about our flight to Heathrow was that it was uneventful. I dozed with my head against the window. Penny fidgeted in the aisle seat. The middle seat remained empty, and I was glad for the invisible buffer between us. It seemed to me that everything the two of us had enjoyed so thoroughly for the past seven days could be overturned if this impulsive jaunt to England turned out to be a disaster.

I kept telling myself to relax and go along for the ride. Penny was a woman on a mission, and I knew there was no stopping her. As liberated as I felt, my role was still the cheerful cosmic DustBuster.

When we trudged through customs this time, Penny was the one who started singing to the officer. He joined in and sang all about the barber taking photographs and the pouring rain.

I stepped up to the window next, and the officer asked if I was traveling with Ms. Penny Lane.

"Yes, I'm with her."

"Will you be paying a visit then to Tony Slavin's?"

"Pardon me?"

"The barbershop. On Penny Lane. It's still there, you know. Will you be paying a visit? Take a photo?"

"I don't know. We might."

He stamped my passport and handed it back. "Make sure you stop by the pub at the bottom of Church Street and have a pint. Tell ol' Reggie that Jon hasn't forgotten about 'im."

"Reggie?"

"Yeah, Reggie's the bartender. You tell that Scouser that Jon hasn't forgotten about that fiver he owes me. You remember now, right, miss?"

I nodded, but I knew I wasn't likely to remember his message and even less likely to go to Reggie's pub.

Penny and I made our way through the long corridors that led to the ground transportation. Marketta's daughter, Elina, had given Penny all the information over the phone that morning, so I didn't know where we were going.

An idea took shape in the back of my mind as we walked. *We should go to Penny Lane. Penny needs a picture of herself standing on Penny Lane.*

I decided there, in that crowded terminal, teeming with travelers from every corner of the world, that I would surprise Penny. There's a first time for everything, and this would be the first time I could surprise her with an early birthday present. She had bought me the gorgeous blue sweater set I was wearing. I could figure out a way to get her to Penny Lane.

All I needed was a tour book.

The disadvantage of not growing up in tune with the popular culture of my generation was that I had no clue where Penny Lane was located. I knew very little about the Beatles.

Penny would know, but then, where would the surprise be?

We exchanged some money and took a train to Paddington Station where we were to change to another train. I convinced Penny to make a quick stop at a newspaper stand inside the charming Victorian train station so I could buy a tour book.

Penny said, "Let's hope we get more use out of this one than we got out of the one on Finland."

I was sure that we would.

Settled on the train for our second ride, I thumbed through the tour book. The index section in the back listed Penny Lane, and that led me right to Liverpool. It was all there. A map, train lines, bus tours. The journey would take us a few hours out of London, but we could do it. Keeping it a surprise would be the tricky part.

"Where are we going?" I asked. Outside the train window I saw we were still in London's suburbs. Billboards along the side of the road that paralleled the train tracks advertised shampoo and designer label clothing. Low clouds hung over the chimney tops from which an occasional spiral of smoke snaked a white rope up to the cushioned heavens.

"We're getting off at some place called Twickenham," Penny said. "Elina said to watch for the station because it sneaks up quickly."

I found Twickenham in the tour book and shared the info. "It says here that Twickenham is by Richmond and Richmond is an 'affluent riverside town along the Thames with alleys full of antique stores and boutiques.' Good. Because if we have time, I need to do some souvenir shopping. I didn't buy much in Finland for anyone else. Kaylee gave me a list, and I definitely want to find something for Joanie."

"Joanie?"

"You remember Joanie from the Clip 'n' Curl."

"Oh yeah, Joanie. Okay. Let's add shopping to the schedule."

I was intrigued with Penny's use of the word *schedule,* so I had to tease her. "And just what else would we have on our schedule?"

"Anything and everything we can fit in. That, and bonding with my cousin. That's at the top of my list."

"Marketta said Elina is our age, right?"

"Right. Hey, this is our stop. Grab your stuff."

All day I'd been carrying my light luggage as well as one of Penny's three bags so she would only have to wrestle with her wheeled suitcase and the oversized gym bag.

"You brought too much stuff, Penny."

"Tell me about it! I'm getting rid of some of this junk tonight. What was I thinking when I packed all this?"

"You probably were thinking you didn't know what to expect."

"Exactly." She looked at me wistfully as the train came to a lurching halt. "I almost wish my luggage had been lost, too, so I could reinvent my wardrobe the way you did."

"Wardrobe? Five or so new items don't exactly constitute a wardrobe."

"But it all works," Penny said. "You look great, and you're traveling light. Look at me. I'm encumbered."

As we stepped off the train, I laughed at Penny's word choice. A woman in a red coat caught our attention and waved to us. I wondered if we obviously looked like tourists to Elina.

Elina wore her straight blond hair short the way her mother, Marketta, did. Her lips were deep red, like her coat. She greeted us with awkward hugs and offered to carry some of the luggage for us. With a bag strapped over each shoulder, Elina led the way through the small train station to where her older model green car was parked in a crowded lot.

It began to rain as we drove away from the station. Elina pulled onto the left side of the road, and Penny pressed her hand against the dashboard and said, "Is this a one-way road?"

"No." Elina put on her blinker and turned again into what would have been oncoming traffic on American roads.

"This is so bizarre!" Penny laughed. "I don't think I can watch."

"Oh yes. It must seem to you that I'm driving on the wrong side of the road," Elina said. "The traffic laws took me a while to grow accustomed to, as well. You'll find this feels normal in a day or two."

Elina's English vocabulary was broader than her mother's. I could see why Marketta had said she would not be good at translating Elsa's letters, but that her smart daughter, Elina, could translate them easily.

Penny asked all the usual questions like, "How long have you lived here?" and "How old are your children?"

Elina responded with short answers and returned the same questions to Penny. I couldn't tell if Elina was uncomfortable with us in general or if she was simply an abrupt person.

If I were Elina, I think I would have been guardedly gracious as well. It's one thing to surprise an older couple like Marketta and Juhani, who have the time to sip coffee at the kitchen table and recount the past for hours on end. It's completely different to show up in the middle of the life of someone our age who is juggling three children, ages eight, eleven, and sixteen, and a husband who works swing shift. Considering, too, that all this had been thrust upon Elina with such short notice, I thought she was being very kind.

"I'm afraid our home is rather small," Elina said.

"Like I told you on the phone, we're happy to stay at a hotel," Penny said.

"It is a little late now to make such arrangements. You might as well stay with us at least this one night. The girls don't mind sleeping in my room. I hope you will be comfortable in their room."

"I'm sure we'll be fine," I said. "Thanks for opening up your home to us."

Elina nodded but didn't say anything. She turned down a straight street with old, two-story homes lined up like matching birthday candles on a cake of someone well over fifty. The houses were different colors, but they were all the same style.

A tiny patch of grass separated the sidewalk from the rounded front window of the house we stopped in front of. Three steps guarded by an iron handrail led to the front door.

Parallel parking appeared to be an impossibility, but Elina expertly maneuvered her car into a space with mere inches between the bumpers. I noticed that all the car bumpers were well dented, as if drivers here actually made use of them for something other than a place to post their children's academic standing or to announce they had a baby on board.

The rain fell at a maddening pace as we pulled our luggage from the trunk and dashed to the house. Elina opened the front door and called out, "William! Cammy! Tara!"

Eight-year-old William was the only child to respond. He bounded down the hardwood stairs in stocking feet. "Mummy, have you brought the imposing cousins with you?"

I watched Elina's face turn as red as her lips and coat.

"William," she said sternly. "This is Mrs. Lane and Mrs.

Andrews. Mrs. Lane is my cousin. Say hello to the kind ladies, will you, son?"

"Hallo!" William held out his hand and shook with both of us. He was the picture of politeness. A sharp pinch twisted my mothering heart as I looked at bright-eyed William. I missed my Joshie. I missed all my kids. I missed Jeff terribly. I was ready to go home. I wanted to close my eyes, and when I opened them again, I wanted to be standing in the entryway of my home with the mud stains that wouldn't come out of the carpet on the second stair and the small chip in the wall where Ben had rammed his remote control Jeep on Christmas morning five years ago.

I blinked, but I was still in England. My brain seemed to be driving on the wrong side of the road. Yesterday at this time, I was bounding along a gravel road in a car that reeked of halibut and listening to Juhani and Marketta argue in Finnish. I wasn't ready for such a quick change in place and culture and sights.

But there I was, standing in the middle of a production of *Peter Pan,* complete with shadows on the wall and a grandfather clock at the end of the hall that was chiming the hour for us. Five-thirty.

I needed to sit down.

Elina rolled on as if none of us had heard William's comment about the "imposing cousins." I knew Penny would only want to stay for a short visit and then call a cab to take us to the nearest hotel.

"Where are your sisters?" Elina asked.

"Upstairs." Turning to Penny, William added, "Would you like to see Miss Molly?"

"Sure." Penny looked over her shoulder at me, as if I knew who Miss Molly was.

"Do wipe your feet when you come back inside, William. It's raining." Elina reached for Penny's largest suitcase. "We can take the luggage upstairs, if you like."

"All right." I followed Elina up the steep, narrow stairway. The door was open to the first room on the right. Bunk beds filled one side of the room. A dozen mismatched posters of kittens and rock bands covered the other side. Obviously the two sisters who shared this room had different tastes.

"Cammy," Elina called out, "please come get your satchel and your shoes."

Eleven-year-old Cammy stepped out from the closet that was hidden by the door. "I'm right here, Mum." She resembled Elina but had long dark hair pulled up in a ponytail. "I'm just collecting my dirty clothes."

"Good. Where's your sister?"

"She's watching the telly in your room."

"Cammy, this is Mrs. Andrews."

Cammy smiled. I tried to make conversation about my children, but Cammy didn't appear interested, so I dropped it and just told her thanks for letting us stay in her room.

"I'm going down to start dinner," Elina said. "Cammy, did you put out clean towels in the loo?"

"Not yet."

"Will you do that, please, and show Mrs. Andrews where everything is located."

I followed Cammy to the loo, where she gave me instructions on how the toilet had to be flushed by pulling on a chain and holding it down until I could hear the sound of the water filling the tank. She introduced me to sixteen-year-old Tara, who had appeared suddenly. Tara had dark hair also. I guessed their father would be the one with the dominant dark genes.

"Sharon!" Penny called from the bottom of the stairs. "Sharon, you have to come down. You won't believe this!"

The two girls got a head start on me and trotted down the stairs. I had to stoop so I wouldn't hit my head on my way down. I followed the girls into the kitchen and there, in the middle of the linoleum floor, stood Penny with a big, fat chicken in her arms. A live chicken. A deep maroon, fluffed-out feathers chicken with dangling feet and a jutted-out neck, nervously looking about.

"Why do you have Miss Molly inside?" Cammy asked.

"It was too wet outside. Mrs. Lane wanted to hold her."

I found it hard to believe that Penny "wanted" to hold any animal at any time. Especially something as jittery as a chicken. My guess was that Penny was doing her usual public relations routine to win over skeptical Elina and the rest of her brood.

"Well, look at you," I said.

"Yes." Penny bit her lower lip. "Look at me!"

I slowly approached Penny and the chicken. "How are you, Miss Molly?"

"She's my favorite," William said.

"Oh, really. How many chickens do you have?"

"Four. Miss Molly is the friendliest."

"Is that right?" I watched as Miss Molly took friendly little pecks at the skin on Penny's hand.

"I think Miss Molly wants to go back to her coop," Penny said with a tight smile. "Here you go, William."

With a flutter of feathers, Miss Molly made the transfer to William's arms. "Would you like to hold her, Mrs. Andrews?"

"No, that's okay. If Miss Molly is ready to go back to her coop, I don't need to hold her."

A wicked grin appeared on Penny's face. "I think Miss

Molly wants you to hold her, Sharon. Go ahead, William. Let Mrs. Andrews hold your favorite chicken. She's so friendly."

I shot Penny a glance that said, "I'm going to get you back for this one." If chickens can sense nervousness in humans, then I'm sure Miss Molly read my thoughts. She wasn't about to roost in my arms. As soon as William tried to hand her to me, Miss Molly clawed my hand and tried to take off flying around the kitchen with a wild flutter of feathers.

"William, get that ridiculous chicken out of here!" Elina called from the sink. "Tara, please set the table, will you? Cammy, see if we have enough milk in the icebox and pour three glasses for the table."

William tackled Miss Molly and took her out the back door. My hand started to bleed. Quietly I excused myself and went upstairs to wash out my wound. Penny followed me.

"I'm sorry, Sharon," she said. "I didn't think Miss Molly would attack you."

"It's not deep," I said, running my hand under the water. "See? The bleeding stopped already."

"I have a first-aid kit in my suitcase," Penny said. "Dave made me pack it. He thought we would need it for blisters. Ha! Won't he be surprised to hear what we needed it for! I'll be right back."

As I cleaned and dressed my wound, Penny said, "Do you think we should make other arrangements for tonight? Obviously we're a big inconvenience to Elina."

"I think it would be awkward if we picked up and left now. What if we stay for dinner, and then if it's still uncomfortable, we can come up with some reason to leave."

"Okay. No matter what, we'll call a taxi in the morning and go somewhere else," Penny said. "Where do you want to go?"

"Where do *I* want to go? Right now, I want to go home."

"Home?"

In one long, run-on sentence I reminded Penny that we hadn't eaten anything since breakfast except for a few pretzels on the plane, and I was furious at the chicken for opening my skin, and since we obviously weren't welcome here, I thought it was absurd for Penny to turn to me at a moment like this and ask where we should go because if it had been up to me, we would still be in Finland, enjoying the soothing tempo of Marketta's life and eating chocolates at her sturdy kitchen table with the green-and-white tablecloth.

"What are you saying, Sharon? Are you saying you want to go back to Finland?"

"No, of course not. I mean, yes, I would. Someday. I'd love to go back to Finland. But not today. It would make no sense to go back there. All I'm trying to say is that I don't know what we should do next."

As an afterthought I added, "Maybe we should pray about these decisions before making them."

Penny leaned against the edge of the sink. "I have been praying. I thought we were supposed to come here, but maybe I misunderstood. Maybe we were supposed to come to England for something other than my cousin."

"Like what?"

"I don't know. I still want to ask Elina to translate my mom's letters. Perhaps I can leave them with her, and she can mail them to me."

"You might find someone in San Francisco who could translate them for you."

I don't know if Penny heard me. She was staring at the shower curtain and seemed to be deep in thought. Or maybe she was deep in prayer. I cleaned up my first-aid clutter and headed for the bedroom. Penny followed me.

"I have an idea," she said.

I almost said, "Of course you do." But my lips were as weary as the rest of me, and they sat this one out.

"What if we visit Monique?"

"Monique who?"

"Don't you remember? Monique. On the plane ride over here. She invited us to come see her if we were ever in England. And look! Here we are in England."

"Where does she live?"

"I don't remember. I have her address and phone number somewhere. Remember? She wrote it on a napkin."

"Do you think she really was inviting us to visit her, or was she just being polite?"

"I think she sincerely wanted us to come visit."

I wasn't convinced. But the thought of seeing Monique again intrigued me. I'm not sure why. Monique was more of a stranger than Elina. It seemed that it had been weeks since we had met her on the plane.

"Here it is." Penny produced a crumpled beverage napkin from her purse. "She lives in some place called Warrington. Is it very far away?"

I pulled out my tour book and found Warrington on the map. With a sly grin I noticed that Warrington was less than a quarter of an inch east of Liverpool.

"Let's go to Warrington," Penny said decidedly.

"Do you think that's going to be okay?" I asked.

"What, leaving? I think they'll be glad to have us gone. Except for William. He said it was 'jolly good' of me to hold his chicken."

"But what about connecting with your cousin? Our time went so fast in Finland. If we leave in the morning, you won't have had much time with Elina at all. That's what you wanted out of this trip, isn't it?"

"Bonding with relatives appears to be more of a two-way street than I realized," Penny said. "It doesn't appear that Elina and I are driving down the same side of the road, so to speak."

"That could change."

"Or not."

I sighed. "Penny, I just want to be sure you take advantage of every opportunity to accomplish what you wanted from this trip. I want you to go home knowing that you tried your best to bond and all that."

"Thanks, Sharon. I know what you're saying, and you're right. I should try harder to connect. I have an in with William. Maybe I could start there and work my way to a closer connection with Elina. Like you said, this is my only chance."

Just then we heard footsteps coming up the stairs.

"Hallo!" William appeared at our open door with a chicken feather in his hand. "Would you like to keep this? It's one of Miss Molly's prettiest feathers."

"Why, thank you." Penny took the spiny quill and gave Will one of her best PR smiles. "Be sure to tell Miss Molly I appreciate it."

William beamed. "Mummy said to let you know we're ready to eat."

"What are we having for dinner?" Penny tapped William on the nose with her feather. "Not chicken, I suppose."

William looked up at Penny, startled. "No, not chicken."

"That was a little joke, William."

His lower lip quivered. He pulled away from Penny and took off down the stairs yelling, "Mummy! Mummy!"

Penny and I looked at each other.

"I'll go call Monique," she said.

"Good idea."

Sixteen

Sweet William seemed to recover quickly from Penny's jest about having chicken for dinner. Elina had prepared a one-dish meal she called shepherd's pie. Although Penny and I both said we had heard of it, neither of us had eaten it before. The bottom layer was ground beef, which Elina called "mince." The beef was mixed in a thick gravy with carrots and peas and then covered with mashed potatoes and sprinkled with cheese on top.

The meal was simple, but the conversation around the table was complex. Cammy said she liked shepherd's pie better when her mum used real mashed potatoes and not the instant kind she had used tonight. Tara argued with her mother about a party she wanted to go to over the weekend. Tara seemed to have waited strategically until we, the guests, were present before she brought up the topic. I recognized the typical teenage ploy to get Mom to say yes.

Elina was a stronger mother than I. She remained firm in her "no" despite Tara's persuasive attempts.

William kept interrupting and was asked repeatedly to wait his turn. When Cammy stood to clear her plate, she said she had homework to do and then reminded her mom that she needed her blouse ironed for school in the morning because they had a special reciting program.

"I can't iron it," Cammy said, "because I still have to work on my piece for the program. I haven't memorized it yet."

Elina looked at her watch. "I have to make several phone calls before it gets too late. William, when you finish, clear the table. Tara, I need you to wash the dishes."

"I can't. I have homework, too," Tara protested.

"Then why were you watching television this afternoon?"

"That was part of my homework. We have to write a paper on a current event in the news."

"She wasn't watching the news. She was watching cartoons," Cammy said.

"So were you," Tara spat. "And you were supposed to be memorizing your speech."

"I wasn't watching the telly," William announced proudly. "I was in my room the whole time you were gone."

Elina's face kept growing deeper shades of red. I thought she was going to blow a fuse. I felt awful for dropping ourselves into her life the way we had. Penny and I were on vacation whereas Elina was obviously on duty. Double duty, since her husband wasn't around.

Elina drew in a deep breath. "All of you go upstairs and do what you need to do. Just go. William, don't forget to take a bath."

"I'm still eating, Mummy." William nibbled off a small bit of carrot from his fork.

"Are you going to iron my blouse then, Mum?" Cammy asked.

I jumped in. "I can iron your blouse, Cammy. I love to iron."

Everyone looked at me.

"I really do." I sheepishly shrugged.

"She does," Penny vouched. "I know. It's kind of strange, but Sharon loves ironing. And I'm an expert on clearing the table and washing dishes. Point us in the right direction, Elina, and we'll cover the bases down here."

Elina was slow to respond. She finally said, "Okay, but don't ever tell my mother I put you to work. I'll only be on the phone for a few minutes."

The liberated ducklings scattered with record speed. Penny and I were alone, playing the roles of the downstairs maids. I didn't mind. I felt it was the least we could do.

We worked swiftly and silently. I don't know what Penny thought about as she worked, but I loved the feeling of doing what was familiar. Rushing through airports was beginning to grow on me, but this—a kitchen, an ironing board, the sound of bathwater running upstairs—this I knew. My thoughts were of my family. I missed them down in a place so deep in my heart that I don't think I'd ever gone there before. My love for them never had been tested like this, and I felt an unfamiliar euphoria over having a husband and children to love. I would never view those relationships as ordinary again.

Tasks completed, Penny sat at the table and we discussed our departure options. As soon as Elina was off the phone, Penny would call Monique.

I joined her, still feeling mushy about my family, and said that our experiences already had surpassed my wildest expectations. I was satisfied. I didn't need any more adventures. "We could take an earlier flight home," I suggested. Aside from my desire to somehow get Penny to Penny Lane, I had no other reason to stay on this side of the world.

Penny, however, seemed addicted to new experiences and sat across from me, growing wild-eyed, looking for her next fix. "We have to go and see all we can while we can," Penny said in a tight voice. "This is our only chance. Life is too short. Don't you get it?"

"Yes, I get it, and I'm content to do whatever you want to do. So you decide. What's next?"

"I want to call Monique."

"Okay. Call Monique, and we'll visit her and then see what happens."

Penny's amber-flecked eyes glazed over. "I also want to go to Scotland. Actually, I really want to go to Switzerland. And Greece. Not necessarily in that order. I always wanted to go to Greece. Have you seen pictures of the Aegean Sea? It's so blue. Can you imagine what it would be like to go swimming in water like that? Or the Nile River. I always wanted to float down the Nile like Cleopatra."

"Penny," I interrupted her stream of crazy travel lore. "Are you listening to yourself? You're not making a whole lot of sense right now."

Penny looked at me with a shadow of sadness veiling her cocoa brown eyes. "I want to do everything, Sharon. I want to see it all. It's like that song back when we were in high school. Remember that song about sailing around the world? I listened to it for weeks after I left Wolf and went home from San Francisco. Remember? Look for gold and dive for pearls?" Penny began to hum and then sang one of the lines about knowing that she would never get to sail around the world.

Elina entered the room and offered to make a pot of tea.

"Sorry to leave you with the dishes," she said. "There's a lot going on right now."

"Don't worry about it." Penny stood up, leaving her song at the table along with her invisible pile of high school memories and travel wishes. "I'm the one who should apologize to you for dropping in the way we did. We plan to leave in the morning because we have someone else to visit. If you wouldn't mind, may I use your phone to give her a call? I'm going to charge it to my phone card, so it won't cost you anything."

"Oh. Certainly." Elina pointed to the phone attached to the kitchen wall. "If you would prefer privacy, you may use the phone upstairs in my bedroom."

"This phone is fine." Penny pulled Monique's number from her pocket and borrowed a piece of paper and a pen.

I could tell by the way Penny spoke into the phone that she had reached Monique's answering system and was leaving a message.

Elina placed three cups on the table. Mine had a bit of dried food or something on the bottom. I tried to scratch at it without being obvious. Elina noticed.

"Sorry," she said, reaching for my cup. "Here, this one looks clean. And I must apologize for the tea. Or should I say the absence of real tea. Loose tea. I didn't get to the market today, and I'm down to my emergency stash of tea bags."

"No need to apologize. I use tea bags at home all the time."

"Do you really?"

Penny hung up the phone. "Monique wasn't home, but we'll still head up that way tomorrow. We can try her again once we get there."

"Where are you going?" Elina asked.

"Scotland," Penny said confidently.

I looked down at my cup and deliberately drowned the teabag, so I didn't catch the exchange of expressions between the cousins. I also didn't want Penny or Elina to notice the inevitable splash of disapproval that was washing across my face. I reminded myself this was Penny's adventure. I was along for the ride. Blazing comets answered to no one.

"Are you taking the train?" Elina asked.

"Yes," Penny said. "Definitely. We'll do better on a train than we would with a rental car."

"I can drive you to the train station," Elina offered.

"That's okay," Penny said briskly. "We'll take a taxi."

Elina shifted in her seat, wrapping her hands around her teacup. We all sank into a pocket of awkward silence.

Rescuing my limp tea bag, I placed it in the hollow of my spoon, the way Elina had, and took a sip of the dark brew. I wished we could politely excuse ourselves, go upstairs, eke out a decent night's sleep, and slip out at first light.

"My mother mentioned that you had some letters you wanted me to translate."

"Actually," Penny said slowly, "I thought I'd take them to someone in San Francisco."

"Do you know a Finnish translator in San Francisco?"

"No, but I thought I could find someone through the university."

"Look." Elina set aside her cup. "I don't think this has been a very good start for us. You and I have gone all these years without knowing each other as cousins."

Penny seemed to flinch at the word *cousins*.

Elina reached across the table and took Penny's hand in hers. "Why don't we start over and try to be friends. Would that not be a better place to begin?"

Penny withdrew her hand but kept her gaze fixed on Elina. "But you see, that's the thing, Elina. We aren't friends. We're cousins. I have enough friends. But I have no other cousins. I have no other relatives that I know of. Only you, your brother, your mother, and your father. That's all. You are one of four people on this huge planet with whom I share the same blood. We don't have to be friends, Elina. But whether we want to be or not, we always will be cousins."

I was stunned at Penny's directness. I was even more stunned at Elina's response. She cried. Not the kind of crying that comes with tidy streams of polite tears down the cheeks. She sobbed with her hands covering her face.

Penny didn't hesitate. She jumped up and wrapped a comforting arm around her cousin and stroked her hair, murmuring gentle words in Elina's ear. The scene mirrored what Marketta had done at her kitchen table, only reenacted with Penny playing the role of the comforter.

"You're right," Elina said, looking up. "We are cousins."

"Yes, but why are you crying like this, Elina? I know a few things about tears, and I'm guessing these have been wanting to come out for a long time."

Elina opened up. The women in Penny's family certainly shared the same propensity toward bursting into tears and blurting out their feelings. "This morning, my husband, Arnie, received a call that some of the men on his shift might be sacked today."

"Sacked? You mean drunk?"

Elina looked at me.

"*Sacked* means laid off, doesn't it?" I said.

"Yes. He said he might be given the boot after work today. He was very upset when he left. I didn't want to bring this into your visit, but I'm afraid I haven't been able to think of anything else. If he loses his job, I don't know what we'll do. We've been living on so little for so long. I had a job for six years, but I was sacked nine months ago. Or what did you call it? Laid off? I was laid off. Nothing has gotten better for us. "

Penny reached for a paper towel and handed it to Elina since no tissue was in sight.

"Well, I guess we picked a pretty awful day to come for a visit," Penny said with lighthearted tenderness.

"Yes," Elina agreed, wiping her eyes and pulling herself together. "It's been a pretty awful day. A pretty awful year, actually."

Penny reached for a chair next to Elina and sat down. With calm, steady words, Penny said to her cousin, "Life can be messy sometimes. But it's okay. You'll be okay. God will work all this out for you. You'll see."

"Mummy?" William, wearing his robe, stood around the corner, peeking into the kitchen.

"Yes, William?"

"I'm ready for bed, Mummy."

"Okay. Good night, son."

"Aren't you going to ask if I brushed my teeth?"

"Did you brush your teeth?"

"Yes, Mummy."

"Good night, then."

"Mummy?"

"Yes, William."

"May I have a kiss?"

"Of course. Come here."

I watched Elina do what mothers all over the world do. She took her son in her arms, kissed him, and buried her nose in a tuft of his hair. Nothing in the universe smells the same as the head of an eight-year-old boy, fresh from the bath.

I also recognized the pattern of what children everywhere do when they sense tension in the family. William wanted to be close to his "mummy."

"Good night," Elina said.

William looked up at her. "Good night. Sleep tight. Don't let the bedbugs bite. If they bite, squeeze them tight, and they'll not bite another night. Good night!"

With a kiss for Elina and a wave for Penny and me, Brave William was off to bed.

"You are rich in many ways," Penny said.

"Yes, but…"

William appeared again. "Cammy and Tara are fighting."

We heard the sound of the front door unlocking and opening.

"That would be Arnie." Elina shook her head. "This can't be good, if he's home already."

"Daddy!" William took off for the front door.

"How's my boy?" the deep voice called from the entryway. We could hear William give a full report of household events including his fighting sisters upstairs. "And the ladies are in the kitchen with Mummy having tea."

"You go on to bed, son."

"All right, Daddy."

Penny turned to Elina and said in a low voice, "Sharon and I can leave so you two can talk. I'll call a cab."

"No, it's okay. Please stay. Arnie won't mind."

A dark-haired man with glasses and a brown corduroy cap stepped into the kitchen with a grin on his face. "Are you ready for the news, Elina? I've been promoted!" He leaned over and gave her a smacking big kiss. Looking up, he gave Penny and me a nod. "Hallo."

"Promoted?"

"That's right. I've been switched to the morning shift, and because of the change, I have off the next three days. With pay. A three-day weekend. That's the first in a long time, isn't it?"

"How did that happen?"

"According to Chester, my number came up for the day shift, and they had an opening. If there hadn't been an opening, I would have been sacked with the other four men on the night shift."

"I can't believe it," Elina said.

"You better believe it! It's about time something good happened to us."

Elina glanced over at Penny. "This is my husband, Arnie. Arnie, this is my cousin, Penny, and her friend Sharon."

Arnie wasn't a large man. He was rugged in a way that suited a man who had made an honest living stuck in the middle of the working class.

"Nice to meet you both. Elina told me you'll be staying with us for a few days."

"Actually, no," Penny said. "We're leaving in the morning."

"The morning? Nonsense! You only arrived this afternoon, did you not? Why don't you stay and keep Elina company for a few days? She could use a bit of a holiday."

"They have plans," Elina said.

"Then you make yourself some plans, love. I'll take over here for a day or two and give you a break."

Elina pulled back and scrutinized her husband. "Have you been drinking, Arnie?"

"Only a pint. I had to celebrate with Pete and the boys."

Elina shook her head. "I can't believe you were promoted."

"Believe it." Arnie pulled up a chair and said to Penny and me, "It's been a rough time for us lately. Did Elina tell you about the new medication the doctor put her on? Ever since the operation she's been on a spin."

"Arnie, I didn't tell them any of that."

"Oh. I thought women always told each other about their female problems."

Elina stared into her empty teacup.

"Hysterectomy?" Penny ventured after the pause seemed to have siphoned all the air from the room.

Elina nodded. "Three months ago."

"Four," Arnie corrected her. "Time for her to feel herself again, wouldn't you say?"

"Not necessarily," Penny said. "A friend of mine from work took a full six months before she was feeling normal, and that was after some creative hormone therapy."

The air didn't seem to be returning to the room because none of us had anything to add to Penny's comment.

Except Penny.

"I have an idea."

I closed my eyes and waited. I didn't even have to check her eyebrows to guess what she was going to say.

"Why don't you come with us, Elina? If Arnie is going to be home for the next few days, why don't the three of us head up to Warrington in the morning?"

Elina said, "You can't be serious."

"Of course I'm serious. A train ride to Warrington would do you good, don't you think? If we feel like it, we might go on up to Scotland." Penny tapped my arm. "What do you think, Sharon?"

I honestly thought it was a good idea. Not necessarily the part about flitting off to Scotland, but the idea of including Elina. After the way Elina had opened up to us, I felt sympathy for her. She was a mom. Everyone depended on her. I knew what that was like. She had been through a lot during the past few months, including surgery and a job loss. If I were Elina, I'd want to get away from home for a few days.

I leaned forward so that Elina looked me in the eye. With a smile I said, "I think it's a great idea. Come on, Elina. Come with us. Just for a few days."

Penny graciously let it be known that she was, of course, paying for the train, meals, and all accommodations. After that announcement, Elina entered into the moment with more animation and sparkle.

"This is crazy!" Elina grinned from ear to ear.

"Yep!" Penny said. "Crazy like a daisy!"

I laughed, knowing oh so well the feeling of having Penny swish into your life and take you on an unexpected escapade. That was Penny's gift to me, and now it would be her gift to her cousin. Elina was being scooped up from the ordinary and catapulted over the moon.

This time, I was the little dog laughing to see such sport.

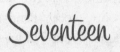

Penny, Elina, and I stayed up until almost midnight discussing our options. Arnie lasted for the first half hour and then went upstairs to bed. Penny tried to call Monique again around ten o'clock. She got the answering machine but didn't leave another message.

"I don't have a problem just heading up to Warrington tomorrow morning," Penny said. "If Monique is home, great. If not, we can get back on the train and keep going until we hit Scotland."

Elina turned to me. "Is this the way the two of you planned your trip over here?"

"Pretty much," I said.

"We're at God's mercy," Penny said.

Elina didn't comment.

"It's not as scary as it sounds," I assured her.

"Have you ever been to Warrington?" Penny asked Elina.

"No."

"What about Scotland?"

221

"Yes, I've been to Glasgow and Edinburgh twice."

"What about Greece?" Penny suddenly popped out.

"What about Greece?" Elina asked.

"Have you ever been to Greece?"

"No."

"Neither have I."

In the short pause that followed, Penny looked at me, and I shook my head ever so slightly.

"What about—" Penny began.

I jumped in. "What about Liverpool?"

"I've not been to Liverpool, either," Elina said.

"What's in Liverpool?" Penny asked.

I pressed my lips together and then decided to spill my idea. A photo in front of Tony Slavin's barbershop couldn't be compared with the Aegean Sea, I knew, but Liverpool was so much more practical.

Practical? Listen to me! As if any part of this trip has been practical!

"Here's my idea," I said looking at Elina, hoping to garner her support in case Penny needed convincing. "I thought of this earlier today at the airport, but I didn't want to tell Penny because I was trying to figure out how I could make it a surprise."

"A surprise?" I definitely had Penny's attention.

"Yes. I wanted to surprise *you* for once. I thought of this while we were going through customs. Do you remember how the officer was singing to you about Penny Lane?"

"Yes, of course."

"Well, that's why I wanted to buy the tour book. I wanted to find out where your street, Penny Lane, is located."

"There's a real Penny Lane?" Penny asked.

"Of course there's a real Penny Lane," Elina said. "The one from the song. It's in Liverpool."

"Liverpool," Penny repeated. "Really? How did I miss that bit of trivia? I thought Abbey Road was real and Penny Lane was made up."

"Apparently Penny Lane is a real street." I felt more hip than I should have. "The customs officer told me that the barbershop is still there, too. You know, the one from the song."

Penny's eyes began to twinkle. "We could go to Liverpool…"

"…and get a picture of you on Penny Lane," I finished the thought for her. "Wouldn't that be a great souvenir?"

Penny started to cry.

I was so surprised I didn't know what to do.

"It's a clever idea," Elina said to me. "Don't you think so, Penny?"

"I love it. It's…it's so fitting for the summary of my life."

I wasn't sure why Penny was being melodramatic. I felt like the only levelheaded woman stuck between two hormone-hyped, premenopausal maidens. I was secretly relieved that Penny loved my idea and wasn't on the phone right now arranging a flight for us to Greece. Or to Egypt for a quick float down the Nile. Liverpool was doable.

The three of us exchanged gleeful grins. Elina's face was lit up with escapade sparkles.

The sparkle remained the next morning after she saw her children out the door on their way to school. Packed and ready, the three of us waited for our taxi to arrive.

I was so proud of Penny. She had trimmed her luggage down to one bag and had left the rest of her things in tidy piles on the floor in the girls' bedroom. One of the stacks of nice clothes, she said, was going to stay with Elina if she wanted it.

I found it soothing to follow someone through the train station who was familiar with the system and knew where she was going. Elina was strong like her mother and took long-legged strides ahead of both of us. She shoved her luggage onto the top shelf of the luggage carrier and settled into a backward facing seat on the train. Penny and I sat across from her. The slight grin on Elina's face hadn't left since the invitation had been extended to her the night before.

As the train started to roll, Elina pulled out a deck of playing cards and challenged Penny to a game of hearts. "You aren't really a true relative," Elina taunted, "unless you can go the distance with one of us in a card game."

Penny agreed. "My mother was a fanatic bridge player. She played solitaire all the time. I remember scrounging in her purse one time when I was eight, looking for gum, but all I found were boxes of cards."

"See?" Elina said. "It's in our blood. We're card-playing women. How about you, Sharon? Are you in?"

"No, that's okay."

"Of course she's playing," Penny said. "Deal her in."

Now I was uncomfortable. My family and Jeff's family were from a breed that shunned card games on the general principle that a person should never appear to be gambling. We stuck to Scrabble and an occasional benign game of Password. I hadn't ever told Penny about the ban on card games in my clan because it never came up. So now I simply said, "No thanks. I'm going to take a nap."

Penny and Elina used the small table that could be propped up under the window between our facing seats and began their game. I closed my eyes, and the steady rhythm of the train rolling over the tracks lulled me into a quiet place of reflection. So far from home, it was easier than it had ever been to take a more objective look at my life. I thought of all the parts of my normal life that usually seemed like such big issues or insurmountable conflicts. From this far away, things looked quite different.

I thought of my mother-in-law. Gloria didn't like me. She never had. That was the truth, and yet I hadn't allowed myself to let that complete thought go through my mind before. I had spent all these years avoiding that truth and telling myself that I needed to try harder to win her favor. I had told myself I was the problem. I was unacceptable for some unknown reason. If I could only figure out what I was doing wrong and change my behavior, then she would see I was a nice person and like me.

But what if Gloria never changed her opinion of me? What if she chose never to like me?

A clear thought came to me. *I can love her through you.*

I opened my eyes and looked around as if someone on the train had spoken those words. No one had spoken them to me. No human, at least.

I can love her through you.

That thought was going to take a while to wrap my emotions around. I understood the concept. Or at least, I thought I understood. On my own power, I might never find it in my heart to genuinely love my mother-in-law. But God loved her. He could demonstrate His love for her through me. I could choose to love Gloria even if she never chose to love me.

The picture that came to my mind was the way Marketta had freely gone to Penny, wrapped her arms around her, and hugged her when she was crying. Nothing was cautious about Marketta's choice to love Penny. Perhaps God had prompted

Marketta with the clear thought, "You can love her through me," when Penny appeared on her doorstep. If so, Marketta ran to the opportunity and embraced Penny with a pure heart.

I wanted to live like that, to be free enough to love and accept others. I wanted to be strong in mind and body. I wanted to grow old with strength and dignity, and I wanted to choose to love with a pure heart.

I can love her through you took on a two-sided meaning. I realized that in my strength and with my emotions, I could never fully love Gloria.

But God could love Gloria through me. And I could love Gloria through God.

At that moment, in that seat, on that train headed for the north of England, a new corner of my heart opened up. I pictured it as a little shop. The Lovin' Gloria shop. The shelves were stocked by the Giver of all good and perfect gifts with everything I needed to love my mother-in-law. The sign in the window read, "Now open for business."

I had no idea how things were going to change in my relationship with Gloria. I only knew that something had changed in me. I was open for business. The Lovin' Gloria business.

I pretended to sleep for the next hour. What I really was doing was letting my personal revelation sink in while Penny and Elina did their cousin bonding.

I heard them talking about their grandparents, whom Penny had never met but of whom Elina had plenty of memories. Elina was relaxing and opening up in ways she never would have been able to at home.

This detour to England was a good idea. Or maybe it was more than a good idea. Maybe it was really a God idea. I thought we had fulfilled Penny's dream by connecting with Marketta in Finland.

That was a big enough miracle. Now Penny is connecting in an amazing way with her cousin.

My awe over God's mercy and His provision grew. I wished once again that I had my Bible with me. I wanted to read His words. I wanted more of Him inside my heart and my mind. I was hungry for God.

The train ride took us out of the London suburbs. I peeked out the window while appearing to be sleeping. We were rolling past an open area of pasture where woolly sheep bowed their heads and nibbled their daily grass.

Elina talked about her hysterectomy and how she had been struggling with terrible mood swings. "It's the worst example of poor planning—I'm having premenopausal trauma at the same time my eleven-year-old daughter is having premenstrual trauma! Poor Arnie, he's living with two insane women. Small wonder he was eager to kick me out of the house for a few days."

Penny talked about how her preteen daughter, Nicole, was going through some of the same emotional loops.

Elina and Penny swapped stories about their children and cooked up a few dreams about them all meeting someday. Penny extended an open invitation to Elina and any of her family to stay with Dave and Penny in San Francisco.

The topic turned to husbands, and I continued to pretend I was asleep so Penny could give Elina an overview of her history with Dave. I noticed that Penny didn't leave out any of the details about their life. Penny seemed as comfortable talking about what her life was like before she became a Christian as she was about after she came to Christ. I realized how shy I was when it came to talking openly about God. He was as real to me as my husband was. I loved God as much as I loved Jeff and our children. Maybe more. So why did I shrink back? Why didn't I openly say it all the way Penny did?

Elina said, "I grew up in the church, as you probably would guess. Then I came to England, and we never connected with a church here. Arnie and I haven't done a good job of giving our children a Christian background, I'm afraid. I think it's not been a good choice for any of us. Especially for the children."

"That's easy enough to turn around," Penny said. "Repent!"

Elina laughed. "You've been talking to my mother, haven't you?"

"Yes, but not about you."

"Sometimes the only thing that keeps me sane is knowing that my mother is praying for me every day."

"So why don't you get yourself back on track with Christ? You know, it's your turn now to start praying for your children every day the way your mother prays for you."

Elina didn't respond.

I wanted to open my eye a pinch to see her expression, but I knew there was a chance they might see me "spying" on them. It never ceased to amaze me the way Penny could be so direct with people yet not offend them.

Elina changed the subject to food. She said this train had a bar car, and so the two of them decided to hunt up some sandwiches. Penny suggested they let me sleep.

As soon as they left, I "woke up" and pulled a brush from my purse. Every day on this trip I'd worn my hair up in a twist with a clip fastening it to the back of my head. This was the way I wore it at home. I thought of how Jeff liked it when I wore my blond hair down and slightly curled on the ends.

I smiled. I missed my husband so much. My Jeff.

Tonight, no matter where we ended up staying, I would call home and tell my wonderful Jeff that I loved him. I pulled out my travel diary and tried to remember as many details of the past few days as I could. I wanted to tell my husband everything when I got home.

Penny and Elina returned and offered me one of the dried-out ham and cream cheese sandwiches along with some hot tea in a paper cup. They were laughing about something Penny apparently had said in the bar car.

I loved watching Penny connect with her cousin.

Our train arrived in Warrington a little after two in the afternoon. Penny called Monique. No answer.

We scanned the train schedule for the next departure to Liverpool and tossed around ideas about staying in Warrington for the night. Penny seemed to have some notion that we needed to arrive in Liverpool in the early morning and take on the city when it was just waking up.

I didn't follow her logic, but this wasn't the first time.

"Warrington doesn't have much to see," Elina said. "But not far from here, in Daresbury, I know of a resort that has a big egg hunt at Easter."

"I've heard of a Lord Daresbury somewhere," Penny said. "Is he a character in a Jane Austen novel?"

"I don't think so," Elina said. "I only know about Daresbury because we have neighbors who came to the hotel for the egg hunt a few years ago."

"They came all this way for an egg hunt?" Penny said.

"They were visiting friends here in Warrington for Easter. They only popped over to the resort with their toddlers for the egg hunt. It's designed for the children, of course. The hotel is near the church where Lewis Carroll's father served as vicar."

Penny and I gave Elina blank stares.

"You know, Lewis Carroll. The author of *Through the Looking-Glass*? Alice, the Mad Hatter, the White Rabbit, and all. That's why the resort hosts the egg hunt."

"Oh," Penny and I said in unison.

Tracking down the resort was easy. Suddenly, we all liked the idea of seeing Liverpool in the morning because a dreary combination of fine raindrops mixed with blotches of sleet had set in.

At my request, Penny called the resort for a reservation before we showed up at their front desk Helsinki-style.

We also had to call for a cab. It took a half hour before a black Mercedes pulled up. Our cabbie started chattering the moment we climbed in. I think he talked the whole way to the hotel. The only problem was that neither Penny nor I could understand a word he said.

He pointed to the river we were crossing. I noticed a small sign that said "Mersey River." The cabbie started singing to us.

"That's a Beatles song," Penny announced.

"No!" the cabbie squawked. He named the band.

"One of the many from the British Invasion," Elina said in a low voice. "Gerry and the Pacemakers. Do you remember them?"

Penny shook her head. "I remember this song, though." She sang about taking a ferry across the Mersey, and the cabbie joined in with renewed enthusiasm.

Elina looked impressed with Penny's singing abilities.

Penny looked impressed with the bridge we were crossing and the murky waters below.

I just tried to look intelligent. The only Beatles song I knew was "I Want to Hold Your Hand." And "Penny Lane," of course.

Beyond that, I was destined always to be the audience when it came to songs from the sixties.

Elina joined in on the chorus, and we rolled along on the slushy roads, filling the chilly cab with song.

It was a good thing Elina was with us because she didn't seem to have difficulty with the cab driver's accent. She interpreted for Penny how much we owed the driver when we arrived at the hotel.

Penny checked us in at the front desk without needing to employ any of her PR techniques. We were pleased with our large room. I flopped on a bed. Elina opened the drapes and looked out on a large grassy area surrounded by trees.

"I have an idea," Penny announced. "Where's the phone?"

Without filling us in, Penny dialed the front desk and asked to be connected to the spa services. Before Elina or I could protest (not that we would have), Penny had scheduled all three of us for a manicure, a pedicure, and a facial.

"Our dinner reservations are for eight," Penny announced. "That gives us four hours to get gorgeous. Come on, the spa awaits us."

"Penny," Elina protested, "you don't have to do this."

"I know," she said.

"If you want to go with Sharon, I don't mind waiting here in the room for you."

"No way! We're going to do this together."

"This is too extravagant," Elina said solemnly.

"Think of it this way: Multiply two dollars and ninety-five cents, plus international postage, by forty-some years. That's what I would have spent on birthday cards for you over the years. Consider this as nothing more than a belated birthday card from your long-lost cousin."

"A very luxurious, belated birthday card," Elina said.

"It's like I always say," Penny added with a flip of her hair. "If you're going to be late, at least be luxuriously late."

Elina and I laughed and followed the fabulous, flashy Penny out the door and downstairs to the spa. We entered the fresh-looking salon, and two young women greeted us. It appeared we were their only clients.

Again, the quick, clipped accent made it challenging for me to understand their English. Elina took over as our spokesperson. We had to decide who wanted which service first.

Penny opted for the pedicure first, saying that was her favorite form of pampering lately. I'd never had a pedicure or a facial. Kaylee had given me several manicures, but this was my first professional pampering.

Elina's experiences were more in line with mine than with Penny's. She told the young women she was new at this and asked their advice. The thinner of the two spa specialists suggested Elina have a manicure first.

At least I think that's what she said.

It didn't matter. We were all treated like queens. Who cared about the order of the pampering?

I was shown to a reclining chair where a cape was draped over me and fastened around my neck. Soft, thin paper was tucked around the cape's neck. A warm, white towel was wrapped around my head, and my flyaway hair was tucked under the towel's edges. The chair slowly reclined. My feet were elevated. Soothing music like wind chimes seemed to float down from the ceiling. The overhead lights were dimmed. Rows of tiny fairy lights twinkled.

"I've never been given such an extravagant gift," I heard

Elina say from a few feet away at the manicure station. "Thanks, Penny. Thanks for showing up in my life yesterday and doing all this. I honestly thought I was going to lose my mind yesterday, and now..." Elina choked up. "Now I feel as if I could take on the world."

"Wait until you have your pedicure." Penny was directly across from me with her feet soaking in a little foot tub that made a contented bubbling sound. "Once your toenails are painted, you *will* be able to take on the world. Barefoot, no less!"

I couldn't stop smiling. *Oh, Penny Girl, look what you've done. You've sprinkled your cousin with your wonder dust, and she will never be the same.*

Eighteen

The spa salon was small enough and cozy enough that the three of us could chat without having to raise our voices. The two beauticians worked inconspicuously as a silent team, moving between the three of us to keep our beautification treatments in sync.

"Sharon," Penny said when I was halfway through my facial. "Let me see your face. Sit up a little."

I had no idea how ridiculous I looked, but I could guess. My cleansed face had been covered with a fragrant, thick cream that had a light blue tinge to it. Two thin slices of cucumber covered my eyes. I pulled myself up slowly like the Bride of Frankenstein emerging from the operating table.

I heard a snap and saw a faint flash.

"Did you just take a picture?"

Penny giggled. "Maybe."

"With my camera?"

"Maybe."

"Leave my camera out," I said. "Your turn for the facial will come soon enough, you know."

I leaned back and listened to Penny tease Elina and snap her picture.

"Did you hear about our experience in the sauna at Anni's house?" Penny asked Elina.

"No. Did my mother take you to Anni's?"

"Yes!" Penny laughed. "Your father drove us there in the Mackerel Mobile."

With plenty of exaggeration, Penny launched into the legend of the night she and I joined the flabby chicks in the Finnish sauna.

I only half listened. In my memory I was reliving the moment when I lay naked and not ashamed in the fresh, white snow. That was the moment when God blew away just enough clouds to open the canopy of this fallen planet. Then, just for me, He uncurled His fingers and held out a single star.

Penny spun a fantastic tale of our sauna night, complete with how "those little grannies" locked us out in the snow. Elina loved it. If laughter is good medicine, then I believe Elina could have been cured of her hormone imbalances and her crazy-making mood swings by the time Penny finished releasing all those healing endorphins through her storytelling abilities.

"You Americans!" Elina said after Penny spooned out the final details of the story like hot fudge on a sundae. "You are so self-conscious of your bodies. We all grow old. Accept it; go with it. You think you are only cool if you look like you're eighteen. Look at my mother! She's cool, and she's in her seventies."

"Your mother is cool," I agreed, rising from the chair. My face felt like it was singing all the high notes. My skin had never tingled before.

"The coolest," Penny agreed.

The three of us traded stations. I moved to the pedicure chair. As soon as I slipped my bare feet into the warm water, I understood why Penny loved pedicures.

"I don't mind if I don't look like I'm eighteen," I said. "But I wish I could always feel like I'm eighteen!"

Penny laughed. "Agreed!" She pulled off her rings and plunged her hands into the soaking bowls for her manicure.

"Your mother couldn't have been much more than nineteen when she left Finland," Elina said. "You knew that, didn't you?"

"Yes, when she left with Hank the Pirate."

"Did my mum actually say that?" Elina asked. "Did she call your father a pirate?"

"Yep."

"I'm surprised she was so blunt with you."

"Hey, we're family," Penny said. "No secrets."

"Did my mum also tell you they suspected Hank of selling secrets from the U.S. government?"

"Yes, I wonder if any hint of that is in the letters Mom wrote to your mother."

"That should be interesting. You will let me translate the letters now, won't you?" Elina reclined in the chair as the specialist covered her face with a warm, wet washcloth.

"Yes, I brought them with me. The sooner you want to work on translating them the better."

Elina said something, but we couldn't understand because

the washcloth muffled her words. When her mouth was free she said, "It's amazing that your mum lived as long as she did, Penny."

"Why do you say that? My mother died when she was forty-six."

"I know. But Grandpa and Grandma were always so worried about her heart."

"Her heart?" Penny repeated. "What do you mean?"

I remembered Marketta saying the same thing in the sauna about the concern over Elsa's heart. I thought at the time that every mother shares that sort of concern for her children. Elina seemed to allude to a bigger issue.

"You know," Elina said. "The problem your mother had."

"What problem?"

"With her heart."

"Her heart?" Penny pulled her soaking fingers from the dish and stood up. "My mother had a problem with her heart? A health problem?"

"Yes, of course a health problem. You know, the hole." Elina sat up and pulled away from the skillful hands of the cosmetician. "Your mother had a hole in her heart."

Penny didn't answer.

"You didn't know that?"

Penny shook her head.

"Why did everyone keep that from you?" Elina asked. "Why didn't your mother tell you?"

Penny seemed to be taking in the information.

"I'm sorry, Penny. I thought you knew. I grew up hearing stories of how your mother was supposed to only live to be ten years old and how she shocked everyone by getting pregnant and marrying your father in such a hurry. No one wanted her to leave Finland, but…"

"…but she had an independent streak in her," Penny said.

"Yes. That's the way I heard it. No one expected your mother to live as long as she did. They couldn't believe she was willing to put such a strain on her weak heart and to risk her life to have a baby."

Penny's face turned pale. "My mother risked her life to have me…"

The room went silent.

I pulled my feet out of the bubble bath and hopped over to Penny. Without a word I put my arm around her shoulders.

Penny tipped up her chin. I could see the reflection of the twinkling fairy lights in her eyes. In a low, steady tone, she said, "I never knew that. Now it makes more sense why she never looked back. She never looked ahead, either. My mother just lived each day as if it might be her last."

"I can't believe she never told you," Elina said. "I feel bad, being the one to spill all this out. I think it would have been better if I hadn't brought up this difficult topic."

"No!" Penny looked at Elina. "Are you kidding? You have given me the truth, and I'm telling you, this truth is going to set me free."

Two tears raced down Penny's cheeks. In barely a whisper, she said, "I have been waiting to die."

Elina glanced at me, as if I could interpret Penny's declaration.

I could not.

The spa specialist had stepped away from the manicure table and pulled the other cosmetologist to the side. They were talking in hushed tones. Elina stood up, her head still wrapped in a towel, and came to Penny's other side.

Penny stared at her hands. "I got it into my head that I would drop dead one day, just like my mother. I thought I would make it to the age of forty-six and that would be it. That's why I had to go somewhere, Sharon. Remember? In the church nursery when our kids were babies? I told myself then that I had to go somewhere before I died. I always felt that my mother carried this unrequited love for Finland. I wanted to come in her stead and see what it was that made her get that far-off look in her eye whenever Finland was mentioned. I had to come before I died. It sounds ridiculous now when I say it aloud, but I thought for sure I only had a few more months or maybe another year before my life would be over. That's why seeing Finland wasn't enough. I craved it all. The whole world! Years and years of life."

I suddenly understood so much.

Elina stroked Penny's hair and dabbed her tears with a tissue. I could tell that Penny was drinking in the womanly touches. Elina and I were the spa specialists ministering to Penny at that moment while the two paid women slipped out of the salon. They seemed to be taking advantage of our "moment" to take a break.

"Why do you suppose my mother never told me about her heart?"

"Would you have treated her differently?" Elina asked.

"Yes."

"Would you have ever left her?"

"Not the way I did when I was seventeen. Not without feeling guilty every time I walked out the door."

"I think," Elina said, "your mother comes from a line of

strong women. Perhaps she didn't want pity. Perhaps she only wanted honest love. It seems to me she loved you enough to let you go rather than force you to stay with her. She didn't want you to put your life on hold so you could wait for her to finish hers."

Penny stopped crying. "You're right." She breathed deeply. "My mother loved me. She loved me enough to risk everything to give me life. I'll never believe anything was wrong with her heart. How could such a heart have holes in it?"

Looping an arm around each of us, Penny drew Elina and me close in an awkward group hug. I understood what her hug meant. It was Penny's way of saying that Elina and I were her women. Penny loved both of us from a strong heart. A heart with no holes.

"Are you okay?" I asked softly.

"Yeah, I'm good. Really, really good."

I smiled.

Penny added, "I'm sure I'll think about all this for a long time before I find a place to put all the feelings I have right now. But I'm good."

"Do you suppose," Elina said, looking around, "that our beauticians felt left out of our conversation? They seem to have vanished."

"We probably scared them away," Penny said.

"What if they don't come back?" Elina asked. "Do you think we will have to complete the treatments ourselves?"

"Sure. Why not?" Penny said with a definite spring to her voice. "We could work on each other. Come on, Elina. I'll goop up your face for you."

"Penny!" I protested, ever the diligent follower of the rules.

"What? We're paying for these services. Did you happen to

notice where they keep the cucumbers?"

"Usually you'll find cucumbers in the teatime sandwiches," Elina said with a laugh. She had returned to the facial chair.

"That's what we need in here. Some teatime sandwiches. Lean back, Elina. I've got the goop ready to go. Upward strokes," Penny said in a high-pitched voice, as if she were teaching a class while she applied the pale blue paste to Elina's face. "One must always work against gravity."

Memories of Lisa Bachman's slumber party loomed before me, that defining night when I decided I was destined to be a facilitator. A fresh tingle tickled my psyche. I didn't have to spend the second half of my life on the sidelines, watching all the girls celebrate being free spirited. I could be just as cool as they were.

Grabbing my camera, I entered into the craziness of the moment and clicked off shots of Penny dotting her own face with blue spots while she was beautifying her laughing cousin. To each blue spot, Penny stuck a cucumber slice.

"Here," Penny said. "You need to be dotted." She touched the middle of my forehead and the end of my nose with a glob of her thick, blue paste. "And cuked," she added, sticking a cucumber slice to the middle of my forehead.

I laughed as Penny took the camera from me. I struck a pose, and she snapped my picture. Then holding the camera out, she snapped a picture of herself.

Elina sat up. "What are you two laughing about? I can't see anything with these cucumbers on my eyes. I'm missing all the fun." She popped out the center of each of her cucumber slices and placed the hollowed-out green rims over her eyes.

Penny busted up and took a bite out of the center of two

more cucumber slices, spitting the seeds into the trash can. Then she placed the hollowed green rims over her eyes and posed with Elina so I could take their picture.

"Do I look like you?" Elina asked.

I knew Elina was referring to the look achieved by the green vegetable glasses. But when I took their picture, cheek to cheek, I realized the similarities between the two women were striking, even camouflaged by the blue goo.

"Here." Penny tossed me a cucumber. "For your nose."

I wasn't ready to catch the flying vegetable slice, and it fell to the floor.

"Wait. There's plenty here. Let me toss you another one."

This time Penny's throw overshot me, and the cucumber slice flew past my head.

"Again." Penny tossed four slices at me at once.

I caught one and spontaneously spun it back at her like a mini flying saucer.

Elina picked up a handful. Penny did the same. Without a countdown, the like-minded cousins threw them at the same time. I ducked to avoid the onslaught of flying cucumber slices.

Just then, Penny and Elina stopped all sound and motion. They were looking past me to the door. I slowly turned to see our two young beauticians taking in the spectacle of our cucumber war. They stood speechless for a moment, and then one of them said, "Sorry 'bout steppin' out like that. But you should know the hotel manager is headin' this way."

I pulled the cucumber off my forehead and wiped the tip of my nose. I was imagining the worst. We would be kicked out of the hotel and made to pay for all the wasted cucumbers.

The door opened, and a striking woman entered. Even in the dimmed light I recognized her. "Monique!"

Penny crossed the floor in five giant steps, losing her facial cucumbers on the way. "Monique!"

"Hello, Penny." Monique said with warm surprise. She looked over at me and Elina. "Hello."

"This is my cousin, Elina. You remember Sharon."

"Yes, Sharon. The brave one. How are you?"

"Fine, thank you."

"You found your relatives, then, Penny?"

"Yes. It's been amazing. I tried to call you last night."

"And now here you are."

"Yes, here we are. We've decided to go to Liverpool tomorrow, but if you don't have plans for the evening, we'd love to have you join us for dinner. We have reservations for the hotel restaurant at eight."

I couldn't believe Penny was standing there, conversing in her steady, professional manner while her face was spotted with a half-dozen blue dots.

"I'll see what I can do." Monique turned to the beauticians, and with a calming nod, she said, "Please continue your services for our guests."

I tucked my camera back into my shoulder bag and returned to the cushy pedicure chair as Monique left. The water had gone cold, but I plunged my feet in the sudsy wet anyway and waited for my pedicure.

"Now I know why I recognized the name Daresbury." Penny wiped her face with a wet cloth one of the beauticians handed her. "Monique mentioned this hotel on the plane."

"Yes, well," Elina said with a grin. "I wouldn't be surprised if Monique chooses not to mention it to Americans on her next plane ride."

"Hey, we didn't cause any permanent damage," Penny said. "Besides, life's too short to…"

Elina and I both looked at Penny.

"Life's too…precious," Penny said. "Whether it's short or long. Life is just too precious not to enjoy every second of it."

An exquisite peace settled over all of us.

Having gone to such a deep low with Penny, followed by an erratic high, and topped off with Monique's unexpected appearance, I was content to sit quietly and let the diligent beautician go to work on my long-neglected feet. I liked the massage with the fragrant lotion the best. My manicure was short. I think it was because I have such short nails. I didn't give the hardworking young woman much to work with.

We talked about a variety of topics during the second half of our beauty treatments. None of our subjects was personal and none of them required much thinking. Penny said she had a headache, and I could see why.

Despite the elevator-like rise and fall of our pampering session, we all agreed that we felt refreshed. We dresssed up for dinner because a placard on the desk in our room told us it was mandatory. At eight o'clock the three of us entered the dining room looking as elegant and refined as any of the other guests who were dining at that respectable hour.

My feet felt happy.

The dining room wasn't very large. Each table was covered with a pale ivory tablecloth. A large buffet occupied the center of the main area, and to the far right was a grand piano. A man in a tuxedo was playing a classical piece. I didn't know

Beethoven from Bach, but I wished I did right then. Such knowledge, along with my happy feet and shiny fingernails, would have helped me feel cultured.

Penny led the way to our table. The waiter announced that they were serving beef Wellington that evening.

"Excuse me," Elina said, as the waiter in his prim white jacket turned to leave. "May we have some menus?"

I was glad she asked because I thought Elina might have some insight into what would be good to order.

The waiter looked perturbed and repeated, "This evening we are serving beef Wellington or the buffet. Those are your choices."

"Oh."

He stepped away. Penny leaned closer to Elina. "Was there something particular you were hoping to have for dinner?"

"It was only a whim," she said with a smile.

"What were you hoping to order?" Penny asked.

"It's silly, but I like to order dishes in a restaurant that I don't prepare at home."

"I'm the same way," I told her. "I love to try foods I would never attempt to make or that might not be what my family would like."

"Yes." Elina pursed her lips together.

"Okay, now I'm curious," Penny said. "What did you want to order?"

Elina's eyes twinkled. "Chicken."

"Yes." Penny appeared to be trying very hard not to burst out laughing. "I would imagine you don't eat a lot of chicken around your house."

I tried to repress my laughter by holding my breath and

biting my lip. I'd been painfully reminded of the infamous Miss Molly when I had my manicure and the bandage was removed so I could get the full lotion massage on my hands.

"It's been over a year," Elina said. "I've forgotten how chicken tastes."

"They might have chicken on the buffet," I suggested.

"Good idea. I'm for the buffet," Elina said.

"Me, too," I said.

"Make that three." Penny looked around. "I hope Monique can join us. Keep an eye out for her."

"You've never met a stranger, have you, Penny?" Elina asked.

"What do you mean?"

"You have a wonderful way of bringing out the best in others. You don't have a narrow view of strangers, the way most people do."

Penny shrugged. "Life is too precious."

I knew that Penny had found a new motto for her life.

Nineteen

Penny, Elina, and I followed each other around the buffet, scooping small bits of this and that. Elina recognized many of the dishes, which was helpful. At church potlucks back in Chinook Springs I never had trouble figuring out what everything was. The same people brought the same dishes each time. My children had grown up experiencing every possible combination of Jell-O salads known to humanity.

This buffet, however, seemed to focus on all the possibilities of what could be done with mayonnaise. Eight of the ten salads seemed to have a base that Elina called "salad cream." It looked like mayonnaise to me.

When we reached the buffet's meat section, Elina filled a second plate with three chicken dishes. A chef in a white jacket and tall white hat stood guard beside a huge slab of prime rib, ready to slice for us on demand.

I was staring at a meat dish that was garnished with thin orange wedges. "Do you suppose this is another variety of chicken?" I asked Elina.

She bent closer.

The chef said, "'at's dowgk, mum."

I looked at him and back at Elina. "What did he say?"

"I think he said 'dog,'" Elina whispered. "But that can't be right. They wouldn't serve dog at a place like this."

The chef apparently heard our murmurings because he spoke up with a louder voice. "Dowgk, mum."

"Pork?" I ventured.

"No!" he spouted just as the pianist ended his piece and a quietness settled over the room. "'at's *dowgk,* ma'am." Tucking his hands in his armpits and flapping, he demonstrated, *"Dowgk!* Qwak, qwak!"

"Oh, duck!" Elina and I said in unison.

Our chef's animated description drew the attention of many of the respectable diners. I passed on the "dowgk" and returned to our table with my eyes straight ahead.

"Dowgk," Penny repeated as she followed behind me. "Quack, quack!" She and Elina spilled their laughter all the way to our table.

Monique was standing beside our table, waiting for us. "You manage to make a party wherever you go, don't you?" she said with a gracious smile.

"We are having a great time," Penny said. "You'll join us, won't you?"

"For a moment, yes." She didn't sit but stood casually and visited with us as if she were out for a stroll rather than in the middle of running a large resort. Her elegant beauty and the warm glow of her dark skin struck me again.

Penny gave Monique one of her business cards and stressed that the next time Monique was in San Francisco, she should give Penny a call. "I'll take you to my favorite Chinese restaurant."

"Sounds lovely. I'll definitely give you a call. How long are you staying with us here?"

"Just tonight," Penny said. "We're going to Liverpool tomorrow and then taking a late train back to London because our plane leaves the next morning at eight."

"That doesn't give you much time," Monique said.

"Enough for us to take a picture at Penny Lane," Penny observed.

"And buy a few last-minute souvenirs," I added.

Monique reached into her pale pink blazer pocket and pulled out one of her business cards. She wrote something on the back and handed it to me. "This will allow you to purchase anything in the hotel for a 20 percent discount."

"Oh, I wasn't trying to—"

"Of course not. I didn't think you were. I would like you all to be my personal guests for the remainder of your stay. I've instructed your waiter to bring your dinner check to me. I'm honored that you decided to stay here."

"Monique," Penny protested, "you don't have to do this."

"Yes, I do," Monique said with a tone in her voice that reminded me of Penny's best PR polish. "You are my guests tonight, and when I come again to San Francisco, I am certain that you, Penny, will be the one who insists on paying for the Chinese food."

Penny laughed. "Agreed." She gave Monique's hand a squeeze. "Thanks."

"You take care." Monique left, and we savored our complimentary dinner. Of course, we had to order coffee and the most decadent chocolate dessert the restaurant offered. It was a seven-layered chocolate cake with thick fudge frosting between each of the thin layers.

We joked about needing to call for a bellman to roll us onto one of the luggage carts to haul us to our room. Strolling slowly, we passed a gift shop in the lobby. I suggested we stop to look for souvenirs. Penny and Elina wanted to go to the room, so I shopped by myself. Aside from the evening alone in the guest room at Marketta's, this was the only time I remembered being by myself. I enjoyed taking my time and looking at everything.

A display of china teacups and saucers caught my eye. They reminded me of the beautiful china and crystal Anni had used to serve us at her home for our presauna dinner.

The glaze on the cups was so smooth I found that I didn't want to put the cup down once my hands wrapped around it. The teacups came in a variety of colors and patterns. A small sign on the glass shelf stated a local artist had designed them.

I decided that every woman on my list would get a china cup and saucer. Picking ones for Kaylee and Joanie was easy. I knew Bonnie liked roses, as did my mom. I bought one set with red roses and one with yellow. The cream-colored set with the sweet blue forget-me-nots came with a matching teapot. I held the cup and thought about getting it for myself.

I don't really need this...

I decided life was too precious to pass up such a rare item, and at 20 percent off, I would be crazy to walk away without the cup and the teapot.

Crazy like a daisy, I told myself. Then a smile played across my lips. In front of me was a teacup with tiny daisies in a chain along the rim. I knew I had to get that one for Penny.

The clerk was attentive and helpful, assuring me that she could pack each cup securely so I would have no problem getting them home without the slightest chip. Since I had only one bag, I could check that single piece of luggage and carry on all the china in a box.

Double-checking my souvenir list, I noticed one name left. Gloria. Returning to the china shelf, I looked carefully at each remaining teacup. One on the top shelf stood out. It was a complex cup in a deep shade of purple with intricate gold trim around the edges. The cup was distinct. Special. This cup refused to be ignored—and was priced at almost three times the other cups and saucers.

With a sense of settled contentment, I picked up the pricey, fragile cup and saucer and smiled. This was the gift I wanted to take home to Gloria.

My assortment of china was so well packed that I didn't want to unwrap it to show Elina and Penny once I returned to our hotel room. They said they would take my word for how beautiful the china was and stop by the gift shop in the morning to see the rest of the assortment.

However, we were up so early the shop wasn't open yet. A cab arrived to take the three of us to the station so we could catch a 7:02 train into Liverpool.

The moment I stepped outside to the waiting taxi, I knew the day was going to be glorious. The ground was covered with a light coat of frost that had come special delivery yesterday afternoon on the rainy sleet express. Puffs of whitened mist floated over the adjoining meadow like the Lady of Shalott set adrift in a whitewashed boat floating down to Camelot.

Overhead, the March sky stretched its pale blue wings and fluttered over our corner of the world, blessing us with crisp, light breezes.

I stopped to stare at a dew-laced spider's web in the potted shrub by the hotel's entrance. Every thread appeared to be spun of silver. Every drop of moisture hung like a diamond—no, like a star. Like single stars compressed and sprinkled as one sprinkles glitter when preparing for a celebration.

I drew in a deep draught of chilled air and watched my exhaled breath turn into a cloud. My breath ruffled the glittery stars strung on the spider's silver thread ever so slightly.

Did You breathe, and it was so?

With such clarity of thought came the sense of my heavenly Father's presence. I felt as if He stood right beside me in that moment, bending over, His magnificent hands clasped behind His back as He examined the tiniest bit of His creation with shared delight.

We are all at Your mercy, aren't we, Lord? Every living creature. We could all be gone in a blink. Yet, in Your love, You gently breathe on us and we live another day.

For the first time on this trip, and maybe in my life, I caught a glimmer of what it meant to be at God's mercy. He speaks, and it is so. He breathes, and we live another day.

"What a gorgeous morning!" Penny held open the taxi's door and waited for me to climb in.

I headed for the cab and then stopped. Digging for my camera, I went back to the potted shrub, leaned close, and snapped a picture of the spider's web.

"Okay, you know what?" Penny said. "I'm not even going to ask what you were taking a picture of back there. But I will ask a favor."

"Sure."

"Will you save enough film for a few shots at Penny Lane?"

"No problem. I have three more rolls of film. I haven't taken as many pictures on this trip as I thought I would."

"So, of course, it makes sense that you would use up that extra film by taking pictures of random hotel shrubbery," Penny said brightly.

Elina chuckled.

For some reason, I thought of Tuija from the department store in Finland. I thought of how she had explained that her name meant "a green bush that is planted in front of a house for beauty."

Feeling cocky, I arched my left eyebrow slightly as I slid past Penny and climbed into the cab. "That wasn't random hotel shrubbery. That was a very special *tuija.*"

"Ah!" Elina's eyes lit up. *"Tuija!"*

I smiled and looked out the window, reveling in the sunlit beauty of this fresh new day.

On our short train ride to Liverpool, we were packed in with dozens of Brits on their way to work. I loved listening to the accents and observing mannerisms and what people were wearing. Kaylee wanted me to bring home some unique clothing for her, and I was certain I could find something in Liverpool.

We hadn't eaten breakfast yet, so our first objective, when we arrived, was to find a nearby restaurant and, as Penny said, "get some protein and caffeine in us, but not necessarily in that order."

Elina was more interested in finding a way to check our luggage so we wouldn't have to carry it all over the city. She found a baggage check station inside the terminal and encouraged us to slim down our shoulder bags to the bare essentials before we took off for the day.

I loved feeling light. I loved the sunshine that came at us outside the train station in iridescent slants across the crowded streets. I loved Liverpool, and the truth was, we barely had been introduced.

We found a small café a few blocks from the station. All three of us moved as one toward the open table in the sunshine by the window. We peeled off our coats and hung them over the chair backs.

"Coffee or tea?" Elina asked us.

"Tea for me," I said.

"Tea for two," Penny replied.

Elina turned to the waitress, who was approaching us with menus. "Tea for three, please. With milk and sugar."

We ordered the full English breakfast. It came with a fat sausage Elina called a "banger," scrambled eggs, baked beans, fried tomato slices, and a stack of white toast served with each slice filed upright in a metal rack. Our table could barely hold all the pots of jam along with our large plates and tea paraphernalia.

The strong tea was delicious. I decided I needed to buy lots that day so I would have authentic British loose tea when I christened my new china teapot.

Our breakfast plates were being cleared when Elina announced a little secret she had kept from us all morning. "I finished them."

"Finished what?" Penny said. "Your eggs?"

"No, your mother's letters."

"You did? Where are they?"

"Here." Elina reached for a dozen folded-up pieces of paper. I noticed the first few pages were written out on hotel stationery from Monique's resort.

"When did you do this?" Penny asked.

"Last night. I couldn't sleep. I'm surprised I didn't wake either of you. I turned the lamp to the lowest setting at the desk and thought I'd translate one or two. Before I knew it, I'd finished all of them."

"Any big secrets?" Penny said cautiously.

Elina shook her head. "No."

"Nothing about my father selling government information to the enemy?"

"No, I think my mother and the rest of the family liked to think there was something more to Hank, so they made up the part about his selling government secrets. It must have made it easier for Grandma to let her daughter go if she could believe the worst about Hank."

"Right," Penny said. "As if it wasn't bad enough that she got pregnant and ran off with him."

"And never returned," Elina added.

Penny glanced at the stack of papers in her hand. They seemed glued to her tight fists. Aside from hugging her aunt Marketta, these translated letters were the biggest chunk of connection to her mother that Penny had held in more than twenty years.

I knew in that moment the power of words, the gift of the written word, and how the importance of those words only increases after the person who wrote them is gone.

I felt a distinct pinch in my heart. Once again, I missed my Bible.

Twenty

Penny?" I asked softly, as she clutched her mother's letters. "Would you like to read them now? I don't mean read them aloud. Just read them to yourself. We don't mind waiting."

Penny reached for her reading glasses. "Sure you don't mind?"

"Not at all."

Penny put on her glasses and pulled her chair back so that she was drenched in sunbeams. Her eyes raced down the page.

Elina ordered another pot of tea.

I quietly pulled out my camera and snapped a picture of Penny blazing her way through a Milky Way of words. Her mother's words. A treasure she once thought unattainable.

I saw Penny's tears before she spoke. "Listen to this:

Baby Penny is sleeping through the night at long last, and so am I. She is a precocious baby. I think she will grow up to have strong opinions, like her mother. The truth is, I can't get enough of her. Every sound, every expression,

*every wiggle has captured my heart. She is perfect, and I
have to admit that I would make all the same choices
again just to see this miracle of life find a place to grow in
this world.*"

Penny looked up, her lower lip quivering.

No words were needed between the three of us. Penny
kept reading to herself as Elina and I sipped our tea.

"These poems," Penny said without looking up.

Elina nodded.

I obviously was the one who sat outside the circle of
understanding.

Penny looked at me. "You have to hear this one, Sharon.
My mom liked Christina Rossetti's poetry. She quoted a poem
in this letter to Marketta when I was only two years old. My
dad was dead. There she was, alone. Listen to this:

I was a cottage maiden
    Hardened by sun and air
Contented with my cottage mates,
    Not mindful I was fair.
Why did a great lord find me out,
    And praise my flaxen hair?
Why did a great lord find me out,
    To fill my heart with care?

He lured me to his palace home—
    Woe's me for joy thereof—
To lead a shameless shameful life,
    His plaything and his love.
He wore me like a silken knot,

He changed me like a glove;
So now I moan, an unclean thing,
Who might have been a dove.

Penny sat, so immersed in the light that it seemed to glow like embers at the ends of her thick, brown hair.

"There is so much I didn't understand," she said softly. "So much I would do differently, if I had my childhood to live over. Despite all her obstacles, my mother made a good life for the two of us. She overcame more than I ever realized."

"Did you read the part about your winning the debate contest at your school?" Elina asked.

"Yes. That was in this one. I was a freshman in high school when my mom wrote this to Aunt Marketta in a Christmas card. Are you ready for this? Her opening line is, 'Penny has surprised me again.'"

I laughed. "Small wonder."

Penny grinned and continued, "'Penny came home with an award from school for her debate team. Her presentation was on returning sacred lands to Native Americans, and she won first place for the district.'"

Penny looked up. "I remember that speech. Guess I was naturally persuasive even way back when."

"Read the next part," Elina said.

"'Sometimes I look at Penny, and I think she is a collection of all that was best in Hank mixed with our mother's deep strength. She has my independent spirit, so we're having difficulty agreeing on anything. We have many arguments, but I love her fiercely, and I pray for her every day. In my heart, I secretly adore her.'"

I reached over and gave Penny's hand a squeeze. "Your mother adored you."

Penny looked up, blinking. "She loved me fiercely."

"And," Elina added, "she prayed for you. Every day."

Penny sighed.

The three of us sat in our silent sunbath, soaking it in, immersed in thoughts that expanded our minds beyond the galaxies, beyond our years. In my mind's eye, I caught a refracted memory. I saw the way the tall candles at the church in Helsinki had given off a reflection in the goblet of wine. The blood. The bread. Broken. All of us broken in some way. All of us invited to come. To receive His eternal life, to cast our nets on the other side of the boat, and to capture all those shimmering bits of glory.

"You know what?" Penny pushed her glasses up on top of her head. "I need some air." She stood, blinking away tears and reaching for her coat. "Don't rush. I just have to go outside."

Elina and I pooled our money to pay the bill. We finished our tea and joined Penny on the noisy street in front of the café. Elina wrapped her arm around her cousin and gave her a hug.

"Are you okay?" I asked.

Penny nodded. Raising her head with strength and dignity, she said, "Onward! Where should we go first?"

The night before we had read in the tour book about the collection of museums and shops at the harbor. We joked about stopping in at the pub at the bottom of Church Street even though I couldn't remember the bartender's name. Then, of course, we would have to take lots of pictures at the barbershop on Penny Lane and find an actual sign that said Penny Lane. That was my goal for the day—lots of pictures.

Tonight we would take a train back to Elina's home, catch a few hours' sleep, and then make another airport dash to catch our flight home in the morning. This was our last hurrah before we jumped back over the moon.

Since Elina wasn't answering, I said, "Penny Lane."

"What?" she answered.

I laughed. "No, not you. Penny Lane. The street Penny Lane. Our first stop should be Penny Lane. Let's grab a taxi and ask the driver to take us there while we still have this glorious sunshine."

Elina held up her hand to hail a cab. We climbed in and took off going the "wrong way" on a narrow street. The driver seemed to be winding us all around town. We wouldn't know if he was ripping us off or not since Penny Lane could have been the next street over from the café, and we would never know.

When he came to an abrupt halt in front of an unimpressive street of shops, I noticed the name painted on the window. "This is the barbershop," I said, as if suddenly I was the master of Beatles trivia. "Tony Slavin's."

We climbed out and stood in front of the white shop with black trim, looking at each other. I noticed a large black and white poster of the Beatles in the shop window next door. The sign painted in black across the top of Tony Slavin's read, "Ladies & Gentlemen's Hairdressing."

"I'll take a picture of the two of you," Elina offered.

The cabbie asked if he should wait. We told him yes and then asked him to take a picture of the three of us. He was the quietest of any of the cab drivers we had encountered on our journeys. If ever we wanted an energetic cab driver, this was the moment. I missed our nightclub-promoting cabbie from Helsinki. This cabbie was old and missing an eyetooth. He wore a frayed tweed cap, which he had pulled down over his forehead while feathers of gray hair stuck out the sides.

"Can you take us to Penny Lane?" Penny said as we got back in the cab.

"This is Penny Lane, love."

"Yes, but isn't there a sign or something that says Penny Lane?" Elina said. "Would you drive us around slowly until we find a sign?"

"I know just the place." He popped the car into gear and made a tight U-turn in the middle of the street. All three of us were taking in an eyeful of narrow houses lined up on either side of the bumpy street.

The driver pulled onto the side of the road and pointed across the street. At a curve in the road, a brick wall that stood about five feet high was marked with a white sign. In straight, plain letters the sign declared, PENNY LANE.

"Perfect!" Penny was the first one out of the cab.

I was right behind her. This is what I had hoped for. As I got closer, I realized the brick wall was thick with green moss growing over the top and moving its way into the crevices. The brick wall was old. The sign was old. It was splintered and worn by weather and showed evidence of faded graffiti.

"Look at that," Penny said, standing close to the sign. "It's falling apart like the rest of us."

"An era gone by," Elina said with a touch of sadness. "I was just thinking about how this will mean nothing to my children when I tell them. We're fast becoming the older generation, aren't we?"

"But, look!" I said, pointing to the sign. After the bold, black letters, was a small number *18* in red. "That's us. Eighteen forever on the inside."

Penny laughed and posed next to the sign, pointing to the number eighteen. I snapped a picture.

The cab driver shuffled over and took a picture of the three of us. Then Elina convinced him to come get in the shot. I took a picture of Elina and Penny on either side of the bemused cabbie.

"Now one of just Sharon and Penny," Elina said.

Penny and I looped our arms around each other and tilted our heads just right so that the magic number *18* appeared in the opening between our necks. I felt the sun coming at us at an angle, pressing warm sunbeams across our foreheads.

"Hold it right there!" Elina said. "Oh. Wait. I have to change the film. Don't move."

Penny and I held the pose.

"Sharon?" Penny said.

"Hmmm?"

"You know how you said you wanted to surprise me by getting me to Penny Lane for a birthday present?"

"Yes."

"Well, thank you."

"You're welcome."

"Now I'm trying to figure out what to get you for your next birthday."

"You already bought me the blue sweater set in Finland."

"I mean for your next birthday. And the one after that, and the one after that."

"How about if we just say that this whole trip covers all my birthdays from here on out?"

"No, I don't think so."

"Okay, the camera is almost ready," Elina said. "Oh. Wait. The film didn't catch. Just a minute."

"Sharon?"

"Hmmm?"

"You know what you are?"

"No, what?"

"You're my best friend."

"And you're *my* best friend, Penny."

"You came on this trip with me."

"You invited me on this trip."

"Yeah, but you came. You did it. You stayed with me. There should be a word for women like you."

"There is. It's *friend.*"

"No, more than a friend," Penny said. "More than a best friend. You're brave. Daring. Close. Caring. Deeply spiritual and forever eighteen on the inside."

"Kindred spirit? Soul mate?"

"No, it's different than that. You're like a sister, but you're—"

"Okay," Elina called out. "The film is all set. Smile!"

"Wait!" Penny held up a hand to the camera. She turned to me. "I know what you are."

"What?"

"You're a sisterchick."

"A sisterchick?" I laughed.

"Yes. Definitely. You're a sisterchick. My sisterchick."

"That makes you the original sisterchick."

"I can live with that." Her face broke into a wide grin. "I can live a really long time with that." Turning back to the camera, Penny said, "Okay. We're ready, Elina."

I opened up my heart and laughed freely as Penny Lane punched her strong arm into the air, right there on Penny Lane, and shouted, "Sisterchicks forever!"

Epilogue

Kiitos Cottage
Maple Leaf Lake, Washington
October 18, 2003

For almost a week I've been blissfully sequestered here at our little cabin that fronts Maple Leaf Lake. I guess you could say this cottage is what Penny gave me for my birthday the year after Helsinki and all the years that followed.

Penny and Dave bought this cozy place nine years ago. Jeff and I have been fixing it up. We named it Kiitos Cottage, and Penny had the name carved on a redwood plaque, which now hangs over the front door. The picture of Penny and me in front of the Penny Lane sign is on the right-hand wall as you enter.

At Penny's insistence and on her dime, her cousin Elina and Elina's husband, Arnie, came to visit her a few years ago. Penny couldn't convince Marketta and Juhani to come, so two summers ago Penny and her whole family returned to Finland. Above the fireplace is a picture of Penny and Marketta on Porosaari. They're both holding up fish.

To the left of that is another photo of a fish. This one is of Joona from the hotel in Helsinki. He took Penny up on her invitation to come visit sometime and came to the U.S. with a few friends. They spent a week here at Kiitos Cottage, and Joona caught the largest fish anyone has ever pulled from Maple Leaf Lake. He sent Penny the photo. On the picture frame are the words, "Joona and the Whale."

Every year, on the weekend that falls closest to my birthday, Penny and I meet here for what our husbands call our "sisterchick weekend." We don't fish. We talk, eat, and laugh. Not always in that order.

I came early this year so I could write our Finland story. The words have tumbled out as I've lowered the bucket deep into the well of my abundant life.

I'd almost forgotten about the wailing nine-month-old who vomited on me. Now I see that incident as a moment that God used to start a new thing in my life. You see, as my children grew older, my heart kept going out to young mothers.

I guess I went from an emerging chick to a mama hen because I started a group called Mom's Monday Mornings. Every week mothers come with their children to our wonderfully practical, multipurpose church for a time of prayer and encouragement. During the past seven years we've involved over a thousand moms and their wee ones. Many of the moms weren't connected with a church, just like Dave and Penny when they first came to Chinook Springs. Dozens and maybe hundreds of women, along with their families, have been loved into God's kingdom.

I guess we don't really choose the things we're good at doing, even if it's as simple as loving new moms and their babies. But we choose whether or not to do something lasting with it. Being in charge of Mom's Monday Mornings energizes and fills me in an extraordinary way. Even with all the challenges and setbacks we've had, I know I could do this for another ten years. Easy. And with joy.

One thing I know is true about finding out what you are gifted to do: Satan divides. God multiplies.

God has multiplied my love for others, especially those in the small circle of my life. Sometimes I think Jeff and I couldn't grow any more in love with each other, but each year brings us closer.

Penny said it's the same with her and Dave. They had a really awful two years right after Finland. The root of the problem seems to have been their schedule—or lack thereof. Both Penny and Dave were working too many hours. All three of their children were on soccer teams and had full social calendars.

I'm certain Marketta's prayers and motherly counsel kept Penny steady through that difficult season. Marketta advised Penny and Dave to cut back their work hours, meet once a week for lunch, and "kiss twice a day, whether you feel like it or not."

Penny says after following that advice, their marriage bloomed like a field of wildflowers. They are closer now than ever.

I've thought many times about what would have happened to Dave and Penny had she not gone to Finland. She wouldn't have resolved her identity struggles before coming into a stretch of marriage struggles. She wouldn't have had access to dear Marketta's loving support and wisdom. She would have felt terribly alone. I think God gave Penny a thimbleful of blood when she needed it most.

When I look back, I realize how many shimmering bits of glory fill our lives now. I'm amazed at how much has happened to both of us after we cast our nets on the other side of the world.

Monique and Penny have become strong friends and see each other whenever Monique comes to San Francisco on hotel business.

Our children are all doing well. Our seven little ones who overwhelmed us in that church nursery so long ago are now grown. Penny became a grandma last summer when her Nicole had a baby girl.

"Our first little sisterchick!" Penny wrote on the back of the photo she sent me.

My Kaylee has been married a year but no babies on the way yet. My relationship with Kaylee took a wonderful turn after Finland. I told her my season of being her facilitator was over, and now she and I were two women figuring out how to be friends. She cried a few glistening tears and slowly began to trust me with her life's complexities, which for several more years came wrapped in layers of wild emotions. By the time Kaylee was eighteen, we were closer than I ever was with my mother. And definitely closer than I was with my mother-in-law.

I'm happy to say that the Lovin' Gloria shop God opened in my heart stayed open. God kept all the shelves stocked with exactly what I needed to love this woman who never loved me back.

Gloria became seriously ill about six years ago. I went to her house every day to care for her and to make dinner for Grandpa Max. Her illness lingered, and she became bedfast. She and Max moved in with us, and I loved on her good for eight months until she had a seizure that sent her into a deep, dark place where she only sang the low notes. Grampa Max and I were with her when she quietly passed away. I've often felt grateful that I made peace with Gloria before she was called upon to make peace with God.

Our son Ben had a rough stretch after the flagpole incident when he broke his wrist. God kept His hand on this "son of my right hand." But Gloria was the one who ministered to him with cakes during his down times and sent him boxes of cookies when he went off to college. Last summer Ben married a fiery, red-haired girl. I adore her.

I've loved just about everything in this season of life. Maybe I really am in the best years now. Penny and I laugh when we look at pictures of ourselves when we were thirty and forty years old and think of how we used to complain that we were getting so old or so fat or that we had too many bulges and wrinkles.

What a joke on us! We were young, and we looked good. Now we *are* getting old, but we feel good. We're free.

Last night I felt so free I did something I'd never done before. All week here at Kiitos Cottage the weather has been perfect. Yesterday was a balmy seventy-two degrees with primrose blue skies. The fingers of Maple Leaf Lake were tap-tapping persistently on the shore all afternoon as I wrote. The water beckoned me to come in and seize the final days of this Indian summer warmth before fall rode in on a chilling wind and took the brilliant colored leaves for a jovial spin.

I decided I was the one who should go for a jovial spin. I'd just finished writing everything I wanted to say about Finland, and I wanted to mark the moment with a little celebration.

Twilight dimmed the lights of day so that all the stars could come out in their bare, shining glory. I wanted to join them. I slipped out of my shorts and sweatshirt and padded down to the water's edge in my elegant black undies. Wading into the cooling waters that had baked all afternoon in the sun, I lifted my arms in an act of solitary worship to the One who made the stars and sent them spinning through the galaxies.

No words were left in me to give Him in that moment. So I gave Him my tears.

That's when He pushed the moon, that eternal night-light, up just over the top of the cedar trees. I lowered myself into the water and stretched out so that I was floating on my back, watching that perfectly round, vastly golden moon as it bobbed in the water beside me.

I imagined that the shivering tickles on the back of my neck were tiny fish that had come to greet me with little fish kisses. As I floated, I noticed that the moon now bobbed on my other side.

"Imagine that!" I said to the stars. "The moon has just jumped over me!"

I slept deep last night. When I woke this morning I tidied the cabin, set out my forget-me-not teapot with matching teacup along with Penny's daisy teacup. Her plane left San Francisco at seven in the morning, which meant I should start listening for her rental car on the gravel road around nine-thirty. As soon as she arrived, I knew we would sit on the front porch and have our traditional pot of tea along with whatever bakery muffins or bagels she had managed to grab on her way to the airport.

With care, I placed the journal of my Finland memoirs on the porch swing where Penny usually sat and went inside to start the teakettle. I couldn't wait for her to read our story and for the two of us to begin our weekend of doing what we did best, which was just being us.

That's when I heard the crush of tires on gravel coming down the long road to Kiitos Cottage. Peeking out the window above the kitchen sink, I spotted a sleek, silver convertible flashing through the row of pine trees. The driver wore sunglasses and a long, hot pink, polka-dotted scarf around her neck that fluttered like a banner declaring wild, wonderful freedom as brightly as possible.

But something was different.

I stepped out on the porch and watched the car come to a pebble-spinning halt. The woman in the pink scarf flipped up her sunglasses and stepped out of the convertible with a large white pastry box.

I stood still for a moment.

Oh, Penny Girl, what have you done?

Her hair was shockingly short, the way the grannies had worn theirs in Finland. It was also white. As bleached white as the pastry box she held in her hand.

"I brought your birthday cake," Penny called out the moment she spotted me. "I figured, why eat muffins with our morning tea when we can eat cake? Chocolate, of course."

"Of course." I wrapped my arms around her and drew in the fresh floral notes of her expensive perfume. She planted her signature greeting kiss on my right cheekbone, and I returned the same.

"Love your hair," I told her.

"Do you? Really? I got tired of fighting the gray, but I thought it might be a little on the wild side."

I laughed. "You, a little on the wild side? Never."

Well," Penny said with a grin, "at least it didn't turn green!"

I laughed with her as we linked arms and headed for the front porch of Kiitos cottage, our breakfast of chocolate cake in hand.

Forever eighteen. Forever knit together by the same hands that dimpled the moon with His thumbprint. Forever sister-chicks.

Watch for *Sister Chicks Do the Hula*
coming in February 2004!

Discussion Questions

1. What do you think Penny meant when Ben broke his wrist and she told Sharon, "This will be the making of him"?

2. How do you think your family and friends would respond if you announced that you were taking a trip like the one Sharon and Penny went on?

3. How would the trip have been different if Penny and Sharon had waited and went after their children were all grown?

4. Do you think Sharon truly resolved her conflicts with Gloria? Why?

5. What relative or acquaintance might God want to love through you? What action could you take to show God's love to that person?

6. Do you think Penny should have told Sharon about Wolf, or would it have been better to leave the past as the past?

7. Why was the communion service in the Helsinki church so different for Sharon, and how do you think it changed her?

8. If you, like Jesus' disciples, cast your net on the other side of your boat of life, what do you think you would catch? What would make that change in your life risky?

9. In what ways could you be clothed in strength and dignity? What new "garb" would you need?

10. Recall a time you've ever been in Elina's position and had "imposing" company arrive at an inconvenient time. Compare how you handled it with how Elina did. Did you or Elina do better?

11. When Penny and Dave were first married, they had very little and lived in substandard housing. When Sharon was without her luggage, she found she could get by with much less than usual. Tell about a time in your life when you lived with just the basics. How did you feel?

12. What were the key elements that drew Sharon and Penny into a friendship and prompted Penny to dub them "sisterchicks"?

13. If you had an opportunity to go on a sisterchick adventure to any place in the world, where would you go and whom would you want to take with you?

The publisher and author would love to hear your comments about this book. *Please contact us at:* www.multnomah.net/robinjonesgunn

Former College Roomies Make Waves on Waikiki

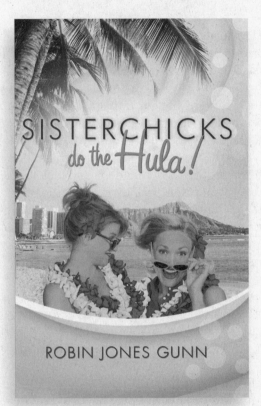

Some dreams take a while before they come true. Best friends Hope and Laurie never made it to Hawaii during their college years. But when they're about to turn forty, the islands still beckon, and off they go—with an unexpected stowaway on board. A little pineapple, a little sunshine, and a surprising little surfing lesson give these two sisterchicks all their crazy hearts could hope for—and more—as they enter the next season of their lives with a splash and with a beautiful vision of what God has dreamed up for them.

ISBN 1-59052-226-5

Sisterchicks Do the Hula
by Robin Jones Gunn

In five days Laurie and I were scheduled to meet up in Honolulu. What triggered my meltdown was an ordinary box that arrived on my doorstep in the snow. Inside was my maternity bathing suit.

Blithely carrying the box upstairs, I drew the curtains, closed the bedroom door, and peeled off layers of warm clothes. Relieved that the back-ordered item had arrived in time, I wiggled my way into the new swimsuit, slowly turned toward the mirror on the back of the bedroom door, and took in the sight of my blessed belly wrapped in swaddling aqua blue spandex.

First the front view. Then the side. Other side. Twisting my head over my shoulder, I got a glimpse of the backside. Then quickly returned to the front view.

I was shocked! Completely shocked!

The woman in the mirror shook her head at me. *"You're not considering going out in public wearing that, are you?"*

"Yes?" I answered with a woeful sigh. "Although, I didn't think it would look like this on me."

"Oh, really? And just what did you think it would look like on you?"

"Well, not like this."

For months I had been riding high on the "blessed-art-thou-among-women" cloud. I considered it a privilege to carry this baby. I told myself I was participating in a calling that was higher than fashion and charm. Who cares about beauty? The truth was, my body was nurturing new life.

However, truth and beauty had crashed head-on in my bedroom mirror.

"I like this shade of blue," I declared, trying to be positive.

"Yeah? Well, from where I'm standing, that shade of blue does not appear to be too fond of you, sweetheart."

"Maybe I could return this one and order the black one instead."

"Right, because everyone knows that black is always so much more slimming."

"There was that black one with the little pleated skirt..."

"Okay, yeah, there you go. Because nothing says dainty like Shamu in a tutu."

"Hey!" I turned away and covered my belly as if to protect Emilee's ears from this audacious woman. "You don't have to be rude about it!"

"Look who's talking."

I glared over my shoulder at the mannerless minx and found I couldn't say anything. I could only stare at her. At myself. At what I had become. How did this happen?

How could it be that my two dreams had intersected this way? Innocent little Emilee Rose was my dream baby come true. A trip to Hawaii with Laurie was a dream that had waited patiently for two decades to come true.

But someone had taken my two best dreams and poured them into a single test tube when I wasn't looking. Now the churning, foaming result bubbled over the top and ended up larger than life in my bedroom mirror. There she stood, defying me to accept the truth.

I was old.

And I was not beautiful. How had those two facts escaped me in the bliss of being a middle-aged life bearer?

Fumbling my way out of the aqua swimsuit and trying to stop the ridiculous flow of big, globby tears, I turned my back on the mirror and plunged into my roomiest maternity clothes. Leaning against the ruffled pillows that lined our bedroom window seat, I inched back the curtains and let the tears gush.

Outside, an icy January snowstorm was elbowing its

way down the eastern seaboard, causing the limbs of our naked elm tree to shiver uncontrollably. Beside me was a tour book of Hawaii. The cover showed shimmering white sand, pristine blue water, and a graceful palm tree stretching toward the ocean as if offering its hand for the waves to kiss. Beautiful people from all over the world came to bask in the sun and stroll along such exotic beaches in this island paradise.

I glanced sympathetically at the quivering elm tree out my window and tried to imagine slender tropical palms in full sunlight, swaying in the breeze, green and full of life.

"That's right. Think about the beautiful beaches, the sunshine, and all the fun you and Laurie are going to have."

I blew my nose and glanced at the mirror.

She was still there, delivering her sugary sass. *"Don't think of the other tourists—those twenty-year-old toothpicks in their bikinis, sauntering down the beach with their long, cellulite-free legs and their flat stomachs. Who cares that you'll be the only woman on the beach looking like a bright blue Easter egg on parade?"*

I picked up a pillow, took aim, and...

The bedroom door swung open, forcing the mirror maven into hiding. My hero entered with a tube of caulking in his hand. "There you are. You okay?"

I clutched the pillow to my middle and nodded.

Darren glanced out the window and then down at the tour book beside me. "I heard this storm is supposed to blow over by Monday. Should be clear sailing when you fly out on Wednesday morning."

"That's what I heard, too." My voice sounded surprisingly steady.

Darren stepped into our bathroom and proceeded to caulk the shower.

"Hope, can you come here and tell me if this looks straight to you?"

I didn't need to go in there to see if his caulking line was straight. Darren's repairs were never straight. But they always worked. That's all that mattered to me.

"Looks good." I tilted my head ever so slightly so that the line along the base of the shower honestly did appear straight.

He glanced up from his kneeling position. With a tender pat on my belly, he said, "And you look good to me."

"Bahwaaaaah!" I burst into tears all over again.

"What's wrong? What did I say?" Darren was on his feet, trying to wrap both arms around me and draw me close. "Why are you crying?"

"How can I possibly look good to you? I'm pregnant! I'm really, really pregnant!"

"Of course you are. Why are you crying?"

"Because I'm going to Hawaii!"

"Yes, you're going to Hawaii. Come on now, pull yourself together."

I kept crying.

Darren looked frantic. He stepped back and, fumbling for his roguish smirk, said, "So, is this a hormone thing?"

"No, it's not a hormone thing! I'm old, Darren! I'm old and pregnant, and I'm going to Hawaii. Can you understand how that makes me feel?"

He couldn't.

How could I possibly expect my husband to understand all the bizarre things that happen to a woman in spirit and flesh when a friendly alien takes over her body? He still couldn't figure out why Laurie and I wanted to fly all the way to Hawaii just to spend a week lounging around a pool, comparing underarm flab, when we could stay home and have the same conversation over the phone for a lot less money.

I took a deep breath. "You know what? I don't care what anyone says. These screaming purple stretch marks running up my biscuit-dough thighs are stripes of honor."

"Exactly."

"I earned every one of those zingers!"

"Of course you did, honey."

"I am a Mother, with a capital *M*."

"Never doubted it for a moment."

"And everyone knows that aqua is the perfect mother-hood color, even in the tropics."

"Especially in the tropics."

"Thank you."

"You're welcome."

What my husband had just observed was a 95 percent hormone-induced solar flare. But there was no way on this blue earth that I would reveal that scientific secret to him.

I concluded my little skit by clearing my throat and saying, "I think your caulking looks good. Very nice."

"Thanks. And I meant what I said. You look good to me, too."

"Thank you." I turned with my chin raised in valor and tried to glide gracefully out of the bathroom, my beach-ball belly exiting a full half a second before the rest of me.

Reaching for the much-debated swimsuit, I rolled it up and tucked it into the corner of my suitcase. Over my shoulder I could feel the mirror maven working up a good sass-and-slash comment. Before she had a chance to deliver it, I turned to face her full on. "Let's see now. One of us is stuck to piece of particle-board, and one of us is leaving for Hawaii on Wednesday. Any guesses as to which one you are?"

She didn't say a word. She knew her place. And I was about to find mine.

Come to Glenbrooke...
"A Quiet Place Where Souls Are Refreshed."

The Glenbrooke Series

TEA AT GLENBROOKE

by *Robin Jones Gunn*

with paintings by *Susan Mink Colclough*

Snuggle into an overstuffed chair, sip your favorite tea, and journey to Glenbrooke…"a quiet place where souls are refreshed." Writing from a tender heart, Robin Jones Gunn transports you to an elegant place of respite, comfort, and serenity—a place you'll never want to leave! Look forward to a joyful reading experience, lavishly illustrated by Susan Mink Colclough, that captures the essence of a peaceful place.

ISBN 1-58860-023-8

CELEBRATE HER BECOMING A WOMAN!

Gentle Passages

Guiding Your Daughter Robin
Jones
into Womanhood Gunn

Every woman who has an adolescent daughter recognizes her own forgotten questions and insecurities mirrored in those bright young eyes. How can she let her know that she understands these changes, too strange and intimate for her daughter to mention? How can she make the passage into womanhood not a shameful, unpleasant experience but a harmonious and joyful one—an invitation to a treasured role in God's eyes? Robin Jones Gunn shares stories of how this uncertain transition can become the loveliest time in the life of a mother and daughter, inspiring women with special traditions to carry on for generations to come.

ISBN 1-57673-943-0

CELEBRATING THE MOMENTS
THAT LAST FOREVER

Focusing upon the special bond between a mother and child, this unique gift book offers lilting poetry, poignant prose, spiritual insights, romantic photographic images, inspiring quotations, and heartwarming journal entries. A delightful companion to women of every age and background celebrating the vast and myriad joys of motherhood!

ISBN 1-57673-914-7

SOMEWHERE BETWEEN WISHES AND REALITY...LIE DREAMS

Autumn Dreams

SEASIDE SEASONS

BOOK THREE

A Novel

GAYLE ROPER

Cassandra Merton, newly forty and never married, is intrigued and intimidated by the rich forty-four-year-old bachelor who arrives at her Seaside, New Jersey, bed-and-breakfast. Management and finance specialist Dan Harmon is there to contemplate his life's significance as a result of witnessing the September 11 tragedy. Meanwhile, Cass dares to resist being the family doormat for the first time in her life, as she struggles to care for her teenage niece and nephew as well as her aging, deteriorating parents. Strengthened by each other, the two baby boomers dedicate themselves to untangling life's puzzles—and a local mystery.

ISBN 1-59052-127-7

A FREE
"BEHIND THE SCENES"
LOOK AT YOUR
FAVORITE
FICTION AUTHORS!

www.letstalkfiction.com

Let's Talk Fiction is a free, four-color mini-magazine created to give readers a "behind the scenes" look at Multnomah Publishers' favorite fiction authors. *Let's Talk Fiction* allows our authors to share a bit about themselves, giving readers an inside peek into their latest releases. To receive your free copy of *Let's Talk Fiction,* get on-line at **www.letstalkfiction.com**. We'd love to hear from you!